WHERE DARKNESS PREYS

Also by Anne Leone

When Snow Falls Like Fire

THE WHITBY REVOLUTION
BOOK 2

WHERE DARKNESS PREYS

ANNE LEONE

LION BOOKS

To the girls I grew up with, especially the two Jennys, Jennifer, Kelly, Carol, and Ann without an *e*.

Thanks for helping me become the woman I am today.

Chapter 1

Mina

IT STARTED ON Halloween, of course.

Night had stolen over me while I was curled up in bed, trying to puzzle out my future. The dark suited my mood. Suited everything really—my future plans, the news, my so-called love life.

Then the dorm room door flew open, and Lucy barreled inside with a pile of clothes in her arms. "Mina! Look what I found!"

I blinked to close the screencast hovering in front of me.

"Are you obsessing over those messages again?" Lucy scolded.

It'd been months since I'd heard from Jonathan, my supposed boyfriend. He had messaged back and forth with me when he first arrived in England, but there had been nothing since. Really, I needed to take a hint. Jonathan was probably having the time of his life and couldn't be bothered with even whisper texting. No matter what I had thought.

"I figured we needed these," Lucy said, unfolding a long black cape around a plastic sword, its tip painted red, along with a matching red bandanna and a witch's hat.

"Did you mug some little kids?"

"No. I found them all in my old dress-up bin back home."

Only Lucy would have a dress-up bin. "For what?" I argued just because I was in that kind of mood. "It's pitch-black out."

"You're sitting in the dark," Lucy pointed out. "Besides, wild fun is on tap tonight. Now—witch or pirate?"

I bit my lip. It was a school night, not to mention after curfew. If we got caught off campus, Irving Academy for Gifted and Talented Students would suspend us, no question. Maybe worse.

But on the other hand, I had spent an entire evening in a dark room, asking existential questions and hating all my answers. I ran my finger along the bloody sword. What if wild fun was exactly what I needed for a change?

"Gimme the hat," I said.

I dressed in all black and tied the cape around my shoulders. Lucy pulled her hair up into a bandanna and laced her sword through a scarf knotted around her waist. Of course she would find a way to add style. She pulled her pillowcase from its pillow and tossed it to me before starting on the other pillow.

"What's this for?"

"Candy." Lucy held up her sack and growled, "Arrr!" like a pirate straight out of that virtual reality adventure she'd been playing.

I frowned, digging my teeth into my lip. So much had changed lately. Sometimes the streets themselves weren't safe, especially after dark. "Does anyone actually trick-or-treat anymore?"

"Maybe not *downstate*." She labeled my part of the state like it had some disease. "But the rich people around here? Definitely. Besides, this is the wild-fun part. I'm starving!"

I laughed. Okay, point to Lucy; I also wasn't sure when I had last eaten.

"Avaunt, me hearties!" Lucy cried, brandishing her sword. "To the back door!"

I rushed after her, Lucy's black cape lifting like wings behind me. My roommate never got caught. It was my senior year. And I was so tired of following all the rules.

But as we ran outside, I tasted blood. I had bitten through my lip. Sometimes I couldn't let myself go.

3

Chapter 2

Mina

OUTSIDE FLORENCE HALL, we sprinted past the streetlight, across the dark commons framed with Gothic buildings like our own, and into the surrounding neighborhood. The downturn started with the pandemic, then the Stagnation—the worst depression since the Great Depression—which led to almost complete urban economic collapse. When city services became unsustainable, people fled the nearby city of Whitby, abandoning houses and increasingly violent neighborhoods. The whole city was designated a Dead Zone and its people noncitizens. So the richest people, businesses, and our school, Irving, had moved here, to the safe suburban bubble of Newholm.

"Look at all the lights!" Lucy cried, gesturing with her sword. "See, it's not *pitch*-black."

A tapestry of light invited us forward, to be part of a crowd of costumed kids. All the houses around

4

campus were new, with square green lawns, shiny white lampposts, and backup generators. We walked to the first house, and Lucy rang the bell.

"Trick or treat," she called. "Give us all your loot."

I shifted my weight to my back foot as the security camera turned in our direction, and then a stranger opened the door. But a wide smile stretched across her face. "A witch and a pirate!" she announced. "How wonderfully traditional."

She didn't study our faces to determine how old we were or question where we came from. She only dropped several mini candy bars into our pillowcases. Then we continued to the next house and the next. Lucy had been right—we were surrounded by other kids, even teenagers. It was as if the whole planet had shifted on its axis and we had stumbled backward into a different, happier time. We headed north, past the gleaming steel-and-glass media center, then along Lyceum Road's string of businesses—the tea bar, the used bookstore, the drugstore, McDonald's. The storefronts were decorated with pumpkins and smiling ghosts, with trays of candy, ice cream, imitation chocolates. Down the road, Newholm Hospital's lights sparkled.

Lucy howled into the night like a wolf, not a pirate. My cheeks hurt from smiling, but I didn't stop. It'd been too long. I'd been so busy being perfect since the school year began, there hadn't been any time for fun.

"This is going to be our best year ever, Mina Bird!" Lucy declared.

I couldn't help but believe her. All my bottled-up fears had melted away.

Lucy grabbed my hand and dragged me across Lyceum into the neighborhood on the other side. As we worked our way down the street, the crowds shifted, died away, and the night grew darker.

"Look at this monstrosity," Lucy said, pointing to the house at the end of the cul-de-sac.

It was huge; wide, but also several stories tall. A black fence wrapped around the yard, encasing a double generator and several actual trees. The windows were dark.

I shook my head. "They're blacked out."

Most homes now used the thick black curtains. They said it was for safety from the protests turned riots, the terrorism spilling over in southern France, and whatever disease was rampaging through Switzerland and now England—thirteen people had died there yesterday according to the news feed. And who knew what the hell was going on in Japan with the bombings. But my dad said the real reason people around here put up the blackout curtains was because they didn't want to see what was really going on.

"Lucy—" I hissed.

But she had already run up to the front door and was jamming her finger on the bell. "Trick or treat," she called.

There was no answer.

Lucy pounded on the door. "Give us all your loot."

"No one's coming." I pulled at her elbow, tried to

guide her away from the security cameras. It was getting late anyway.

She lightly kicked the door with her stiletto boots. "Fine. Be a curmudgeon in your big, fancy house. We've got plenty of other options to satisfy our sugar high. We're—"

The door swung open. From a darkened hallway, a man stared down at us.

"IDs?" he barked.

"It's Halloween!" Lucy countered. "Trick or treat." She held open her bag, nudged me to do the same.

But I froze as the man's eyes zeroed in on me.

"I don't care if it's Christmas," the man said. "You're required. Show 'em."

My ID wasn't in my back pocket. It was in the jeans I had taken off before I changed. I had forgotten to bring it with me.

"I'm calling the police," he said, reaching for the receiver behind his ear.

I grabbed Lucy's hand, tried to pull her away, but she stood her ground.

"Really? On Halloween? If you don't want to give us candy, fine. But you don't have to get all establishment."

Establishment was Lucy's word for the ID checkers at the soccer games, the police, US President Pro Tempore Evans, who had somehow managed to hold on to his "temporary" position for several years now. Lucy even called Jonathan establishment when he was getting political about something. But establishment or not, the man was right. It was the law. The IDs confirmed our citizenship, noted our immigration status, religious practice, and DNA code. On mine, the man would have seen I was a second-generation immigrant of Asian descent. Dad wasn't born here. Of course, the man already suspected—he could see it in my hair, my eyes. But no ID meant the police, suspension for sure, and who knew what next.

I never should have gone out into the streets. I was different—anyone could tell. It wasn't safe.

I had screwed up *everything*.

I yanked Lucy, sent her stumbling. "C'mon," I hissed in her ear, and finally we were off.

"Hey! Stop!" the man yelled after us. "Stop them!"

Lucy took the lead even in her stiletto boots, ducking between two houses, into a backyard, then another, then bursting onto a different street.

"I don't have my card," I told her in spurts of breath.

"You are so antiestablishment, Mina."

"I don't have it!" I protested, angry at her for not getting it, angry at myself for even being in this mess.

Lucy swiveled, studied me in the dim light. It lasted only seconds, but she must have seen my blotchy, teary face, how if I could just catch my breath, I might throw up everywhere.

"Let's get the hell out of here," she said, grabbing my hand as we sprinted out of the neighborhood. She wobbled in her boots, but we held tightly to each other and kept running down Lyceum.

Most of the trick-or-treaters had gone in, the businesses had turned out their lights, and more and more blackout curtains were pulled over shop windows and upstairs apartments. Only the yellow-and-red McDonald's sign glowed as we raced past. Everything was quiet.

"Hold on," I gasped. I ducked into the doorway of the tea bar, behind faux columns, and pulled Lucy after me. Other than the ever-present surveillance cameras above our heads, we were hidden.

"No sirens," Lucy whispered.

"No police."

We caught our breath. Lucy finger-combed her hair. It was almost funny. We had run more tonight than we had in years of PE. I wasn't much of an athlete, and somehow Lucy was always coming down with a stomach bug right before class.

Then we heard the thud of boots.

I froze again, but this time Lucy grabbed me, pulled me deeper into the shadows of the columns.

Somehow, under the pounding feet—so many—and my racing heart, I heard the chant.

"Fighting keeps our country strong, hunting those who don't belong."

It was a brigade troop. From our hiding place, we could see dozens of people marching down the street in formation, boots stomping together, heads lifted high, chanting in time. The brigade troops were nongovernment, nonmilitary, free of any rules but their own. They pooled money to buy guns, body armor, even uniforms. This troop blended into the night with their all-black gear, but I could see the triangular A insignia on their chests: Alphas. They wore guns strapped to their backs, knives sheathed at their sides. Their movements were stiff with the bulky armor but still efficient, deadly.

I pulled farther into the darkness, pressed my back against the tea bar's door, pulled my black cape around my shoulders.

Had the man at the house called them? The brigade could march me to the police station for a payout. But they could also just as soon thrash me. There would be no discussion, no equivocation for a person of color without ID. My heart raced like a rat about to be flushed out by wild dogs.

"Fan out!" someone at the front called in time with the chant.

The formation broke open as the members jogged to their right and left, creating a giant spade down the street. But they were about ten steps too late to find us as they sprinted diagonally across my field of vision and toward the hospital.

I sank to a crouch, my hands around my knees, my head buried.

Lucy joined me, wrapped her arms around me. "It's going to be okay," she murmured. "Bunch of stupid brigaders."

I meant to say something, but the words were clogged in my throat, overwhelmed by my pounding heart and rushing breath.

We stayed that way for minutes, maybe hours, until Lucy pulled me to my feet. "Coast is clear."

I still couldn't say anything. Lucy was wrong. It wasn't the brigade that was stupid. We had gotten insanely lucky. I'd sacrificed everything for a night of fun and candy. Never mind suspension, even expulsion. I could have been swept up, deported. Then Dad would be investigated, probably Mom too.

We weaved through the neighborhood and returned to Florence Hall without incident. We sneaked in through the back door; last year I had programmed my dad's birthdate as an access code. Our entrance wouldn't be recorded, the surveillance cameras over the doorway wouldn't be checked.

As Lucy scanned her thumb at our dorm room door, I finally found the words. "I'm sorry."

"What?" Lucy said, an edge to her voice.

I repeated myself, louder. "I'm sorry I got us into this whole mess. I'm sorry I was so stupid. I'm sorry—"

"No," Lucy said. "It's the stupid establishment, the stupid brigade."

"Stupid Mina for forgetting her card."

"No." Lucy pulled me to her, pressed our sweaty faces together. "No such thing as stupid Mina. It's a stupid racist establishment."

She had gotten it after all.

Chapter 3

Mina

IT HAD BEEN more than two months ago, on a hot, sticky day in late August, when Jonathan left for his internship.

His first message had come through my xphone the very next morning. I was holed up in Rickman Hall, in the school's air-conditioned finance and operations office, trying to get as many hours of work in as I could before school started up again. When Jonathan's message sounded, I was up to my eyeballs in digital receipts, trying to figure out who bought what, whether it was allowed, and what the school owed them. I dropped everything to cast my screen.

Jonathan's face appeared, his dark hair more of a tousled mess than usual. "Arrived at Heathrow Airport," he announced, grinning.

"What's it like?" It would already be midafternoon

there, five hours ahead of me. I'd never even been on an airplane, let alone in another country. "Tell me everything!"

"Well, I haven't made it much farther than the bathroom, but that seemed nice."

"Not *everything!*" I said, laughing. It was good to hear his voice again.

He told me about the flight, how he could see a grid of streets and buildings, then, higher up, a sky full of clouds. The plane had been mostly empty, so Jonathan had been free to get up and stretch his long legs. He hadn't even needed to wear his mask. But he was still feeling restless, anxious to continue his journey.

"I'll message you along the way," he promised before we said our goodbyes.

The internship was something his mom had worked out for him through her firm—he would help collate immigration papers for some old guy in the English countryside who wasn't comfortable with modern technology. It meant traveling to Europe, but the area seemed safe enough. Plus Irving Academy had granted credits for the experience, waiving the fall semester of his senior year. Jonathan figured the "law internship" would look great on his college applications regardless of what he actually wanted to do with his life. Mom would've jumped at that kind of opportunity for me.

Half an hour later, Jonathan messaged more.

I cast a screen to read, "London is a mess. There's a line of people circling the terminal, trying to get in. Of course, they've got cameras everywhere, but still an armed guard had to escort me and the other passengers out."

I grew cold at his words. I had started a spreadsheet listing staff and payments, but it was instantly forgotten. "What kind of people?" I whispered back, the receiver at my ear translating my words into text.

"All different types," his message read. "Mostly English, but some French, maybe Spanish? Some are young like us, there're some families, a few older people. But they're almost all people of color. They've all got masks, gloves, and lots of luggage. I think they're trying to leave."

"Where?"

"For the US. They've got blankets and coolers, even tents. They look like they've been here a while."

After that he was quiet. I got as far as tallying all the receipts, but none of my numbers were matching. Instead, I thought about a line of people, desperate to escape their country, willing to come here, even when they knew what might await them. More than five hundred people had died of the Bloodless Syndrome this year in England alone, and most of them were people of color. The local news kept downplaying the disease: the risk of contagion was low; there had been no reported cases in the US. In other words, it wasn't such a big deal since it didn't apply to white people or Americans. The media refused to call it another pandemic. But most countries had closed their borders to try to stop the infection. Or maybe it was an excuse to keep out immigrants, especially people of color, the so-called "race terrorists" who had been blamed for the massive protests last year. Now people were calling them RATs for short, like people of color were dirty, disease-carrying animals. My family had been keeping their heads down for years, staying out of trouble, avoiding large crowds, and never calling the police. But it all turned my stomach.

Regardless, the disease was real enough. Most died instantly. And in death, all victims looked the same: desiccated, with every drop of blood drained from their skeletal bodies. Researchers hadn't yet figured out the cause, how the disease was transmitted, or who might be next.

"On the train now," Jonathan messaged. "Ready for the long haul."

I remembered us poring over his travel plans together, how the journey from London to York would take six hours, how gradually night would settle over the country. Neither of us had ever been on a train before—they were still used occasionally in Europe, but my dad said track maintenance had been completely abandoned in the US. Nowadays if you really needed to go anywhere, most everyone took driverless shuttles.

"Tell me what you're up to," he said.

So I whisper-texted back, told him about my folder of receipts, about Lucy's plans for one final, wild party before school started. I told him about my increasing

15

anxiety regarding my valedictorian status. "Everyone says senior year is the best, but I have so much riding on it."

"You're the smartest person I know," he said. "And the teachers will ease off a bit in the spring, you'll see. We'll be graduating before you know it."

Who knew what would come next. College, of course. Mom had been planning for years, saving every cent to get me, the baby of the family, the so-called smart one, into Irving. She'd banked on it being a springboard to university no matter my immigration status. But what about me and Jonathan? We'd only known each other for a few months, yet I already couldn't imagine the semester without him.

We messaged on and off for the next few hours. Jonathan narrated the countryside—rolling hills, sheep, stone walls. The train was mostly empty, though this time Jonathan kept his mask on. He said people must not be traveling much anymore except to London. The only activity was in Birmingham, when a military regiment boarded to check IDs again. Jonathan felt lucky to be holding his American ID along with his introductory letter from Mr. Anghen.

I thought he'd finally fallen asleep. I hadn't heard anything in over an hour, and I knew it was getting late there. The receipts had finally added up, but I had a stack of other work to get to. Soon Jonathan would arrive in York, catch a driverless shuttle to this Anghen's house. He'd already warned me the man didn't believe in technology, that his connections might be pretty slow. I'd have to get used to minimal contact from then on out.

"Mina?" Jonathan messaged suddenly. "What's the difference between a dog and a wolf?"

Some people still kept dogs as pets, but the only dogs I remembered ever seeing were the wild packs around Whitby. As for wolves, I didn't even know they were around anymore.

"I suppose wolves are bigger," I messaged back.

"Did I say you're the smartest person I know?" But a minute later he wrote again. "I think there's a pack of wolves running alongside the train."

"Wolves? In England?" I couldn't tell his tone from his words. Was he teasing?

"I could've sworn... But it's dark."

It didn't sound like a joke. "You sure you're not dreaming?"

Maybe he was. I checked my xphone, turned the volume up. After several minutes of silence, I returned to my work, though I never stopped listening. All the way back to Florence Hall I checked, and all the next day.

Finally, around lunch, there was another message: all positive, no wolves, nothing to worry about. He had arrived, the house was nice, Mr. Anghen was too, and Jonathan would write more soon.

I hadn't heard from him since.

Chapter 4

WHIT News

BLOODLESS ORIGINS
Oct 28, 2---

RESIDENTS FIRST NOTICED the smell during an early summer heat wave in Geneva, Switzerland. Initially they blamed the cramped, crowded apartment on the top floor, which housed recent migrants. No one answered repeated knocking. Finally the landlord called the police. Inside, twelve dead, their bodies pale and skeletal, bloodless except for a red, gory warning painted on the nearby wall: IT'S COMING!

If only the rest of the world had paid attention.

At the outset, the incident was dismissed as random, migrant violence. But scientists now believe it to be

Europe's first-known cases of the Bloodless Syndrome. As the disease continues to rampage through Switzerland, France, and England and more people mask up again, we reexamine the case that started it all. Our series will trace the course of the disease, from its potential origins in bats, mosquitoes, or an as-yet-unknown parasite; to treatments that were tried and failed; to hospitals and labs where researchers continue to battle against this novel, deadly illness. Can it be stopped before it becomes the next worldwide pandemic?

Chapter 5

Jonathan

Sunday, August 26

I THINK I'M in danger here.

That sounds as melodramatic as some text-message novel. But it feels good to write it down, to see the words on my notebook page. I'll explain everything. Maybe the words will help me see the logic behind it all. Or serve as evidence for whatever happens. But I'm getting ahead of myself.

Let me start again.

I arrived in Yorkshire to a storybook English house with towers and stone walls. An older man in a suit stood in the front drive.

"Please come in, come in. You are my guest," he said, beckoning me to the open doorway. "You may enter freely."

I was struck by his old-fashioned words, his slightly foreign accent. "Mr. Anghen?" I asked, getting out of my driverless shuttle. Then I wondered if he didn't want his name spread around. Maybe I was supposed to bow? He was some sort of minor aristocrat.

Instead, Mr. Anghen bowed to me. "Count Anghen," he said, correcting me.

Count, that was it! Like the guys that wore the capes—or maybe not.

His hair was wispy gray, his face thin and sunken with age, and he smelled. But after traveling the past several hours in darkness, I was so pleased to see a brightly lit house ahead of me.

While Count Anghen paid for the shuttle, I gathered my luggage. But then Anghen was there. He took my backpack, threw it onto his own shoulder, and picked up my suitcase.

"I can get that—" I protested.

"No, no. You are my guest." He led me through the front door and down a hallway with thick wooden beams overhead. He didn't struggle with the luggage. In fact, I had to rush to keep up with him.

I got little sense of the house from the inside, only a sprawling hodgepodge of stone walls intermixed with modern plaster. He didn't have any blackout curtains— I guess the man lived in the middle of nowhere—but there was the occasional mounted receiver or camera. The technology relaxed me. He wasn't as tech ignorant as he had implied. I followed him through the house, ducking to fit through a doorway, then weaving several flights up a worn staircase before turning in to another hallway. He threw open a door, let me pass in front of him. A red easy chair sat in front of a stone hearth with a blazing fire. There was a table set with a plate, silverware, and a spread of covered dishes.

Beyond was a bedroom with a giant bed covered with blankets and throw pillows. I stepped inside, Anghen following after me and placing my things on the floor beside the bed. He opened a final door into an adjoining bathroom.

"Welcome to Bram Manor," he said, returning to the bedroom door. "I know you've had a long day. Take your time, make yourself comfortable. When you are ready, I can serve you dinner."

I changed clothes, washed my face with a plush towel, and hoped I looked presentable enough. I returned to what I imagined as the sitting room to find Anghen pulling golden covers off serving dishes filled with chicken, rolls, and green beans. There were even two lit candles.

"Please forgive me for not joining you," he said, gesturing toward a chair. "I already dined tonight."

I paused. It wasn't as if I had met any other nobility, but the sight of Count Anghen uncovering those golden platters threw me. He was rich. Didn't he have anyone to do these things for him? It reminded me of those text-message novels Mina loves, the ones about fairies. The rule was you could never eat food a

22

fairy served you, otherwise you'd be trapped in their realm forever. Not that I thought Count Anghen was anything more than human, not then. But the way he had invited me to eat, his strange accent... I hesitated.

But I was starving, so of course I sat down and ate like a pig. I mean, the chicken was real, not imitation, and even the beans didn't have that salty, canned flavor. They must have been fresh.

Meanwhile, Anghen kept up polite conversation, asking after my home, my family, any siblings.

"I'm the only child," I told him. "It's just me and Mom." Actually, it was mostly just me and Grandma in our old house in Whitby—until Grandma died a handful of years ago. I also didn't mention my sperm donor dad whom Mom had picked out of a catalog. People could get a little weird about that.

But Anghen noted it anyway. "So you've always been the man of the house?"

I imagined I could hear Mom cackling all the way from our condo in the suburbs. Mom had always been the man, the woman, my sole provider. She wanted the world for me.

But before I could figure out how to explain any of that, Anghen frowned, looking over my head. The sky had begun to lighten ever so slightly.

"Please forgive me," he announced, standing. "I had not realized it was so late—almost dawn. I will leave you to finish up and make yourself comfortable for a sleep." Then he was gone.

23

My plate was empty. The golden platters in front of me offered more food, but I was no longer hungry. I covered the platters, tidied up as best I could. The leftovers alone had to be worth a fortune. But I was achingly tired. How many hours had I been up? I returned to the bedroom, closed the door behind me.

I pulled the curtains to block out the dawning sun. I changed into my T-shirt and boxers and nestled deep in my bed, which was as comfortable as it looked. I cast my xphone screen, but as Anghen had warned, there was no reception. Bram Manor must be seriously isolated. Regardless, I had my Triangle Connection activated, so it would track down any available signal over dozens of miles. But even as I waited for it to establish service, I was fighting to keep my eyes open. I unhooked my earpiece and placed it on the small table next to my bed. It would wait until tomorrow.

In the distance, over the hum of the house's generator, I could have sworn I heard something howl. Maybe those wolves running alongside the train hadn't been my imagination after all.

Or maybe I was already dreaming.

Chapter 6

Jonathan

Monday, August 27

WHEN I WOKE, it was already late afternoon. In the absence of blackout curtains, I peered out my bedroom window. Several stories below was the circular drive and front door. I gripped the windowsill as vertigo washed over me. I'd never been good with heights. Not that there was much to look at: the day was gray with clouds, maybe rain, and there were no neighbors, only rocky, windswept fields. In my sitting room, dinner had been cleared away and in its place was a hot plate with bacon and eggs (could they possibly be real?), platters of bread and fruit, and even more impressive, a coffee machine bubbling away. Hardly anyone could afford coffee these days.

An actual paper note was propped on the table:

"Dear Mr. Harker,

I am sorry to be away on business for your first day, but please eat and make yourself comfortable."

I pushed aside the disquiet of the night before and poured myself my first cup of coffee. At least he was feeding me. Hell, it looked like he was feeding my whole soccer team! And yes, the coffee was definitely real, as was the bacon. I settled down in a chair.

I wasn't here to like Count Anghen. I was here to do a job, to prove myself to Mom.

After gorging myself on breakfast, I cleaned myself with a real shower (not just absorbing gel!) and dressed. The guest room must not have been used much. Not only was it sparkling clean, there were no mirrors anywhere. I used the xphone behind my ear to cast a screen. Still no reception, but at least I could use the camera to comb my hair.

By the time I was done, my xphone found service, so I sent a quick message to Mom and another to Mina. I opened my virtual reality Dreamscapes game, but the reception wasn't *that* good.

Already I wasn't sure what else to do with myself. I pulled out the folder with the count's paperwork, though everything was in order, the papers clean and unwrinkled. I was a good errand boy. Mom had suggested Anghen wanted more than a courier. He supposedly had questions to ask, information he wanted conveyed to the firm personally, securely. I knew this was great legal experience, and working with a foreign dignitary would look good on my college apps. I just couldn't imagine what more the man expected of me and why it would take a whole semester to do it.

There was another door in the sitting room. It was opposite the door to my bedroom, perpendicular to the room's entrance. I didn't want to go exploring without the count's permission, but it was right there. I cracked open the door.

Books. Everywhere. Bookshelves circled the room, floor to ceiling, like an old-fashioned library. There was another easy chair, a table in the center stacked with newspapers: the *New York Times*, the *Washington Post*, England's *Guardian*, *die Zeit*. I didn't even know they printed newspapers anymore! I moved to the stacks and ran my fingers over rows of worn leather tomes. I even recognized some: *Jane Eyre*, *The Art of War*, *Frankenstein*. Tucked away in another set of shelves were more recent works—bestsellers, critically acclaimed novels with silver awards, nonfiction about the downfall of Detroit, the history of Whitby, the National Park service—all physical books. There were multiple rows of dictionaries—English, Hungarian, Mandarin, Welsh— and so many other books that I didn't recognize, from different cultures, languages. It smelled faintly like him, but who cared? It had to be almost as big as Newholm's media center. I could spend my whole semester reading.

"Good day," Anghen's strange voice announced behind me.

I started but rearranged my face into a smile. "Hello!" My words tumbled over each other. "I hope you don't mind—"

Anghen waved his hand. "No, of course not. I only regret I forgot to mention that you must have free rein of my library."

I exhaled. At least I had the library.

"It's impressive," I said. "You must have spent years collecting it all."

"Hundreds," Anghen said with a smile. "I'm glad you understand its importance. It's a mark of a good student."

My face warmed at the compliment. Not that I was a good student. School was all soccer, video games, and goofing around... but every so often my inner nerd emerged.

Anghen continued. "A good library is especially important for a man like me, trying to immigrate to a new land. I must understand the language, the culture."

"You speak English well." It was true, but I guess I was trying to return the compliment.

Anghen shook his head. "I am pleased to count English citizenship among my accolades, yet I could never be mistaken for a native English speaker."

I had been right. It was on the tip of my tongue to ask—was he Russian? Some other Eastern European country? Mina hates being asked "Where are you

28

from," but sometimes a guy wants to know.

"Well, I hope you don't mind learning a bit of American English," I said instead.

"That's exactly what I had in mind."

"Deal," I said, like I was making a bet with the other guys on my team.

Unexpectedly, Count Anghen offered his hand. Since the pandemic, people didn't really do handshakes. His hands were large and ghostly pale, spotted with thick black hair. His nails were filed to points. I let him grab hold of my hand—after all, he lived in the middle of nowhere. How many germs could the old man be carrying? But I couldn't help a shudder moving through my body. A wave of nausea passed over me. I fought it off, swallowed, smiled as my eyes watered.

But Anghen must have seen. He loosened his grip on my hand, stepped back.

"Why don't I get your papers?" I skirted around him and hurried to my bathroom. Outside my bedroom window, the sun was beginning to set, leaving the room a glowing orange. I ran a towel over my face, shuddered again in private. It hadn't been the handshake itself but something more, something about his hands. And his smell—musky, like something from the Mayfield Zoo. No. I straightened my back, dried my face. *Don't screw up*, I told myself.

I grabbed Anghen's folder and returned to the library.

Anghen was paging through a newspaper. "I am so

appreciative of your coming, Mr. Harker," he said, folding the newspaper. "I am eager to travel to America. I feel lucky not only to have you to double-check I sign my forms correctly but also that you are a young American who can teach me all of your homeland's customs and cultures. I want to be accepted as part of this American experiment, this melting pot, as they call it."

Anghen didn't mention my disappearance at all. Outside of school and close personal friends, people didn't often share their last names. But I wasn't going to get into that with him, not now. And I couldn't imagine calling the count by a first name! Instead, I smiled, this time meeting his eyes. "Call me Jonathan. It's a privilege to be here. I will do whatever I can to help."

"Well then, sit down, sit down. You're too tall to keep standing up."

Anghen and I sat at the table, and he talked me through his business as if I weren't some teenage errand boy but a trusted partner. He told me he intended to put an offer on property in the Whitby area (he kept calling the Midwest "the Heartland") but also rental properties on the East Coast (Boston or New York) and somewhere in Nevada—far enough inland to be safe. Mom's firm had power of attorney to sign purchase agreements, but if he intended to stay long-term, he would also appreciate the firm's help to acquire a visa.

I still didn't understand why he needed me. He seemed to have enough money to buy dozens of lawyers' time, and he already had a firm grasp on the bureaucracy involved. But then he started to ask questions. For example, if he stayed for ninety days without a visa but returned a week later, would that be considered the start of a new ninety days? If a condo association had a homeowner's policy preventing foreign ownership, could he submit a counteroffer? And would any of these rules apply if he settled directly in Whitby, the official Dead Zone? Mom had prepped me to answer those questions and had me study countless articles. Anghen and I talked late into the night about real estate, immigration, Whitby's layout; and I answered his questions as best I could.

"What about the president pro tempore?" Anghen said. "I admit the current complexities of the American democratic experiment have left me quite adrift."

"Well, some think the democracy of it all is a little questionable..." After the president and his entire cabinet were impeached, for some obscure legal reason the same party got to nominate the next president, who would oversee a corruption investigation. It'd been five years since President Pro Tempore Evans was "elected," and of course the investigation still hadn't been completed.

We continued our conversation over dinner in my sitting room and late into the night.

"I apologize that business will take me away again

31

tomorrow," Anghen said. "But please make yourself feel at home, Mr. Harker."

He must have gotten my name from the school's paperwork. I could not get him to call me Jonathan, but I wasn't going to fight it, not tonight.

"Thank you," I said. "It's a beautiful home."

"Some of my doors are locked, but you do not need to worry yourself with them. There is nothing to see behind those doors. It's an old home, and I have not been able to modernize every room."

"Of course," I said. I certainly hadn't planned on prying.

Shortly afterward, Anghen excused himself. In only a few hours, the sun would rise again. I was becoming a nocturnal creature.

Maybe that explained the tremble in my fingers as I remembered Anghen's hands, his locked doors. I needed to get a grip.

Tomorrow I was determined to get up earlier.

Chapter 7

Mina

THE MORNING AFTER Halloween, I was up early. Morning was the best time at Irving: no schedule requirements, no teachers. Newholm's media center would be deserted. I had a quiz in history to review for and calculus homework to double-check. Plus I was already wide awake, my brain running at triple speed, replaying trick-or-treating, the man demanding to see my ID, the brigade, the two thousand ways I had screwed up.

I sneaked into the still-quiet hallway, slipped outside. The moon was bright, peeking out from the smog-covered sky.

A dark shape raced toward me. Muscular, tight clothes, black.

I fell into Florence's doorway, threw myself against the generator. The brigade! They had followed me, had lain in wait. I ducked into the shadows even as I knew it was too late.

"Mimi?"

"Quincey?" I gasped at the familiar voice. "What the hell are you doing?"

"Uh, running?" Quincey offered a hand to pull me to my feet. "I haven't seen you since Lucy's party in September."

Quincey and I had known each other from the first day of Irving Academy. He was Irving's token local black kid, one of the only other students of color in the whole school. We had found each other immediately. He showed me around Whitby; it hadn't always been a Dead Zone. We studied together, commiserated together. Somewhere along the way, he started calling me Mimi, as if I weren't the total opposite of a Mimi.

Last spring, when Dad lost his government job and Mom had to scramble to pay for the rest of the semester, it was Quincey I told. When all those "random" fires started in Whitby, right near his uncle's neighborhood, Quincey and I had watched the newscasts together, contrasted them with what his uncle said was actually happening on the ground. As the years passed, we found our own groups, our own friends, but he had always been there for me.

Except as I took his hand, I found myself staring at his black running clothes, the golden pin on his lapel. "Why are you dressed like a brigader?"

"It's good training."

"You're in the brigade?" I asked, dumbfounded.

"A brigade."

Everything from last night cascaded over me again: the thudding boots; that horrible, racist chant; the way my heart beat as they hunted me like an animal. My hands curled into fists at my side.

"Why?" I hissed, my voice like a gunshot in the early morning.

"Why should only the bad guys train?"

"It's the brigade! The whole point is racism, usurping government services so they can get away with whatever the hell they want. Arresting people, assaulting them, getting them deported so they lose their whole lives!" I couldn't hold back. I jabbed my fist into his side, hard enough that he stumbled against the wall.

"That's why we need to fight back," Quincey said. "The Omegas are a group from Whitby, from my parents' old neighborhood. They're taking a stand against the government, and they need everyone they can get. They're going to protect people like us."

"You don't join the enemy's team!" I yelled. Surely he of all people should understand that.

"We're not joining the enemy, Mimi. We're our own team."

"You're using their tactics!"

He only looked at me as we stood at a silent impasse.

"I thought you'd understand," he murmured.

I hesitated. I wanted to. I trusted Quincey. But as I studied his omega-shaped pin, his black gear, his muscular frame revealing months of hard work, I only thought of huddling in that doorway, shivering with fear, and how it had all happened for no other reason than the color of my skin. I'd been thinking about it all night. I shook my head.

"Okay," Quincey said, stepping back. "I get it. But it doesn't change us."

I nodded. I wanted that to be true. But I wasn't sure it was.

"I need to finish my run," Quincey said.

"I was headed to the media center." We both had places to be, things to do.

"Tell Lucy hello for me."

Lucy and Quincey had always gotten along surprisingly well, like co-conspirators from some virtual reality heist game.

"I will."

But before I turned back to the media center, I watched Quincey run into the darkness ahead.

Chapter 8

Quincey

As QUINCEY RAN, the thoughts crept back on him. His parents and siblings were safe in the suburbs, but his uncle insisted on staying in Whitby's Dead Zone. There'd been a CMS raid—the federal government's Citizen & Migrant Security, though there was nothing secure about them—two blocks from his uncle's house last night. Last month there'd been another fire in the neighborhood down the street—the third in the past year. Of course the Omega Brigade was blamed, but everyone knew it was CMS. As a Dead Zone, Whitby didn't have police, fire, or emergency services; its entire governance was reliant on nearby Newholm. So when a building burned, it burned. Clearly the federal government was determined to destroy the Omegas even if it meant they destroyed all of Whitby in the process.

And Whitby wasn't alone. There were Dead Zones throughout the country—all former large cities, all filled with people of color, and all those people no longer counted as citizens, no longer held any basic rights. But maybe, if they all joined the fight, maybe they could win.

He lengthened his stride, flew faster. As if he could outrun it all. After all, in his brigade gear, no one ever harassed him. The police ignored him as long as they didn't get close enough to notice the Omega pin or his black skin.

He thought of Mina's darting eyes, her panic as he approached. He got it, even as he knew he was right about the Omegas. But would it be enough?

He pushed himself harder, faster. He wouldn't think about any of it. He imagined each step was a beat of a poem, accelerating like his heartbeat. If he could be fast enough, he'd be free.

He thought about Lucy instead. He flew along the road, above it, as if his feet had grown wings.

She was altogether too white for him, too privileged. But he didn't feel that way when he was around her. She listened. She asked questions. She made him feel like he could be anyone.

Lucy.

Chapter 9

Jonathan

Tuesday, August 28

OF COURSE I forgot to set the alarm on my xphone. I hurried to eat breakfast, shower. When I got out, I heard someone in the other room. Probably Anghen, cleaning up breakfast even while wearing his suit. I felt bad that the old man was always cleaning up after me, especially since he never joined me for meals. I pulled on my cozy pants again and threw on a T-shirt, then leaned out of the bathroom. Anghen was in the doorway across the room.

"Don't worry," I called. "I'll be out in a minute. I can clean up."

Anghen nodded but continued to stack dishes. I shook my head, returned to the bathroom. I needed to shave, but then I would be right out. I cast my screen

39

against the wall, above the sink, in place of a mirror. I started to close the door, but it was strange: I couldn't see Anghen's reflection behind me. I could see the door, the other door, the table Anghen had been standing over—everything but him.

I turned around, thinking he'd left, but he said, "Take your time, Mr. Harker."

I stared back at the screen. No reflection. Maybe it was something about the technology, the distance, or the lack of reception.

Whatever it was didn't matter. I shaved quickly, only half paying attention, so I nicked myself. Not bad, but bad enough that blood welled up. I fumbled for tissue in my toiletries kit. When I couldn't find any, I grabbed some toilet paper.

I heard something. I glanced at the screen, but nothing was there.

Then Anghen was right behind me. I heard a low murmur—a growl?—and spun around. My hand absently poked at my cut with toilet paper.

Anghen towered over me, his arms outstretched. His mouth gaped open, revealing teeth like knives. I stumbled back, tripped over my toiletries kit, then fell to the tile floor.

My heart raced; my brain couldn't keep up. Anghen didn't look like himself. He didn't look human—more like an animal. His scent overpowered me—musky, wild. *Move!* something inside me screamed. But I couldn't even blink.

Then he was on me. His fingers wrapped around my neck. My whole body felt limp in his arms. I might have closed my eyes. I was shaking,

But he froze. I opened my eyes, saw a drop of blood on the white tile. But Anghen was staring at my chest. He had shrunk back to his regular self, somehow frailer, whiter, his hair gray. His hands dropped to his side.

"What is that?" he whispered.

I looked at my own chest as best I could. My necklace must have escaped from my shirt. I kept it hidden for obvious reasons, but I'd worn it since I turned thirteen, since my grandmother had hung it around my neck and told me I was grown up now. "My Star of David."

Anghen shook his head vigorously like a wild dog, but then he was himself. His eyes moved from the blood on the floor back to my face. I imagined he saw tears, more blood, terror. I pressed the toilet paper into my neck.

"Be careful with cuts," Anghen murmured. "Even the smallest cut can be more dangerous than you can imagine." He started to leave but stopped at the screencast opposite, showing the sink, the door, the door beyond, everything but Anghen.

"ARE YOU RECORDING ME?" Anghen screamed. He grabbed for my ear, yanked the xphone receiver. "You will not use your technology against me."

He stormed out of the bathroom.

"Wait!" Somehow I made it to my feet even as my whole body shook. He couldn't take my xphone! "Count Anghen!" I called. "I wasn't recording you!" He wasn't listening, even as I charged after him. "I'll put it away, you'll never see it again—"

He pushed open a window so hard it rattled in its frame. Then he pulled back his arm and threw my earpiece like some old-fashioned baseball player. I jolted forward only in time to watch my xphone fly into the sunset.

Anghen slammed the window shut and strode from my room.

Chapter 10

Mina

WHEN MY XPHONE chimed before study hall, I knew who it was.

"You got a C on a test?" Mom demanded.

"A quiz," I started to explain. "I got up early to study, but—" I hesitated. I knew Mom would get the fear, my fury at Quincey. But would she understand how, even as I had tried to study, the words had swum in front of my eyes? How I'd been unable to concentrate on any dates or names? I knew what she would say about my sneaking out last night, forgetting my ID, almost ruining everything. And she'd be right.

"Do you know how much your father and I have sacrificed to keep you in that school?"

I settled on my bed. Never mind what I told her—it was going to be one of those conversations.

Of course I knew what they had sacrificed. When

43

President Pro Tempore Evans, in an effort to increase economic opportunities for "hardworking Americans," had eliminated all government positions for non-white or immigrant Americans, Dad had lost his job. It was the same department he'd been working at for decades, the same place he had been when he first met Mom. Mom signed up for every extra project or overtime possible at the insurance agency where she worked while Dad found custodial work plus some neighborhood handyman jobs. There were so few secondary schools left, and none near home. I was the smart one in the family, the youngest with two much older brothers. Mom and Dad had pinned all their hopes on me. But Irving Academy didn't come cheap.

"You need an education," Mom continued. "If you want to get anywhere in this country, you need to prove to them that you're the best."

Of course she was right. It wasn't that one quiz was so important, but there couldn't be any mistakes. Irving Academy was selective, competitive. It would be easy enough for Mark or Deborah to slide into my valedictorian slot. It was my only shot at college, maybe a stable, nongovernment job in one of the tech towns. For a girl like me, there was no prize for second best.

"I'll be better," I promised. "I'll work hard. I'll keep valedictorian. I'll make it all worth it."

***

"Why of course I'll have this dance."

44

I was jolted from my history reading. My screen cast a circle of light around me. Otherwise everything was pitch-black. I could barely make out the shadow of Lucy's bed.

She tittered again. "I dance with all the boys, you know. I like to keep my eye on them."

Lucy was dancing in her dreams.

I hadn't been focused on my history anyway. I had been desperate to catch up, drill into my head everything I'd missed. But instead, I'd been thinking about Quincey's brigade, my promise to Mom to work harder, the newscast about how someone had tied a dead rat to an Asian immigrant's front door. Somehow, amid all that, Jonathan's final whisper text had once again appeared in my screencast.

"Be careful. It's cold over here," Lucy murmured into the dark.

Lucy talked in her sleep sometimes. It was weird, especially since I was one of those people who never even remembered my dreams. Lucy said it happened when she was stressed or coming down with something. Sometimes, she claimed, she even walked around. But in all our years together, I hadn't seen anything and had never heard anything more than the occasional nonsense word. Until tonight.

Marking where I had drifted off in my history reading, I closed my screencast and let my eyes adjust to the darkness. Lucy shifted in her sleep, rolled to her side. It was late, and I needed sleep too. School could wait until tomorrow.

I heard a creak at the end of the hall. It must have been Mrs. Holmes, Florence Hall's dorm mother, on patrol. Frequently she was checking up on Lucy, who was forever hosting late-night parties or video game marathons or sneaking out. Thankfully Lucy was equally good at talking herself out of trouble. Everyone adored Lucy. It would be incredibly annoying if she weren't also my best friend. Even though Lucy was the type to dream about dancing and I was the type to stay up late getting ahead in history, somehow, since the beginning of freshman year when we were randomly thrown together, we had always made the perfect team.

"It's because of the war. When it comes, we won't dance anymore. Everyone will be dead."

Lucy turned once more in her sleep, and as my own breathing settled, I could hear a faint whistling snore.

I lay down, tried to force myself to sleep. But I heard Lucy's ghostly whisper over and over in my head: "We won't dance anymore. Everyone will be dead."

Chapter 11

Mina

THE NEXT MORNING when my xphone alarm chirped and I rolled over, Lucy was gone. I threw on a sweatshirt, grabbed my toiletries bag, and hurried to the dorm bathroom.

"You're up," I said, spotting her at the far sink.

"Hair," she murmured around the hair tie in her mouth as she wove a French braid.

I watched her for a moment too long. Her eyes met mine in the mirror.

"Teeth," I said, searching for my toothbrush. "Why are you up anyway?"

Lucy frowned at the mirror, tugging a strand of hair at the very top and then loosening the whole braid. "Breakfast," she said, spitting out her hair tie. "I'm hungry."

Lucy was never up this early. I grabbed hold of my

47

toothbrush, squirted some toothpaste on it. "Did I keep you up?"

Lucy shook her head. "How late were you up doing history?"

"Not too long. You don't remember anything else?"

Lucy finished her braid and looked at me. "What?"

"You were talking in your sleep."

Lucy groaned. "I didn't say anything too weird, did I?"

"Do you remember what you were dreaming?"

Lucy shook her head. "C'mon, say it. Was it really horrible?"

"You said everyone would die."

Lucy spat out a laugh. "That *is* horrible!"

"You said there wouldn't be anyone left to dance."

Lucy snorted. "What a drama queen!" She inspected her braid in the mirror one last time. "You coming to breakfast with me?"

I watched her in the mirror. "You sure you're okay?"

"Did I scare you? Mom says it's really creepy." Lucy wrapped an arm around my side, leaned in close. She talked to our reflection in the mirror. "But I didn't jump off any staircases, okay? I don't even remember my dream. Seriously, if I was dancing, how bad could it be?" She squeezed me tightly. "C'mon, do breakfast with me. You're my favorite roomie!"

"Your only roomie," I said, rolling my eyes. But I agreed. History could wait.

It wasn't until we were rounding the last set of stairs into Florence's basement cafeteria that I realized Lucy had never fully answered my question. "Wait... Why are you really up? You never eat breakfast."

A sneaky smile crept onto Lucy's face. "Let's just say it's been a new thing lately."

"Lucy Westin, you tell me right now what's going on."

Her smile grew wider. "Better, I'll show you. Now get your breakfast."

I grabbed a bowl of cereal while Lucy inspected the imitation eggs, sausages, and even the waffle station before helping herself to some toast and canned fruit. Lucy had hardly ever eaten breakfast before, but honestly I couldn't think of the last time I had made it there myself. I had been getting up early each morning to get more work done, to get a little further ahead. I had wanted to start senior year off on the right foot, to make sure there was no questioning my valedictorian status, but now I felt like I was running just to stay in place. *One breakfast won't kill you*, I reminded myself. I filled a cup of milk and followed Lucy. She slid into a seat opposite a chiseled, tanned blond.

"Morning, Arthur," she said in a cheerful voice.

"Morning, Lucy," he said, lighting up like a screencast.

Ah. Got it.

I slid into the seat next to her.

"You know Mina?" Lucy asked.

"A bit," Arthur said, turning his full attention on me. "Arthur Godalming."

Last name and everything, like he had nothing to hide. "Morning," I said, nodding to Lucy's latest prey. At least he was polite, if a bit officious.

"Mina's my absolutely incredible roomie," Lucy said by way of introduction. "An inspiration. Someday she's going to change the world, you just watch. And Arthur"—she gestured to him—"Arthur and I were friends in elementary school, but this year we've got the school news together and we started talking again." Lucy grinned. "He's been working these graveyard shifts at the hospital's detention center, so it's easiest if we meet for breakfast."

"Detention center?" I couldn't imagine why anyone would want to work there. Technically the detention centers were medical facilities for people with drug addictions or mental health problems. In reality, they were usually a holding pen for any person of color, immigrant, or revolutionary the government wanted to disappear.

"He wants to be a doctor," Lucy gushed.

Arthur and I had probably never talked before, but I recognized him. He had played soccer with Jonathan. Instead of the typical xphone earpiece, he had a pair of expensive specrays propped in his hair. And of course he was ridiculously handsome. I could see why Lucy was, at that very moment, seductively sucking on her spoon.

"I missed you yesterday," he murmured to Lucy like she was the only girl in the world. Exactly how many breakfasts had I skipped?

"We had a Halloween adventure," Lucy said. "I couldn't bear to get up."

"Really?" Arthur raised his eyebrows.

I bit my lip. I hadn't expected Lucy to spread my gossip all around.

"Mina was a witch and I was a pirate, like in that Dreamscapes adventure."

I sat back on the bench as she described our costumes, the mound of candy we had collected, and how we had blended in with all the other, younger trick-or-treaters. Nothing else. I should have trusted her.

"We even got some exercise!" Lucy cackled. She and the PE department had never seen eye to eye.

Lucy was practically glowing. There were no visible effects of last night's dreams or whatever might have triggered them. Hell, had I known breakfast would be this awkward, I wouldn't have bothered.

I leaned into Lucy, whispered, "I think you've got this covered."

"Wait, Mina," Arthur said. "I wanted to ask… how's Jonathan?"

I was surprised, but I guess Arthur probably remembered me the same way I remembered him.

"He's…" I stopped, unsure what to say. "He actually hasn't been in touch much, so it's hard to say."

Arthur frowned. "Really? But he was wild about you."

I shrugged like it was nothing.

But Arthur peppered me with more questions. "He's in England, right? Or Scotland? With the earl or something? Has he bumped into any of the pandemic mess over there?"

"I'm not sure," I said. "Maybe Mr. Anghen is a count?"

Arthur shook his head. "I don't know the name."

I remembered Jonathan once saying that Arthur equaled money. His dad was some bigwig in the military, stationed in Europe.

"When did Jonathan leave?" Arthur asked.

"Late August."

"Weird," Arthur said. But then his eyes shifted back to Lucy, and my xphone whispered the time in my ear.

I could still get to class early, maybe finish the history reading. "I think I'm going to head out."

"See you," Lucy said.

"I'll ask some of the guys on the team," Arthur said. "Someone's bound to have heard from him."

"Thanks." As I left, their conversation bubbled up again. A little sadness rushed through me. For a brief moment in time, Jonathan and I had been like that. I hadn't mentioned it to Arthur, or even Lucy, but Jonathan was scheduled to return in just a few days. November 5. But I hadn't heard a thing.

***

Jonathan and I had only met last spring.

I had just started working for the finance and operations office most days after classes. One afternoon my boss left early and asked if I'd close the door on my way out. I finished my work for the day and had my coat on before I realized how quiet it was. Perfect math homework conditions. I sank back to my desk, cast my screen, and started puzzling through my assignment.

The office was in the basement of Rickman Hall, an old brick building. The upstairs, with all the administrative offices, was elegant—tall windows, columns, a vaulted ceiling. The basement was more cramped with funky carpet and wood paneling. Only when I finished my math did I realize the building had grown dark with the setting sun. It was almost seven. I'd already missed dinner and was about to be late for study hall.

I returned to my screen, whisper-texted Lucy. "Tell Mrs. Holmes I had to work late. I'm coming." I wouldn't have a pass, but if I hurried, I could make it in the next five minutes.

I gathered my stuff, closed the door behind me, and started upstairs. Then I froze. A voice was chanting.

It was singsongy; speeding up, slowing down. But the language was unfamiliar. Plus I hadn't thought anyone was there.

I gripped the banister, steadied myself. "Hello?"

Nothing. No answer, but no more voices either.

Maybe it had been music from outside? I continued up the stairs. The lobby was dark. I made it to the front door before I noticed the candlelight in a side alcove.

Someone was having a picnic of some sort. He had a blanket spread out with little containers of various things. He wore a black beanie on his head and studied an open book, then recited again in that other language, part song, part words.

It looked like some kind of one-person religious service. I hadn't realized there was such a thing. I thought you needed a group—a congregation, that was the word. But then again, I'd only been inside a church once and never a synagogue or mosque or anything. The government had closed the latter before I was born. Christianity was still technically legal, but ever since the Lansing Marches, when those Michigan pastors had dared to protest outside the state capitol, any religious affiliation would be noted on your ID card and tracked in a government database.

The ritual didn't seem as silly as I would've imagined. The guy kept reading, stopped occasionally to drink or eat, then returned to the text. It was strangely mesmerizing.

Jewish, I decided. I had seen pictures of the hat before. I reflexively cast my screen, pulled up images of Jewish ceremonies. Yep, there was the hat: a yarmulke. And the time. I was officially *late* late for study hall. "Shit."

"Shit!" he echoed in surprise. He jumped up,

scattering a bowl of something or other. A jug tipped dangerously before he snatched it. "Sorry," he murmured. "I didn't realize anyone was here."

I should have hurried out the door. But I had questions. "Rosh Hashanah or Yom Kippur?"

"Huh?"

"Those are the two main Jewish ceremonies, right?" I was pretty sure I had read that somewhere. There was another one I remembered, but that sounded complicated, with children and costumes, and there was no evidence of that.

He didn't answer my question, but of course, why would he? No one wanted their name on government radar.

"I didn't mean to disturb anyone. I thought the old synagogue would be empty—" He snapped his mouth shut. Instead, he knelt on the floor, closed his book, and started shoveling what looked like apple chunks back into one of the containers. "I'm on my way out."

"Rickman Hall is an old synagogue?" I asked. But as my eyes ran along the arch above him to the design in the cement roof, I could see it was kind of churchy.

He kept fumbling with the various containers, fitting on their lids. He had said too much and he knew it.

I knelt beside him, picking up one of the lids and searching for its matching bowl. "You don't have to leave," I said. "I'm not anyone important. Besides, I've got to get to study hall."

"Is it seven already?" he asked, standing upright.

He must have been a student, but I didn't recognize him. I also didn't move. He was taller than I had realized at first, with broad shoulders and dark, tousled hair.

"What ceremony?" I asked again. I'm nosy, okay? I like to know things.

He looked at me. His eyes were a startling blue. "It's Pesach. Passover."

"What is it all about?"

"It commemorates freeing the Israelites from slavery. There was Moses, then ten plagues. They survived because God passed over their homes, then they left Egypt."

I prided myself on my memory, on reading everything. But I had never heard of any of this.

"Sorry." He bent down for the last of the containers. "I have to go. No one can know. I shouldn't have come. I shouldn't have—"

I rose to my feet so he could pick up the blanket. Except I hadn't realized I was so close. When I stood, we were only inches apart.

"I won't tell anyone," I whispered. There was something mysterious about him, something dangerous. "Do you believe in it?"

"Yes," he whispered back.

"Explain it to me."

He only hesitated for a second. "Sit down. I'll show you."

We finished the ceremony together. Jonathan answered my questions, and then we kept talking, about religion, school, life. He showed me his grandmother's old book, which had the prayers and services written out along with the transliterated Hebrew. He talked about how she had left it to him secretly, without telling his mom, because she wanted him to choose for himself whether to believe. He hadn't known what to think about this secret religion, but when he had missed her, he had studied her book. I told him about my dad, who wasn't religious at all but would still light incense at the New Year to remember his parents.

When we finally made it outside, the sky was velvety black. It was like everything had colluded; the trees had decided to whisper in the breeze, the moon to shine through the smog. Our bodies were so close together, almost touching. Like magic. I leaned into him. His lips brushed across my own. I opened my mouth. We kissed again.

When I made it to Florence Hall, my xphone showed a screen full of Lucy's messages. But before I could even read them, I had to report to Mrs. Holmes. I would serve my first-ever detention. I stuck to the math homework story. I couldn't have explained anything else even if I had tried.

But all night I smiled with my magical secret.

It had happened astoundingly fast. But somehow it had stuck. Maybe because I knew a side of Jonathan no one else had ever seen. We had been together ever since.

Or so I had thought.

Chapter 12

Jonathan

Tuesday, August 28–Saturday, September 1

SOME PEOPLE THOUGHT I was reckless for going to Europe for the summer. *Don't you follow the news?* they had asked. I explained how that was Switzerland mostly. The Filipino terrorists were in Japan, halfway across the world. London might be dangerous with the sickness, but not northern England. Especially not the remote county of Yorkshire. *There're no minibuses out there. I have to take a driverless shuttle to get to his house*, I had told them. Mom hadn't been afraid. She had only talked about the opportunity. If Mina had been scared for me, she had kept it to herself. We had wanted to spend the rest of our time exploring other things.

Now I was afraid. It wasn't something simple like heights or some terrorist army or unidentified disease.

It was Anghen himself. He had shifted, become someone darker than I had realized. Someone dangerous. And without a phone, I had no news, no connections, no communication with Mina or Mom or anyone.

"Would it be possible to go outside tomorrow?" I asked that night at dinner. I started abruptly, before I had quite realized the words were coming out of my mouth. But I had to see what was left of my phone, maybe even get reception, let Mina know— "I haven't had a chance to walk, to see any of the grounds."

"I'm afraid the grounds aren't much to speak of," Anghen said. "They're rocky, remote, and the wolves..." He shook his head.

"Wolves?" I echoed. I thought that had only been in my dreams.

"They are numerous and quite wild in this region. I would not recommend any exploration. But of course, you must go wherever you wish. Make yourself at home here. *Mi casa es su casa*, isn't that what they say?"

I nodded blandly.

"However, please make sure you sleep only in your bedroom. The house is old and carries many strange memories. I would hate for you to fall asleep elsewhere and be troubled by dreams. Especially ones from which you may not wake."

He smiled again, wide and toothy, then took his leave.

I returned to the window. Without blackout

curtains, I could stare into the nothingness for a long time. I couldn't see any pieces of my xphone. After the sun set, I could barely see the front drive. It wasn't as scary being high in the darkness. Apparently, my brain was stupid enough to only be afraid of the things I could see.

I pushed at the window, but it didn't move. I pushed harder, putting my whole body into it. I couldn't see any locks or screws. But however Anghen had opened the window, I couldn't do it. I slammed my fist against the glass. Nothing broke, but my knuckles cracked and blood welled up. I sucked my fist, closed my eyes. Then, remembering what Anghen had said, I dug through my toiletries for the box of Band-Aids Mom had made me pack.

My hands were shaking so badly I could hardly get the Band-Aid on. I pressed them together, as if in prayer.

Sudden movement caught my eye. Outside, toward the back of the house, I could see one of the old towers rising above the roof. Then I saw the shadows move.

I pressed my face against the glass, cupped my hands to block out the light behind me.

It was him! Anghen stuck his face out the tower window. For a brief moment, I smiled with dark humor. Maybe he was trying to escape too? But my smile fell, my breath caught in my throat as I watched the man pull his entire body out the window and climb down, headfirst.

He moved like a lizard, his hands clenching at the rough stonework, somehow supporting his entire body. His boots dug into the stone, pushing him down the side of the wall. He wore a black trench coat that billowed out behind him like black wings.

Stumbling, I backed away from the window. So many things were rushing through my mind: Anghen never joining me at meals, how he had carried my suitcase quickly upstairs, as if it weighed nothing, his body like a reptile as it scaled the wall. And the way he had been drawn to my blood— What if Anghen was not a man at all? A vampire?

I tried to laugh, but the sound choked in my throat. My hands twitched, desperate for action, but what?

I had to capture it, every piece of information, make some sense of it all.

I searched for the mini-notebook Mom had dug up for me, back when our biggest worry had been Anghen's disuse of technology. I flipped to the first page and started writing.

Chapter 13

Jonathan

Wednesday, October 3

I HAVEN'T BEEN keeping this notebook as updated as I should in the past weeks. I've tried every door and window in the house. Although I haven't found any way to escape should it come to that, in my head, I have a layout of Bram Manor's interior as well as the exterior. The tower room from which Anghen exited that night faces northeast, the back corner of the house. I stood outside what must be the tower door for several minutes, listening intently, hardly daring to draw breath, but I heard nothing.

One night I kept watch at a hall window where I could see the tower better. Sure enough, after dinner, as dusk set, the window opened and Anghen emerged. Without hesitation, he descended the house wall. My stomach twisted, but I kept watching until his figure disappeared in shadows.

I returned to a door at the base of the other back tower. The door was wedged shut but not locked. With some careful maneuvering, I pulled it open and climbed the stairs. The door at the top opened to another room. I checked the window. It faced the back of the house, exactly as I had expected. When Anghen returned to his tower, I would have a better view, might be able to figure out what his errand had been, get a sense of his routine.

The room was thick with dust, the furniture draped in cloths. But somehow it was strangely pretty. A cloth-covered chair sat positioned in front of a stone fireplace. Elegant curtains hung to the floor. A wooden desk in the corner had remained uncovered. The room obviously wasn't in use, but I could imagine some woman from long ago sitting at the desk, writing poems or love letters or Gothic thrillers for all I knew. I liked it. I moved the chair to the window and sat down. I pulled my notebook from my pocket, and while I kept watch, I reread what I had written.

I was sure, like my xphone, my notebook was contraband. If Anghen ever discovered it, he'd destroy it. If I wanted Mina to read it, I'd have to keep it safe.

Focus, Jonathan. I looked out the window—Anghen had not appeared below.

It was a clear night. In this rural area, without any of the US's factory farms, I could even see stars. But

they looked different than I expected. More colorful.
Maybe I was tired, but the stars had auras of green,
pink, blue. I could have sworn they were moving ever
so slightly. Or was I shaking? The window seemed
hazy, like a mist had settled over it. I finished my last
sentence and jammed my notebook deep into my
pocket.

I closed my eyes as if I could reset my vision. I
must have been tired. My eyes felt heavy when I
opened them again. The colorful stars were still there.
They moved past me, right through the glass, into the
room.

I felt like my head was too thick, my thoughts
muddled. The stars were coalescing into shapes. Long,
slender, feminine shapes. I thought of Mina. I hardly
dare to write what happened next. But I know I have
to.

The stars grew more numerous, formed into
sparkling eyes, ruby mouths. Before I understood what
was happening, there were three naked women in the
room with me. I jolted in my chair. One was tall and
thin with long dark hair. The hair reminded me of
Mina. The woman was beautiful. Her eyes sparkled as
they settled on me. But I was so afraid.

For all her beauty, there was something terrible
about her. Her lips were red, as if they were painted
with blood, not lipstick. She held her mouth slightly
open, breathed through it. The teeth biting into her lip
were pointed. *Vampire!* my brain insisted. But I couldn't

stop looking. My eyes traveled down her body.

No. I darted one last glance at the window. I didn't see Anghen, but the glass was so thick with condensation I'm not sure I could have seen anything. I turned to the two other women, both blond. One was petite, the other curvy. I couldn't stop staring. I'd seen naked women before of course: in paintings, videos, Mom dressing. But never this close, never in person. Mina and I had never gone this far. I had wanted to save something, wait until we were older. My whole face burned. I needed to use the opportunity to ask my questions about Anghen, the house, escape.

A throaty growl interrupted my thoughts. The sound echoed in my ears, pulsed through my body.

The dark-haired woman hunched over me. No— not like a human at all. Her body was arched, the muscles in her arms flexed, her fingers spread like claws. The other two were behind her, circling, like wild cats stalking their prey. Me.

When the dark-haired one growled again, it was long, deep, raised all the hairs on my body.

I gripped the armrests, stuck in the chair before her. I needed to get up, to move, to fight, but I couldn't make my body obey. My legs felt heavy as concrete. It was like trying to run in a swimming pool. Or a dream.

The creature slunk closer. A thick, musky smell filled my senses. Like Anghen. Her eyes flashed a glowing red.

I closed my eyes.

Her hand sprang out, grabbed my neck. I jerked back. My whole body shivered uncontrollably. My brain too was buzzing out of control.

But she held me in place, trapped against the chair. Her skin was cold, like something dead, frozen.

Her tongue tasted my jaw.

I squeezed my hands, screamed.

Teeth pressed against my boiling skin.

Suddenly feet pounded up the stairs. There was another growl, loud, deep. The creature in front of me jumped back.

A giant black wolf burst into the room. Another growl rumbled in its chest as it came closer.

I fell back in my seat, my pulse racing. I squeezed my knees to my chest, buried my eyes like a child hiding.

But the next voice I heard was Anghen's. "Did you touch him?"

"No, we left him alone," one of the creatures spat out. I couldn't distinguish between their voices.

Human footsteps pounded right to my chair. I kept my eyes closed tight. It felt as if the night itself had approached, was staring me down.

"The boy belongs to me," Anghen announced. "I told you. If you touch him, you will be damned to hell for all eternity in the space it takes me to slice through your heart. Stay away from the boy." He slammed something, maybe a fist, against the wall. The room echoed with his anger.

"But we're hungry!" one of the creatures growled, more noise than words.

"I brought you dinner," Anghen said.

There was another voice, a cry. My eyes darted open. A white carrier box was in the corner. Something inside was moving, thrashing against its lid. It cried again. A human cry.

I squeezed the armrests harder, my blood pulsing in my ears. What was in that box?

It screamed, a bloodcurdling, never-ending scream. That's the last thing I remember.

Chapter 14

Mina

IT WAS AFTER calculus, a few days since the awkward breakfast, that I ran into Arthur outside of class. Literally.

"Whoa, whoa." He put his hands out to catch me.

I stepped back, righted myself, face blazing. "Sorry."

"I was hoping I'd bump into you again," Arthur said without missing a beat.

I couldn't help smiling. Point to Lucy—he was charming.

"No, really," Arthur said. "Can I walk with you?"

"Uh, sure." Was this about Lucy?

We walked out of the modern Lovelace Hall, along the sidewalk toward Rickman. I would get in some work hours before dinner. The air was wet, the sky a slate gray.

Arthur kept his specrays propped on his head, his eyes clear. "You haven't heard any more from Jonathan, have you?"

I shook my head, braced myself. Today had been the day Jonathan was supposed to return. Of course, I hadn't heard a thing. But Arthur clearly had news. Maybe Jonathan had run off with someone from London. Or he had joined some heroic cause, like the fight against that white supremacist army in France. But more than likely, he was just enjoying his work, learning a ton, having even more fun, and was too busy to bother with me.

"I chatted with some of the guys on the team, then a few others, and no one's heard from him. So I messaged Tom. You remember him?"

I nodded even though I couldn't picture a specific face for the name. I wanted to hear what came next.

"Tom graduated last year, ended up being a walk-on for Michigan's team. Jonathan knew it was going to look bad, him not playing his senior year, but he had told Tom he'd be back in November. There're so few people who have the money and education to go on to college anymore. Tom had offered to have Jonathan come up, take in a game, some practice with the team, maybe even a chance to play in front of the coach, you know?"

I did vaguely remember something about that.

"But Jonathan hasn't been in touch. He's not answering calls, messages, nothing."

"The place he's staying has bad reception," I murmured, as I'd told myself daily. "He has to rely on one of those connection apps."

"But Tom hasn't heard anything from him. I mean, the coach even offered to fly Jonathan out for a long weekend. Nothing."

I stared at Arthur, taking it all in.

"Look, I know it's none of my business. It's not like Jonathan and I were super close, but Lucy's been worried about you, and... it's weird, right? You should check with the headmaster, or even Jonathan's parents, just to make sure he's okay."

I had never actually met Jonathan's mom. But I could ask the administration, I supposed. Surely they had to know if Jonathan's circumstances had changed.

"Because here's the thing," Arthur continued. "That name, Anghen. It's not familiar at all. There's only so many old, noble families left. So I did some research, asked my dad, he asked some people around England, Scotland, France... No one's ever heard of an Anghen."

"What?" I stopped walking. "But this was an internship. His mom's firm set it up."

"Right," Arthur said. "It's weird."

A shiver started up my back as Arthur continued. "Everyone I've spoken to, everything I've looked up, there's no trace of the man."

Chapter 15

Arthur

November 6, Newholm Detention Center

Patient 562:
    Age: 47
    Ethnicity: African American
    Gender: Male
    Condition: Stable
    Heart rate: 72
    Blood pressure: 122/74

WHILE PATIENT 562 slept, Arthur double-checked the screencasts and updated the records.

He hoped he hadn't sounded like a complete creeper with Mina. Between Tom and the rest of the team and Dad, who knew everyone, and then the people Dad reached out to—it was weird. Plus Lucy had been anxious for Mina. But Jonathan could take care of himself. And Mina—she seemed like she could take care of herself too. Except when some random guy sneaked up on her after class.

Yep, complete creeper.

Really, it was about Lucy. She'd told Mina she and Arthur recently reconnected, but honestly, he'd been obsessed with Lucy since they were both five years old. Lucy was the happiest person he'd ever met.

Focus. Arthur looked back at the patient, who was still sleeping. Mr. Renfield, according to the detention center records. It was a government facility, so there was no secrecy around patients' last names.

No one had believed Arthur when he first got the job at the DetCen: not his dad, not his mom, not her girlfriend, not even any of his friends. It wasn't like Arthur was interested in politics or needed the money. Everyone knew Godalmings were strictly military. But Arthur liked taking care of people. He liked finding out their stories, how they had ended up in the DetCen, maybe in a small way helping them get better. It was a small DetCen with intake limited to Newholm and a few long-term cases, so there hadn't been much action. Mostly his job seemed to be watching people sleep. Apparently not many other people signed up for the graveyard shift, especially at a detention center.

"Fly."

Arthur jerked from his chair. His eyes darted around, settled on Mr. Renfield smiling in the dim light.

Mr. Renfield pointed toward the ceiling and the steel ductwork running across it. Now that he mentioned it, Arthur could hear a faint buzzing.

"Is it bothering you?" Arthur said.

Mr. Renfield shook his head. "Is it bothering you, Doctor?"

As much as Arthur wanted to help, he didn't always know what to say to the patients. Especially Renfield. He was a tall, angular man, middle-aged, with terrible dreams that kept him up at all hours. But at times he was also like a little brother who knew Arthur's every weak point and poked at them constantly. It was like he knew Arthur was only playing doctor.

The fly came out of the duct.

"Doctor?"

"I'm not your doctor, Mr. Renfield."

"Only a 'ward monitor,'" he said, making air quotes with his fingers. "Only a high school student. Sorry. I forget."

Arthur mindlessly cracked his knuckles. It was better to ignore Mr. Renfield and his little jokes, stay polite, professional.

Mr. Renfield moved his head with the fly, watching. Suddenly he shot out his hand and grabbed the fly in a fist. Arthur stared at where the fly had been, but the buzzing had stopped. Impressive.

"I've got him, Doctor," Mr. Renfield said. Then he jammed his fist in his mouth, opened his fingers, and swallowed.

"Did you—?"

"I ate him, Doctor." Mr. Renfield stuck out his tongue to show nothing was left.

Arthur looked at the ceiling again. This had to be another joke. Surely he hadn't really eaten a fly.

"Protein," Mr. Renfield said. "Life."

"Life?"

"Every little bit helps if I'm going to become strong again."

Arthur figured he'd better update the patient's record.

Condition: Stable
Heart rate: 72
Blood pressure: 122/74
Ate 1 fly.

Chapter 16

Mina

WHEN I ARRIVED at work that afternoon, my boss was on her way out.

"Meeting with the headmaster," she said. "Not sure how long I'll be." The headmaster, Dr. Stoker, had the reputation of being a talker.

I was only in the office alone for a few minutes before I slid into her seat and used a backdoor code to hack into her account.

Computers had always made sense to me. I was usually good enough not to leave any trace. Not that I did anything criminal, just small things like granting Lucy and me an access code to Florence at any time of night. Besides, there wasn't anything especially damning in the staff view of the student records; basically an ID number, home address, phone number, class schedule, and grades. I searched for Jonathan. There was a file on his internship, but it only contained a brief job description signed by the head lawyer at his mom's firm and another document with dates and credit hours proposed, signed by Dr. Stoker.

November, I read. His official return date had been November 5, just as I had marked it in my calendar. Today. And I had heard nothing.

There was a file for recommendation letters, but it contained only one, from Dr. Abigail Helsinger.

She had been Jonathan's historical religion teacher. Jonathan had been forced to take her class to fulfill a requirement before he graduated. He hadn't said anything bad about her, but I couldn't remember him saying anything good either. After the Stagnation, when the government tried to increase the labor force by changing education requirements to only eighth grade, a number of high schools were forced to close and there were hardly any universities left. She wasn't the only professor who had ended up teaching high school.

"Dear Mr. Anghen," Dr. Helsinger's letter began. Like he was a real person. Like he did exist after all.

"Time?" I whispered into my xphone.

It wasn't four yet. Classes were done for the day, but Dr. Helsinger might be in her office. I erased my footprints and signed off the computer. I'd make up the work time tomorrow.

Dr. Helsinger and the rest of the humanities people were in the basement of Slains. Jonathan had complained about how it was right next to the furnace and always boiling, whereas the math and science building, Lovelace, got all the modern heating and cooling technology. I cut across the commons, through the main door, and downstairs. The teachers' office door was closed. I raised my hand to knock.

"Who are you looking for?"

A tall woman with a mask and work boots stood behind me, her head cocked like one of those video game dogs.

"Dr. Helsinger."

"Well, come in. Or rather, I'm not there, I'm here, but please, let me show you in," the woman said in a rush. "I'm Dr. H." Then she threw her head back and laughed.

It was so ridiculous I found myself smiling too. She squeezed in front of me and opened the door. I followed her inside.

The basement office was utilitarian. All the desks faced the cement block wall and were interspersed with old-fashioned, mostly empty bookshelves. None of the other teachers were there. Opposite the door, along the ceiling, was a small basement window with a fan balanced precariously inside and no blackout curtain.

"This one," Dr. H said, navigating around several piles of books to pull a chair out from a desk and gesturing for me to sit down. "I apologize for the mess. I'm one of these Luddites who still deals with paper."

She stacked folders into a pile and pulled open a drawer. I could see a framed photo inside—why would a photo be hidden in a drawer instead of on top of a desk? She crammed the folders on top of it and shoved the drawer shut. Only then did she settle into the chair opposite me.

"Apologies for the heat too. Hot as Hades in here. Now, who are you?"

"Mina," I said, like Dr. H, not announcing my full name.

"And which class do I have you for?"

"I'm not one of your students. I hope you might have a moment though—" She knew something, I reminded myself. You couldn't write a reference letter to a ghost.

Her laugh boomed out again, even through her mask. "Oh good. I couldn't place your face and wondered whether I should feel guilty."

"You taught my friend, Jonathan…" I couldn't decide whether to call him my boyfriend or friend. I could feel my cheeks flush, and it wasn't just the heat.

"Jonathan," Dr. H repeated, her voice suddenly serious like a funeral. "How is he?"

I bit my lip, fiddled with my glasses. Used, so the fit was never quite right. "Well, I… I haven't… I mean…"

"Shit."

"Excuse me?" I was sure I had misheard her, but she didn't repeat herself. "Is something wrong?" I whispered.

"You tell me," she shot back.

I didn't know what to say, so I asked my question.

"Do you know Mr. Anghen?"

Dr. H looked first at the door, still slightly open. She looked at the window behind her—without a blackout curtain. She reached for the desk drawer with the photo, but she didn't open it, only held the knob in her hand. Then she was on her feet. "Let's go on a walk."

* * *

The air was cold. I pulled my sweater tightly around me and wished I had thought to bring a coat.

We walked behind Slains. Beyond was the rec center, overlooking the Esk River. Dr. H hurried a step ahead of me, crossed the wooden bridge to the island with the abandoned field house.

"Sorry," she said, lowering her mask to her neck. "The walls have ears."

Jonathan had said she was a little weird. But this wasn't just weird—she was scared. I tucked my fingers into my sleeves and wrapped my arms around my body. I wasn't sure I wanted to hear whatever came next.

She gestured down a narrow footpath past the field house, along the trees' edge. As I followed her, she started to tell her story. "I do some work with Avett, Lucent, and Rogers."

Jonathan's mother's firm in Newholm. I nodded to show I was with her so far.

"In this day and age, it's important to keep my passport up to date and make sure no bureaucracy ever hinders my personal life."

I had no idea what secrets she was hiding, but I nodded again. Lots of people felt similarly, whether they were immigrants like my dad or religious or queer. The government had grown increasingly strict, so more people hung blackout curtains in their windows and planned every step in case they needed to run.

"Avett, Lucent, and Rogers have been good to me. Professional, reliable, discreet… So when they mentioned a client of theirs, a Count Anghen, I was willing to do what I could to help." She swallowed but continued walking. "They suggested Jonathan for some sort of internship. His name came up because of his mother's connections, but he happened to be in my class last spring. I said I would recommend him. To avoid any trappings of nepotism, the firm asked me to communicate with Anghen directly."

"So he is real," I mumbled.

"I have no reason to question his existence. But he is a very hidden man. The firm didn't provide me with any digital address or number, only an office address in York in the United Kingdom. So I sent a letter via mail service. I included a reference for Jonathan, all positive. The next week there was a letter waiting for me on my desk."

I stayed silent, encouraging her to continue her story.

"The next week there was a letter waiting for me," she repeated.

"I don't—"

"Let me explain," she said. "You may be too young to have much experience with mail carriers. But given all the violence in Europe, the virus spreading, not to mention the distance, it should have taken my letter several days, if not over a week, to reach York. A return letter would take just as long. But there was this response, a letter with all my questions answered, and several additional questions if I would be so kind as to answer." Dr. H snorted. "Maybe I should have never opened the thing. You see, it didn't have any addresses or codes on it. It wasn't left at my door. It was waiting on my desk. Only days later. The questions seemed innocent enough at first. Anghen wondered about Jonathan's work ethic, how he might tolerate being away from home. Anghen warned me that his manor had little connection to the outside world. He wanted to know more about Jonathan too—his background, his interests. At the time I only thought Anghen was thorough. I answered his questions as best I could and continued to recommend Jonathan for the position. All our students should have some chance to see the world after all. Two days later, there was another letter on my desk. He must have someone, if not multiple someones, stationed in Whitby, maybe even at Irving."

A cold wind blew across my neck, down my back. *The walls have ears*, I remembered, spooked.

"He asked more questions. He wanted to know if Jonathan had a lot of friends, how he responded to stress, how responsible he was… At first I thought it meant he had changed his mind about Jonathan and he was trying to find a gentle way to say he didn't measure up. Since Jonathan left, I've worried about those questions more. They were entirely too personal."

We circled past the abandoned field house. Dr. H brushed a branch to the side as she continued ahead. "In my previous research life, I studied folktales, superstition, and coincidence. I still collect articles from around the world with strange stories, unexplainable phenomena. There have been a lot lately."

I followed her along the path, not sure what her research background had to do with anything other than explaining all the paper and books. Honestly, it sounded a little kooky to me.

She stopped so abruptly I almost bumped into her.

"Everything suggests something is happening," she said. "Something horrible."

"To Jonathan?"

"Let's hope I'm wrong." But Dr. H sounded pretty sure of herself.

Chapter 17

Mina

AFTER MY VISIT with Dr. Helsinger, it was almost past dinner.

But I wasn't hungry or ready to explain everything to Lucy. Instead, I went back to Rickman. I ensconced myself in one of the synagogue's alcoves, hidden from the front door. I cast my xphone screen to Avett, Lucent, and Rogers's site. Under a tab labeled Our People, I skimmed through the list of names, stopping at Nancy Harker.

I studied her picture for a moment. Her face was the same as Jonathan's. Rounded but with intense blue eyes, massive eyebrows. I dialed her number. She was a lawyer. Unlike me, she'd still be working.

She answered on the first chime: "Nancy speaking."

She frowned at my image—whether it was my youth, my Asian face, or something entirely different, I couldn't tell.

I took a deep breath. "Hi. My name is Mina. I'm a friend of Jonathan's at Irving."

"Yes?"

I bit my lip but pressed ahead. "I'm trying to figure out where he is."

"He's on his way home," she said.

I hadn't realized I was holding my breath until it rushed out of me like a deflating balloon. "Good. That's really good to hear."

"I'm glad I could help. Now, if that's everything—"

She was going to disconnect me. "Wait! Do you mean on his way home like he just stepped out, or is he on his way from Europe? I haven't heard anything from him in ages." I didn't care how desperate my voice sounded.

"His flight from London is scheduled for today. He'll return to school for the spring semester."

"But have you heard from him?"

"I assume he's been busy doing his job. He's well aware how expensive those plane tickets were—"

"You haven't heard anything else?" I pushed, my heart sinking. "We were close. I thought he'd stay in touch, but— You haven't heard anything?"

"I'm sorry, dear," Nancy murmured. For a moment, the lawyer slipped out of her voice as she half whispered, half cried, "I haven't heard anything else."

***

He's on his way home, I told myself.

But why wouldn't he message me? Nancy's final words reverberated in my head. What if Dr. Helsinger was right? What if something horrible had happened?

My xphone chimed; five minutes to study hall. *He's on his way home*, I insisted. I closed my screen and hurried back to Florence.

Lucy was at study hall already, surrounded by a bunch of other girls. I slipped into a seat at the end of the long table. She glanced at me, asking a question with her eyes. I nodded. I was fine. Jonathan had probably done something stupid like send his xphone through the laundry.

While Mrs. Holmes walked up and down the rows of tables, her heels clicking across the wooden floor, I cast my screen and pulled up my calculus. I was in the mood to solve problems. Especially problems with only one answer, with no mysterious details and no crying mothers.

I worked through the whole chapter, problem by problem, figured out the patterns, the method. Next week would be easier; I'd know how to do all the basics. I didn't even jump when I felt a hand on my shoulder.

"Time for bed, Mina," Mrs. Holmes said. While I had worked, everyone else at my long table had already left.

***

I couldn't sleep that night. No matter how much I insisted. Why hadn't Jonathan been in touch? I pulled up our last conversation even though I had already memorized every line. The light flickered on in the darkness.

I jumped back, cried out, before I recognized Lucy standing in the middle of the room.

Her head whipped toward me, her mouth curled into a snarl.

"Lucy?" I whispered.

"Hungry," she growled.

"Lucy?" I said again, louder. "You okay?"

But she wasn't staring at me. She was staring at nothing, her eyes perfectly blank.

"You're asleep." The pieces clicked together in my brain. "It's a bad dream. You're sleepwalking."

"He's coming," she announced. "He'll destroy them all." She pivoted, raced for the door.

I jumped to meet her, locked the bolt, then wrapped an arm around her.

"Lucy, Lucy." I shook her, tried to wake her.

She rattled the doorknob, cursed under her breath.

Then suddenly she stopped, sank into my arms. We fell to the floor in a tangle of Mina and Lucy. Lucy woke, laughing.

"Holy cows! Mina? Where am I?"

"You had a dream. You were talking and walking, and you tried to get out the door. I had to lock it."

Lucy buried her head in her hands. "How

embarrassing! I must have woken you up! Did I say anything?"

"Um, you said he was going to destroy them all." I could hear the words in my head, chilling me.

She used my bed to pull herself back to her feet. Her hand trembled ever so slightly.

"Lucy?" I pressed.

"I did have the most horrible dream," she said, more to herself than me. "I was in the airport."

"The airport?" That didn't sound too scary, though I had never flown. But how bizarre—today was supposed to be Jonathan's flight.

"There were the rows of screens, and the falafel place with the waffle fries, and those scary long escalators. Definitely Caine County Airport."

"We should get back to bed," I said, casting my screen to check the time. It was later than I had realized.

"He was cold. I know that doesn't sound horrible, but his hands were like ice and everything was dark and he was so hungry—" As she talked, Lucy crawled into her bed, nestled deep under the comforter.

"Who?" I asked.

"Who knows." Lucy sounded as if she were already half-asleep. "Good night, Mina Bird."

"Good night," I murmured.

Unfortunately, I was as wide awake as if the nightmare had been my own. I watched Lucy for several minutes, but she was quiet, her breath even.

Then I cast my screen, checked all the flights that had come into the airport that day. I checked all the flights leaving Heathrow. I figured out which flight Jonathan had to be on. But my xphone stayed silent. Jonathan didn't contact me.

Chapter 18

Mina

THE NEXT NIGHT, I had still heard nothing from Jonathan. I didn't even try to sleep. As soon as I finished my homework, I cast my screen.

I started with Jonathan's last messages. They were exactly as I remembered.

Next I searched the net under his name. Only the usual stuff came up: soccer, school, a class production of *Hamlet*.

I stared at the empty search box. What had Dr. Helsinger said about coincidences? "Caine County Airport," I whispered.

There was the number, the map, the site. But below that, my screen filled. I clicked on a link.

"Police are investigating the death of two baggage handlers at Caine County Airport yesterday evening."

Yesterday? It coincided with Lucy's dream,

Jonathan's supposed flight.

"The deaths occurred in the American Airlines Baggage Claim Office, part of a restricted area where lost or leftover luggage is stored. Individuals with further information should contact airport security."

I returned to the search results, clicked another. A video popped up.

"It was a black dog," a woman in an airline uniform said, the sound channeling through my xphone earpiece. "I saw it wandering through the terminal. We were mostly empty, so there was no mistake. I pressed the call button, but then it started running. Galloping out the back. Ain't no security going to catch that."

"Can you describe the dog, ma'am?"

"Well, it was big. More like a wolf. Not that I've ever seen a wolf before, but it was hairy, with a long tail. Black all over. Big."

"And you think this dog had something to do with the baggage handlers' deaths?"

"I ain't never seen no dog in the terminal before."

"That is Ramona, an airline attendant at the scene—"

I clicked on another site and jumped back at the surveillance footage that appeared. But I couldn't look away. It was bodies, dead from the Bloodless Syndrome. Right in Whitby! Blue body bags had been pulled over them, so only their heads showed. But their faces were sunken, skeletal, like all the blood had been drained away. *They must have been cold*, I thought. Just like

Lucy had said.

But none of the other news sites mentioned the Bloodless Syndrome, there were no precautions suggested, no warnings on the state health page.

I clicked on another video.

"The weirdest thing was the boxes," a different crew member, a man, said. "I mean, we're used to the drugs coming in, but these boxes were filled with dirt."

"Dirt?" repeated someone off-screen.

"Huge boxes of dirt. Maybe for a sandbox? But who would pay to send dirt from England?"

My body was shivering. I couldn't make it stop.

I closed my screen, crawled under my comforter, pulled it over my head. But I kept shaking.

It was all so random. Boxes of dirt? But Lucy had known.

There had to be a logical explanation. I didn't think I had mentioned Jonathan's flight. But maybe Lucy had been thinking about the airport... she was planning a trip... or her mom was traveling for business. Or maybe she had heard something about the deaths right before she went to sleep; she talked in her sleep when she was stressed or upset. Or maybe... Jonathan had mentioned a wolf.

None of it made any sense; none of it connected. *It's random coincidence*, I told myself. I turned in my bed, looked once more at Lucy: sound asleep.

I got up, tugged at the blackout curtains to make sure they were closed. In their folds, I saw a face at the window.

I stumbled backward. I could see white skin. Red eyes flashed in the darkness. My heart raced ahead of my brain.

I cast my screen, called campus security. But by the time someone answered and I dared to look again, the face was gone. By the time I explained what I had seen, I sounded like an idiot. I returned to the window, stared out. The night was quiet. For now. I carefully closed the curtains again.

Chapter 19

WHIT News

DEADLY JAPANESE TERRORIST ATTACK
Nov 7, 2---

AT LEAST A dozen has been killed and hundreds more wounded after a terrorist offensive in Kagoshima, Japan. Estimates are based on aerial footage of the strike, as since the outbreak of the Bloodless Syndrome, Japan has closed its borders to most Western commercial trade and news media organizations. The perpetrators have not yet been identified, but experts believe this incident is a new front in the ongoing offensive carried out by the Filipino organization Wahash.

Wahash has been perpetrating attacks with renewed intensity since they seized Osaka this past spring.

Rumors indicate the army's size has increased exponentially, its victims often becoming recruits in its ranks. Experts say Wahash's tactics must be exceptionally persuasive, if not violent. Survivors, however, say their neighbors are hardly recognizable. They have transformed into monsters overnight.

Chapter 20

Jonathan

Wednesday, October 17–Sunday, November 4

THE DAYS BLEND together. I write madly, determined to capture all that has happened, to prove to myself that I'm not losing my mind. Because sometimes I wonder. Sometimes I'm no longer sure what's real.

Like the woman who stood outside my window, screaming, threatening, begging for her child—all the while, I knew what had happened. I tried to get her attention, to make her understand. But I was too late. The wolves were on her almost instantly.

Only a few days ago, a moving van appeared. The workers transported six enormous boxes from the house to their truck, using several men to haul each. During one of their breaks, as they guzzled rehydration drinks and dried sweat from their faces, I tried to get their attention. Just like the woman outside my window, I begged the movers, showed them money, pounded at the glass. But they completely ignored me. Anghen must have already gotten to them.

So I continue to work for the monster. What choice do I have? Whenever I fight back, whenever I resist, he's there, stronger than any human should be, a red glint in his eyes. So I answer his legal questions as well as all his questions about Whitby and the Midwest as a whole. I can find no other way to survive.

But the writing is comforting. I dream about giving the notebook to Mina. My handwriting is mostly indecipherable, cramped on the tiny pages. But I imagine Mina diving in, doing her best to listen, to understand, to evaluate. She will tell me the truth. So I keep writing.

On the night before my "internship" was supposed to finish—arranged back when I worried about things like internships, résumés, and college applications—there was a knock on my sitting room door.

"Good evening, friend," Anghen said, inviting himself in.

I stared at him in horror, my whole body turning to ice. Instead of his usual suit, he wore jeans, a hooded sweatshirt, even had an xphone behind his ear. He looked American. With numbed fingers, I felt for my back pocket. Even in the middle of the countryside, I had tried to keep my ID handy. Maybe the habit was too ingrained. Or it had been some small reminder of my previous life. But now my pocket was empty. My ID was missing.

"I stopped by to say goodbye," Anghen said, as if nothing had changed between us, as if he weren't dressed like a teenager. "I assume you saw the movers out front? You have sold me on Whitby! With their help, I'll be off tomorrow at first light. I've already put an offer on my American castle. Thanks to you, I hope to be settled within the next few days."

My spit caught in my throat. I coughed. The monster was coming. Not to me, not trapped here, but to my friends, my mom, my school. To Mina.

Anghen got me something to drink, patiently waited while I choked, my hands shaking, the buzzing starting in my brain.

"You'll kill them all!" I cried when I was able to breathe again.

"Surely not all of them," Anghen said, as if we were discussing his vacation plans, not murder. "I'll need to eat, of course, to keep my strength up. But there're always plenty of available victims—the homeless, the addicts, anyone who is disenfranchised. No one notices their absence. Yes, I'm anxious to see what America has to offer me."

"I'll stop you!"

He only laughed. "No, I have no intention of your interfering with my plans. With your ID, I can keep my own name clean and should arrive without any problems. Perhaps I'll look up your... Mina."

He hesitated before pronouncing her name and added no title, even though I was always Mr. Harker to him. It was as if her very name, her race, left a foul taste in his mouth. But how did he know Mina? Had he read my journal? Maybe I had said her name in my sleep? It didn't matter. Blood surged through my body like red-hot lava. I flew to him, swung my fist at his face.

Anghen spun like lightning, grabbed my hand. I couldn't move. He squeezed so tightly I thought my hand might crumble to ash and bone. My eyes filled with tears.

The monster continued. "You have performed an admirable service for me, Mr. Harker. Even if our friendship must end like this."

I couldn't see through my tears, the pain in my hand.

"I had hoped for my sisters to enjoy you upon my departure, but of course I can take care of you myself."

Outside, a wolf howled. Others joined. Then Anghen howled back, his voice echoing like thunder in the small room: throaty, deep, inhuman.

"It seems I am called away. Goodbye, Mr. Harker." His words were a growl in my ear. Then the pressure left my hand and I tumbled to the floor, holding my hand between my legs, tears flowing in streams down my face.

He returned to the sitting room door and showed himself out. I heard the key turn in the lock.

***

Whether minutes passed or hours, I wasn't sure. But I forced myself to sit up, to dry my face, to look out into the night. Perhaps the monster was preoccupied. Perhaps this would be the only chance I had before those female creatures descended on me.

If the monster could crawl out his own window, why can't I? I ignored the drop in my stomach, the catch in my throat. There are far worse things than height.

I packed my backpack with only the essentials. Just like that poor mother, I have no one else, no other options. If I ever want to see my own mother, I have to be brave.

I recited the only Hebrew I could remember. Then I called out to God directly, over and over again. I begged to survive.

Before I could second-guess myself, I grabbed a chair and threw it with all my strength against the window. The glass shattered, spilling over the ledge and out the window.

Carefully placing my hands, I climbed outside.

Chapter 21

Jonathan

Monday, November 5

THE CLIMB WAS horrible. The stones were worn, but they had been rebuilt over the years, so there were handholds between the mortar. I forced my fingers to move, to ignore the throbbing in my right hand. I told myself it was like the climbing wall in the rec center or one of my video games. But my eyes couldn't focus, sweeping from one thing to the next; dizzy, my heart pounding. I didn't know if it was better or worse that I couldn't see far in the moonless night, couldn't even see the ground below me. Sometimes I had to close my eyes and press my whole body against the wall while I waited, shaking, before I could start again.

But I had no choices left. If I wanted a home to return to, I needed to stop Anghen. Whatever it took.

101

The night was still dark when I reached Anghen's window. I stared into black nothingness, sensing no movement. I propped my elbows on the sill and pulled open the window. It slid easily, like it had been well-oiled and used for years. I tumbled inside.

I landed on my feet but then fell forward, hard, on my already injured hand. I wouldn't let myself think about it. Instead, my eyes hurried from dark corner to dark corner. The room appeared empty, disused even. I had thought it was Anghen's bedroom, but there was no bed, only a staircase in the middle of the room. The fireplace was thick with cobwebs. Actually, the whole room—the desk, a set of built-in shelves, the chairs, everything—was thick with dust. Except in one corner was a metal table, shiny and clean, topped with a console, threaded with wires to other machines, pulsing with blinking lights, humming with power. It must have been connected to Anghen's receivers, his cameras. There had probably been reception all along. He had purposely kept me isolated. Mina would have known what to do; she would have known how to hack into it, how to get a wireless code or even how to decimate the whole system. If I had time, or if I had only found it earlier maybe— But no. Once again, I was completely useless!

Instead, I crept downstairs, toward the base of the tower, and discovered two doors. The first, positioned toward the hallway, was locked tight even from the inside. I would need a key to escape. The second door was unlocked, but there were only more stairs, continuing to spiral downward.

I traveled deeper into darkness, my feet inching forward step by step. My heart began to race; panic bubbled up. I imagined a wolf silently creeping toward me. But with the next curve, I felt dirt below me. I had made it to the basement of the house.

There must have been a window somewhere because I could see faintly again even though the air was thick and musky like an animal's lair. But the light meant dawn was coming and I was running out of time.

The basement was divided into small rooms, like stables. I could make out wooden benches, a fireplace. Then I saw the coffins. Perhaps this was an old chapel and family burial ground? But unlike the room upstairs, there was no dust, not even spiderwebs. In fact, some of the coffins were open, empty except for dirt piled inside. There was dirt outside too, earth thick against the stone walls. As if they had been used for planters, or—I remembered the boxes the movers had carried out earlier: large, rectangular, person-shaped. My whole body began to shake. Vampires slept in coffins—the movers were transporting the dirt, the monsters' beds, to my home.

I peered into the next stall. The earth around this coffin was thick, rooting it to the ground. It too was open, but not empty. There was a blond woman inside, looking more asleep than dead. I traveled to the next room, the next. I saw the brunette, the one who had initiated the attack on me upstairs. She was in a cardboard box, waiting for her trip. I ran to the next stable and found Anghen.

I stumbled on the floor, my hand grabbing at the wall so I wouldn't fall. But Anghen didn't move. My hands shook, my heart raced, but against all my instincts I stepped forward.

Anghen was resting on a mound of dirt in a wooden coffin. More easily transportable too, I guessed. He looked fifty years younger. His hair was jet-black, his lips red. Worse, he was bloated, puffed up like he had gorged on his last meal before his trip. This was the monster that planned to make his home in Whitby.

I reached the edge of his coffin, then jerked backward. His eyes were wide open.

But they were sightless. I kept breathing, forcing air in and out. He was asleep. Or dead. I had no idea how the hell vampires worked. But motionless, that was the important thing.

I kept breathing. I clutched my Star of David.

One of the workers had left a shovel lying nearby. I picked it up, held its solid, reassuring weight in both hands. I raised it above my head. I would make sure this monster never stirred again. I threw the shovel down, aimed the point of the blade directly at his face.

His head turned. His eyes stared at me. I cried out. The shovel twisted in my hands. It struck his forehead, burying itself into his flesh, but not deep enough to kill.

The useless shovel fell from my hands. I stumbled backward, tripping over myself, falling to the ground. I gasped out. A thousand apologies and excuses came to my mouth. I scrambled to my knees, intending to beg for my life. But he didn't move.

I crept backward. Anghen's red eyes stayed motionless, like a hornet pinned to a board. I kept backing up, farther and farther away from all of them, all the monsters. When I could no longer see his eyes, I ran upstairs.

Outside Anghen's tower window, I saw the movers' truck approach. It was over. I failed.

I heard them below, gathering the final two boxes, the female monster's and Anghen's wooden coffin, sealing them shut. Whatever this monster does, wherever he goes next, I know I'm responsible.

There is only one thing left for me to do: I have to escape, to tell the world what I know before it's too late.

If these notes are ever read by anyone else, please pass them on to Mina Muto. I have thought of her all this time as I have written. I know she will listen. Goodbye.

Jonathan Harker

Chapter 22

Mina

IT WAS TWO days after Jonathan's supposed arrival when I woke to my xphone chiming. I grabbed for my earpiece, cast my screen.

It was Nancy Harker, Jonathan's mom. Thankfully I had kept my video off. "Jonathan is back but has been hospitalized. Visiting hours are at Newholm this afternoon, ninth floor. Can you come?"

"Of course I'll be there. Is he okay?"

But she had already disconnected the call.

It wasn't until I was properly awake that I started second-guessing everything.

"I can't just leave," I said to Lucy between classes. "Remember Halloween?" I remembered the sickening feeling in my stomach when I didn't have my ID. My fear of losing everything I had worked so hard for.

"So take your ID. But he's in the hospital! You have

to see him. Today!"

Of course she was right. Lucy was always right when it came to people. I had to find out what was wrong. But I also had to know what had happened. Everything about it tied my stomach up in knots.

Lucy created a whole scheme; I would sneak out of activity period. We were creating a "memory portfolio" for our senior year. Mostly it involved Lucy pulling up billions of pictures and me captioning them with snarky comments. We would wait until everyone else was engaged in their work, until the art teacher was hunched over his own tablet, sketching away. Lucy swore campus would be deserted and no one would notice my absence until at least study hall.

Except we didn't need to bother. Mrs. Holmes herself handed me a pass at lunch for that afternoon.

"Your friend's mom called. You've been excused," she said. "Good luck."

"Thanks." I had no idea if she was referring to Jonathan's health, my getting to the hospital, or our relationship. Maybe all of the above.

***

I'd never been to Newholm Hospital before. In fact, I'd never been in a hospital since my birth. Thankfully, I had avoided any expensive emergencies, no broken bones or middle-of-the-night panics. My family never had enough money to pay for insurance. As I started down Lyceum Road, past the McDonald's, the gray building towered over the street. A giant yellow generator nestled against its side. The hospital had to be big enough to serve Newholm, Whitby, and much of the surrounding area.

Sirens sounded in the distance. *A patient*, I thought. But instead, a black truck flew around the corner with its triangular *A* insignia: the Alpha Brigade.

I bit my lip, forced myself to keep walking. Newholm Hospital housed a detention center, the one Arthur worked at. When there was unrest on the streets, fighting, public intoxication, unauthorized demonstrations—even people who could not show their IDs, I reminded myself—someone would often call the local brigade. They were nongovernment, but since the Stagnation depleted government funding, the police and military offered payment for brigade services. Like dropping people off at the local DetCen.

This was what Quincey had aligned himself with.

I was close enough to watch the black truck pull into a side drive. I stopped, leaned against a sign outside the pharmacy, too afraid to cross the street.

Alphas poured from the van—so many, each armed with a giant black gun. A shiver went down my spine. My family had always had a gun—just in case—but it was different watching someone in real life hold it, threaten another person's life. I wrapped my hands around the sign's solid metal. The Alphas were a chain operation, one of the country's biggest brigades. They circled around the side of the truck. The door slowly opened. They raised their guns.

"No!" cried a woman. She was handcuffed. Some Alphas grabbed her from the van while the others kept their guns trained on the action. I closed my eyes.

"Please!" the woman cried again. "My daughter will come home, and she won't know where I am. And I'm legal! I wasn't doing anything! You can't let—"

I heard a scuffle, mumbled warnings. Someone yelled, "Shut up, RAT!" Then silence.

When I opened my eyes, the DetCen's door was swishing closed. The van circled in the drive and turned back down Lyceum. The mounted surveillance camera followed its movement, then returned to center.

But I didn't move. I tasted blood in my mouth. I licked my lips, tried to staunch the bleeding.

Quincey thought he could stop this from happening. Save everyone. But no one had saved anyone today. Next time it could be his uncle. Or my dad.

My xphone chimed with a message. I welcomed the distraction, casting my screen. It was Lucy. "You get there okay? Find him?"

A family passed me on the street. I heard the pharmacy door beep behind me as customers entered. Dim sunlight glimmered on the pavement.

"Getting there," I messaged back to Lucy.

"Take your time," she wrote. "Might as well milk that Get out of Jail Free card for all it's worth."

She was right. *So move*, I thought. *It wasn't you.* I

crossed the street.

Newholm Hospital was ice-cold, the air circulating around an enormous lobby with a cathedral ceiling. Potted plants were dotted around the area.

"ID, please?" said a woman at the front guard desk, her lower face covered with a mask, the desk itself surrounded in reinforced glass.

I pulled my ID from my back pocket, felt its hard, plastic edge in my palm. My mind ran every scenario: expulsion from school, detention, deportation to a country I didn't even know.

"Miss?"

I held out my ID, and with gloved hands the guard plucked the card from me. Out of my control.

"Any chest pain, headache, disorientation, or shortness of breath?" the guard rattled off the most common symptoms from the previous pandemic. I guessed the only reported symptom of the current Bloodless Syndrome was death. The news had said there was no indication of casual physical contact or even airborne transmission, but the news almost certainly wasn't reporting the full story from Caine County Airport either.

I shook my head as she checked my temperature with her remote sensor, then scanned my ID. She made a note on a tablet and gestured me through the metal detector.

On the other side, she handed my ID back to me. "There's a map straight ahead, elevators on the left wall."

I barely heard her. I was safe. Free.
I could find Jonathan.

Chapter 23

Mina

I WALKED TO the ninth floor in a daze. PSYCHIATRIC EMERGENCY SERVICES, an overhead sign read. Psychiatric? But I didn't think about what it meant, all the implications. I was counting fingers, toes, trying to assure myself that I was here, my ID safely in my pocket. *Jonathan*, I reminded myself.

I checked in at another desk, stiffened my shoulders, reached for my ID, but the receptionist didn't take it from me. "Room number 928, love. At the end of the hall."

There was a man in the waiting room. He sat up, his eyes following me as I walked past. But I stopped paying attention when I saw room 928. The door was open. My eyes skimmed over empty beds, curtains, a bathroom, finally stopping at a figure staring out the window. Jonathan! He looked exactly as I remembered—a little skinnier, but it was his ridiculous height, his rounded shoulders, his intense focus.

He must have heard me. He turned around. We found each other midway across the room. Jonathan wrapped me in his arms, and I held on so tight I couldn't have said where one of us started and the other ended. Whatever was between us vanished, and it was as if we were right back where we had been.

It was several minutes before either of us tried to talk, and then we both spoke at once.

"What happened?" I said. "You're so thin."

"You're here!" he said. "Mom said she messaged you, but I thought—"

We laughed.

Jonathan squeezed my hands. "You first."

Someone behind me coughed. I recognized the woman in the bedside chair—Nancy Harker—from the firm's site. Jonathan dropped my hands.

"You two talk, get reacquainted. I should stretch my legs anyway." She stood, but before she left she said, "Remember our discussion, Jonathan." Then she was heading down the hallway.

I turned back to Jonathan. "Discussion? What's going on?"

"I..." Jonathan stared at the door as he stumbled over his words. "I had a rough trip. Toward the end I wasn't even sure I'd make it out alive. But Mom..." His eyes moved to the wall, staring over my head. "She wanted to get me checked out, make sure I wasn't misremembering things or anything like that. She doesn't want me talking about it."

I stared at him, rethinking Psychiatric Emergency Services. "*Misremembering* things?"

"They put me on some medication. But the doctor says I'm fine now. I can go home soon. I should get my new ID card any day now. I just wanted to see you…" He ran his fingers through his messy, too-long hair, flattened on one side. Then he plopped on the bed, smiled as if he had pushed everything to the back of his mind. "Tell me about something else. How is school? Did you have any issues getting here? I told Mom she'd have to call you out."

My mind buzzed with questions—not only what had happened but why he hadn't been in touch, why he hadn't answered any of my messages, whether he knew that man in the waiting room. And why did he need a new ID? But instead, I settled next to him on the bed and let him change the subject.

"Getting here was a mess." I told him about the truck, the Alpha Brigade, that poor woman and her daughter.

"It's okay," Jonathan said. "You're safe. I'll keep you safe."

His arms wrapped around me so tightly I wanted to believe it. Even though practically I knew: if they came for me there would be nothing anyone could do.

Not to mention how thin he was. Now that I was closer, I could see the shadows under his eyes. For some reason he had a splint around two of his fingers. He didn't look right. Like he couldn't even keep himself safe.

"How much longer did you say you're here?" I asked.

Jonathan shrugged. "Only a few more days, I think. Mom had to threaten to sue, but the insurance agreed to cover it. It's not like another patient needs the bed." He gestured at the empty room.

Empty. It was as if we both had the same thought at the same moment. His too-long hair fell in his eyes, and I brushed it away. He took my fingers, kissed them. I moved to his lips. We kissed slowly, gently, until all my insides were thrumming.

But I forced myself to pull back. I eyed the open door, Nancy Harker's chair. "What if your mom comes back?"

"She'll come back," he said, shrugging. His eyes danced. How could I argue with that logic? We kissed again.

Eventually we were interrupted, not by Nancy Harker but by a nurse who thankfully knocked before she came in with a dinner tray.

Jonathan let me munch on the grilled "cheese" sandwich, which had been vaguely heated up, while he picked at the canned fruit cup. But we weren't really hungry. There was so much to say, so much to catch up on. Too much of each other to drink in.

But before I lost myself completely, the thought

was still nagging at me. "What happened to you?" I asked again.

"Nothing," Jonathan said. "The doctor says I'm fine: eating, sleeping, blood tests, everything. I'd rather—" He ran his fingers along my face.

I gave in, leaning back onto his hospital bed. He lay down next to me, brushed his hand along my neck.

He jerked his hand back.

"Jonathan?"

I opened my eyes. He clasped his hand against his chest, trembling as if with some terrible memory.

"Hey," I whispered, pulling him closer, into my body, as I kissed him once more.

He came back to himself. He wrapped both arms around me, squeezed me tight.

We kissed again and again and again. I forgot about the hospital, the nurses, the time. Jonathan was as I remembered him. Whatever had happened, nothing had changed between us.

We fit together like a puzzle, like two sides of an equation equaling each other. I only wanted more, more, more.

Chapter 24

Mina

As DAWN STARTED to lighten the sky, I hurried upstairs to the dorm room and slipped open the door. Lucy stood in her cozy pants and T-shirt, her comforter draped around her shoulders.

"Are you okay?" I asked. It was a stupid question—of course she wasn't okay. Her eyes were sunken, surrounded by dark circles I didn't remember from yesterday.

"I didn't sleep well at all," Lucy said. "I dreamed I was cold again. I can't seem to warm up."

I took in her bed, the sheets a mess, pillows strewn every which way. Then I saw the blackout curtains gaping wide, the exposed window open right above her bed. "Did you open the window?"

"Did I?" Lucy turned.

I crossed the room into an icy breeze and slammed

the window shut.

Lucy's question hung between us. She must have been walking in her sleep again.

"I'm going back to bed." Lucy pulled the sheets and comforter tight and burrowed inside.

But class would start soon. "Should I call the clinic, tell them you're not feeling well?" Unlike hospitals and doctors' offices, the campus health clinic in Rickman was free for students even if they didn't have insurance. Lucy probably did have insurance—her mom was fairly well off—but I knew things had been tight after her dad died in Korea. Regardless, the clinic would be a start. Between the dreams, the sleeplessness, opening the window and freezing... I had no idea what any of it meant, but hopefully the on-duty nurse would.

"I'll get up in a minute," Lucy murmured, though not very convincingly. "I'm supposed to be at breakfast with Arthur—" Lucy bolted upright. "Mina! I can't believe I forgot Jonathan! Did you just get home?" A sly smile slid across Lucy's face. "Did you and Jonathan—?"

"Not in the hospital!" I said even as my face flushed. "But... there was a lot of kissing. And some other stuff."

"Hurrah for kissing and other stuff! So what happened to him? Did aliens steal his xphone? Or was it something serious? Is he okay?"

I bit my lip, not sure how to explain. "He didn't really want to talk about it."

"But how many months has it been since you've heard from him? How can he not talk about it?"

"He hasn't been feeling well. He says he's not *sick* sick, but..." I drifted off, not wanting to explain Psychiatric Emergency Services. Or to admit I didn't understand any of it myself.

"Boys!" Lucy exclaimed like a curse.

"Is something going on with Arthur?" I asked, gently shifting the conversation.

"No, not really. But he definitely wants more. I mean, we've messed around a bit, but he wants to go out, to do things, be a proper couple. Then yesterday my lab partner asked me out, and last night Luke from French slipped an invitation to Midwinter Ball under my door. I mean, seriously. Midwinter Ball isn't until January."

"And you're not interested?"

Lucy sighed like she was staring down some complicated physics homework set. "I just want this to be the best year ever, you know? It's our last year of high school, and I don't want to be tied down to Arthur or Luke or anyone. I want to have fun! I want to kiss twenty boys!" She stopped. "Do I sound like one of those girls in a text-message novel?"

I laughed. "No."

"Well, that's something! Of course, Arthur's superhot. And we both come from military families and we've known each other forever, so we always have plenty to talk about."

In other words, they were both typical Irving Academy students: from money.

"But?"

"But at the moment I'm horny like a cow, and I don't want to settle!"

"A cow?" I spat out.

"They have horns, right? Or an antelope, isn't that a thing? I'll be horny like an antelope!"

We were both laughing.

"No. Triceratops!" Lucy cried, falling back in her bed.

It was only then that I remembered. "You know, Quincey was asking after you the other day too."

"Mina Bird!" She threw a pillow at me, missing by a mile. "Stop! You're distracting me. Now, do you want to tell me what happened with Jonathan?"

But I had just noticed her hand, swollen and red. "What happened to you?" I gestured at her fist.

Lucy shook her head. "It's nothing. Just that same dream. I keep trying to open the window. I'm desperate to get out and join them."

"Who?"

"The people dancing. And him... A man. Last night he asked after you. 'How is Jonathan's Mina?' That's what he said."

Something hard and cold settled in the pit of my stomach. Jonathan's Mina? Who would think of me like that?

"That's what I told him," Lucy said, noting the

expression on my face. "Stop being a creeper! I wanted to dance and have fun, but the window wouldn't open. And to be honest, I wasn't sure I wanted it to open. Something about the man's voice was scary. But I couldn't stop fighting with the latch. Then I woke up, freezing and scared, my hand hurt, and the window was open."

"And I was gone!"

"No, no, no," Lucy said. "You found Jonathan! Besides, I'm far too old to need a babysitter."

I remembered those eyes outside the window. Security had never found him, but I was sure someone had been there.

"He's trying to stop you from being happy," Lucy said.

"What?"

"He doesn't want you to be happy. That's why he attacked last night. He wants you to doubt yourself and your relationship with Jonathan."

I stared at her as my heart began to gallop. "I thought you were only having bad dreams. Who attacked you?"

Lucy shook her head as if clearing fog. "I don't know." She still clutched the comforter around her.

"Are you sure you don't want me to call the clinic?" I asked. "Maybe your mom? Or security. If someone is trying to get in—"

Lucy yawned. "No, Mom's all the way out in Mayfield. And no one's really trying to get in, I'm sure.

It was just a bad dream. I should get a wiggle on." She cast her screen to check her hair and inspected something on her neck. "Ugh. Just my luck, I popped a pimple."

She ran her finger across the red spot, examined the blood on her finger. "I'm a wreck!"

I kept staring at her. Lucy was typically upbeat, but this was ridiculous.

"I promise I'll hit the clinic after classes. Today."

Chapter 25

Arthur

November 8, Newholm Detention Center

Patient 562:
　　Age: 47
　　Ethnicity: African American
　　Gender: Male
　　Condition: Stable
　　Heart rate: 81
　　Blood pressure: 127/86

WHILE PATIENT 562 slept, Arthur kept himself awake by playing doctor.

Lucy wasn't herself. He could tell right away that morning at breakfast. It wasn't just the makeup, hiding who knows what, but her quietness, her heavy eyes. He had tried to draw her out like he might a patient. She told him about the dreams, the sleepwalking. The nurse who had seen Lucy at the clinic that afternoon had suggested melatonin and told her to come back in a week if it wasn't working to get something stronger. Of course the nurse was the expert, and melatonin could improve Lucy's sleep patterns. But it didn't explain the underlying cause of her nightmares.

Arthur racked his brain, determined to figure it out. For Lucy.

The nurse had said something about stress at school, but Lucy said she was "perfectly happy" other than not sleeping. Lucy was always perfectly happy. She made the most out of every day, reached out and grabbed exactly what she wanted out of life.

Not that Arthur had anything to complain about. Even from home in DC, Mom was always there for him, only a screencast or a flight away. She kept things quiet with her girlfriend, but of course his dad's job provided them some leeway and privacy too. Meanwhile, Arthur was getting an excellent education along with numerous Midwest contacts, and he'd soon be off to a military academy of his choice. But lately he'd started to think about medical school instead. No matter what happened with the current government, the country would always need doctors. Even more so if the Bloodless Syndrome made its way to the US. Maybe helping people, fixing them, could be exactly what he wanted out of life. If only his dad agreed.

These night shifts got too quiet. Arthur squeezed

his eyes shut, then stretched them wide open to stay awake, sick of only himself and his thoughts for company.

The nurse was right that increased stress could lead to sleepwalking, but Arthur wondered if there might be another root cause. It could be a compound problem, the sleeplessness leading to the sleepwalking. Or perhaps a chemical intolerance or a digestive problem. He would talk more with Lucy that weekend.

Arthur's eyes closed again. Slowly his chin slipped to his chest as sleep overtook him.

***

Arthur woke to a string of drool hanging from his mouth, pooling on his shirt. Ugh. He swiveled his head around. The door was closed. Had any of the other staff seen him asleep? He could lose his job, and he'd barely started. Arthur checked on his patient and jumped to his feet. Mr. Renfield was sitting in bed, dangling a spider over his lips.

"Mr. Renfield!"

The patient offered him a wide smile. Then he popped the spider in his mouth, chewed, and swallowed.

"What are you doing?" Arthur demanded. "Where did you get that? What if it's poisonous?"

Mr. Renfield shook his head. "There are no poisonous spiders in Newholm, let alone its hospital and detention center. We live in the modern world now."

"Still," Arthur argued. "You don't know what germs it carries, or where it's been, or— What else have you been eating?"

Mr. Renfield's face was covered with something that looked like dusty white cotton candy with flecks of black and— Oh.

"Spiderweb. That's where I found all these." Mr. Renfield pointed at his stomach, making his fingers dance as if to suggest he'd eaten multiple bugs and they were all running around inside him. "Lots of life."

Arthur studied each corner of Mr. Renfield's room, but everything looked clean. His heart began to race. "Where did you get it all?"

"Room 220, room 117, the stairwell, the window in the bathroom that is never opened."

Arthur's heart beat faster. "You escaped?"

Renfield shook his head. "I came back. You see, I have such terrible dreams. I promised the king I'd visit him in person instead. Prove that I can do his favors. He doesn't need to rely on those other men of his. Only me."

"Rely on you for what?" Arthur asked. If he could just understand what the patient was saying, maybe he could help.

But Renfield shook his head. "Never mind. I won't tell anyone about your falling asleep, Dr. Godalming."

How the hell had the patient learned his last name? It must have been written somewhere, maybe on the records while he was sleeping.

"I'm not a doctor," Arthur grumbled for the billionth time.

"But you want to be. So you'll have to keep my secret too."

Renfield smiled with his blackmail, his lips thick with spiderweb.

Chapter 26

WHIT News

THE VILLAGE THAT DID NOT WAKE UP
Nov 10, 2---

ESPUI, A SMALL village tucked in the mountains of Northwestern Spain, did not wake up yesterday. The news started when commuters failed to arrive for their jobs. Teachers did not meet their pupils at the village school one town over. After a mother-in-law didn't answer the phone the previous night, her daughter drove up early in the morning to check on her. Upon arriving, she found the entire town was quiet, as if asleep. The market was empty, the police station shuttered. She found her mother, Abene Garcia, dead, a victim of the Bloodless Syndrome.

Later that day, as authorities arrived at the small town,

more victims of the Bloodless Syndrome were discovered. As of yet, no survivors have been found.

Experts are unable to explain the death of an entire village. Scientists have described the disease as a novel parasitosis, meaning its transmission is caused by a parasite, such as a worm or fly, preying on its host. The Bloodless Syndrome is not considered contagious. One researcher speculated that perhaps one of these parasites became trapped and contaminated the village water supply, but he quickly clarified. "We don't know yet. We'll run tests, diagnostics. This should not happen."

For weeks, people throughout the region have been complaining about wolves roaming the Pyrenees. While sightings are not unusual, the wolves have been described as surprisingly fearless. Two hikers' bodies were found mauled on a popular trail, and numerous livestock have been lost. Meanwhile, on the other side of the border in France, the antigovernment, white supremacist organization the Sphinx Army has been increasingly vocal, inciting violence in its regular demonstrations. While none of these events are connected to Espui's tragedy, conspiracy theorists have been hard at work stringing them into a unifying theory. "It's not a disease," one local insisted. "It's a monster."

Regardless of the cause, it seems everyone in this small

town has paid the price in this tragedy.

Chapter 27

Mina

I WORKED HARD the rest of the week. I read, then reread, my history, answered the review questions, and defined all the bold-faced words in my notes. At least I'd ace the test. I finished *Frankenstein* for English, then doubled down on calculus and physics.

I had time. The vitamins the clinic had given Lucy helped her sleep, but she still spent the night pacing the room, reaching for the window with each pass. I got into the habit of locking both it and the door. I wired a motion detector to her bedside lamp so the light would wake me every time she moved across the room. It worked so well I lost track of how many times each night I had to get up and bring her back to bed.

By Sunday, I was exhausted. But I was caught up on my homework, and Jonathan had been released from the hospital. He had permission to visit that afternoon, though of course not to my room. We spent our time wandering around campus, talking about nothing important. Jonathan held my hand. We visited a secluded gazebo.

But I had questions, and by the time dinner rolled around, I couldn't hold them in any longer. "What happened in England?"

Across the cafeteria table, a shadow darkened Jonathan's face. "I don't want to talk about it."

"Not even to me?"

Jonathan threw up his hands. "There's nothing to talk about! It was all made up!"

Clearly it still bothered him. But it wasn't just that. "I didn't know where you were, what was going on. I wondered if you weren't interested in me anymore." I bit my lip.

Jonathan leaned over the table, took my hands. "It was never about you. I was scared. I—" He closed his eyes as if to keep back whatever he was seeing in his mind. "I didn't even know if I'd make it back to you, but I wanted to. It was thinking about you that kept me going."

He kissed my hands. I let him. He was clearly working through some mental health issues, so I buried my questions deep inside. Not forgotten but on ice. For Jonathan, I could wait.

Instead, I told him about Lucy's dreams, the sleepwalking. "The dreams are random, some about dancing and parties, once it was about the airport.

Maybe they're all from her video games or something. But then—" I hesitated. This was where it stopped making sense.

"Go on."

I mashed my fork into a chicken salad that was about three-quarters mayonnaise, the rest a mush of canned vegetables and imitation meat. I wasn't hungry anyway.

"After she dreamed about the airport, there were all these news stories about a dog—maybe a wolf? Two people died of the Bloodless Syndrome, or that's what it looked like from the photographs, but the news didn't say anything. I know it's just a coincidence, but—"

Jonathan was holding on to the table, his knuckles white, like he was on a roller coaster about to take off. "When?"

"The airport?" I cast my screen and searched through the cache of news articles I had already read. I pulled up one. Jonathan read silently, motionless, only his eyes moving across the lines of text. I pulled up another. Jonathan didn't say anything. I pulled up a third, a fourth, a video.

"She didn't tell me," Jonathan murmured.

I had no idea what he was talking about. "Who?"

But he wasn't listening to me anymore. "The doctor said nothing had happened, that it was a hallucinatory episode, but Mom—she must have known. I asked. I was so afraid he'd come, but Mom didn't say anything."

"Who?" I pressed again. "Who has come?"

"Anghen," Jonathan said. "He must be in Whitby, just like he said."

"The guy you did your internship with?"

"He's a vampire. He traps people, and I think he drinks their blood, though he kept me safe for some reason. He can climb buildings upside down like a lizard, and he's strong, stronger than any human should be."

"In your hallucination?"

Jonathan shook his head. "Don't you see, Mina? This is no hallucination!"

It was like I was solving one of those story problems from calculus; I couldn't get a sense of my constants, let alone figure out any of my variables.

But Jonathan careened on as if I wasn't even there. "He can control wolves, maybe even turn into a wolf. The women could slide through the windows like mist—I don't know why he couldn't do the same. I knew there were men in the hospital, watching me, but Mom said—"

"You think your guy—Anghen—is a vampire?" I said, trying to connect the dots. "And he's in Whitby?"

"Yes!" Jonathan cried, suddenly beaming at me. "I knew you'd listen, I knew you'd believe me. I kept a notebook, tried to write everything down, but I didn't trust myself. I thought, *I'll let Mina figure it all out, tell me I'm sane.*"

"But what if you're not?" I whispered. A vampire?

None of this sounded sane to me. It sounded like one of his video games or a text-message novel, nothing real.

Jonathan froze. "You don't believe me?"

"I don't understand a word you're saying." Maybe I should have asked him more when I first saw him, pressed him harder, but his mom hadn't wanted him to talk, and he had been so quiet. And frankly, it had been easier to lose myself in kissing him.

"You have to read the notebook," Jonathan said. "I'm not explaining it well, but you'll see. It all connects. Lucy's dreams, the wolf— He wanted to come, said he had found his castle, and now he's here."

Jonathan was so certain. But I couldn't turn my brain off. "What does Lucy have to do with this? She's always been prone to sleepwalking and bad dreams. And maybe that dog or wolf or whatever was just a coincidence. They say we've destroyed habitats all over, maybe it was scavenging for food?"

"You don't believe me," Jonathan said again.

"You're talking about werewolves—"

"Vampires."

Didn't he hear himself? But his face remained impassive. If he had expected to drop this all on me, have me read some notes and believe in vampires... he didn't know me as well as he thought. "I guess I'm not really a believing sort of girl."

Jonathan rose to his feet. His face was doing this funny thing, like it wasn't quite holding together. Like it was about to crack, fall apart.

"Jonathan?" What if he was sick again? Having another mental health episode? I needed to call the hospital—

"Good night, Mina."

I got up too, scrambling. "But—"

"I need to leave before I say anything I'll regret."

"I'm willing to listen," I called to his back. "Let's talk about this."

It was as if he didn't hear me. Jonathan continued out of the cafeteria, past the nearby people staring at us, past the farthest tables of people just eating dinner, talking, doing homework, and then he was out of sight.

Before I could figure out what any of it meant, my xphone chimed with a message. I cast a screen instantly, hoping it would be Lucy or another friend or even my mom, someone to distract me from what just happened. But it was an unfamiliar number. I stared blankly at the screen.

"Mina, please come visit me for study hall. Slains 13, basement. Dr. H."

Chapter 28

Mina

WHEN I ARRIVED at Dr. Helsinger's basement office, she looked up from twelve different screencasts circling her desk, a mask over her nose and mouth. "I understand Jonathan Harker has returned."

"Uh, yeah." My mind swirled with our heated words. "He was sick."

Dr. H waved me aside like she already knew. "Sit down," she said, directing me to the chair opposite her desk. She cast another screen, directly in front of me, and opened a maze of digital folders. "Since we last spoke, there have been a plethora of strange activities, primarily concentrated in the Whitby area. I would like to understand if there's an overarching connection."

I had wandered from one incomprehensible conversation right into another.

"Now, two baggage handlers were found dead at

Caine County Airport." She had a screenshot of the article as well as a link to the news site. She switched to the next article. "A security guard is missing from Newholm Hospital."

It was weird, I'd give both Dr. H and Jonathan that. But how often do people die? Go missing? Maybe it wasn't weird at all.

"Did you happen to see pictures of the baggage handlers before WHIT News pulled them?" Dr. H asked.

"The Bloodless Syndrome," I whispered, too afraid to say the words any louder.

"Exactly like in Switzerland and England," Dr. H confirmed. "And now the Pyrenees."

"But the news— Why haven't they said anything? Why hasn't—I don't know—the health department warned anyone?"

"I suspect they know more than they wish to reveal. In truth, it may not even be a disease."

"What?"

But Dr. H continued, ignoring me. "I'm also looking into the handlers' backgrounds to figure out how it might have been transmitted. Maybe they were in Europe recently for work."

"My roommate hasn't been sleeping well," I said, my heart racing ahead. "Could she have the same thing?"

Dr. H shook her head. "The news out of Europe is scattered and sometimes conflicting, but there haven't

138

been reports of sleeplessness. In fact, any illness at all is unusual. The Syndrome's most common symptom is death."

She didn't wait for any comment before switching to the next article. "On Wednesday, a wolf maimed three, killed two," Dr. Helsinger read. "The nearest zoo is out in Mayfield, and they report no escapes."

I sat upright in my seat. I remembered my suggestion that the wolf population was looking for new homes, more food. I could still be right. But I could also be terribly wrong. "What do you think is going on?" I couldn't bring myself to say the word *vampire*. "Is Anghen here? Has he followed Jonathan?"

Dr. H abruptly closed out of her folder. The screencasts around us blinked away. "The firm has given me no reason to distrust Count Anghen."

"What? But what about all the coincidences? What does it mean?"

Her hand rested on her desk drawer, but she didn't pull it out, only squeezed its handle. "Someone should probably look into that."

Was it my imagination, or had she purposely emphasized the word *someone?*

Dr. H cocked her head. "I've kept my files for years. Sometimes a number of strange things happen all at once. Sometimes it's a full moon or a shady politician or a sudden weather change. Sometimes it's never explained." Her mouth said the words, but her eyes said something very different as they stared into my own.

139

"So... you're not going to do anything?" I asked, desperately trying to keep up.

"There isn't anything to do until we understand the pattern."

Understand the pattern, she seemed to be telling me.

"Now, it's getting late, and I promised tonight wouldn't be another late night," Dr. H said, standing up.

I couldn't tell if she meant she had promised me (she hadn't) or someone else. There was no ring on her finger. She issued a pass for me to study hall.

I messaged Lucy as I walked back to Florence. I couldn't afford to get in any more trouble. "Tell Mrs. Holmes I'm on my way."

"Aye, aye, cap'n." Lucy had apparently reverted to pirate mode. She was obsessed with that Dreamscapes pirate adventure.

"Enjoying study hall?" I messaged.

"Quincey stopped by to help me review for English. Do you know how buff he's gotten?"

I rolled my eyes. "He probably exercises!" I messaged back. Then I remembered exactly the exercise he had been doing. "Did you ask him about his brigade?"

"He's so passionate about it," Lucy whispered right back.

At least someone was having a good evening.

An old-fashioned driver-required car pulled out of the parking lot behind Slains. Probably Dr. H. I could just hear her insisting that in an electric car, anyone might be listening. But the gas had to cost a fortune, especially on a teacher's salary. I glanced back at Slains, its windows exposed without blackout curtains. They were all dark. I changed direction.

***

Slains Hall unlocked with my ID, and Dr. Helsinger hadn't bothered to lock the basement office. I slipped inside. There were surveillance cameras, but I doubted anyone was going to check the footage. And it's not like I was going to do anything wrong.

Understand the pattern, I whispered to myself. I didn't understand anything at the moment, certainly not vampires, but between Lucy and Jonathan, something was wrong, and I needed to get to the bottom of it.

Everything was dark, silent. I went straight to Dr. H's desk, slid open the bottom drawer, and pulled out the framed photo.

It was old, a true photograph, the color having yellowed over time. Dr. H looked young, even pretty. She was holding another woman in her arms, the other's feet clear off the ground. The women were kissing. It was all legal—for now. But rumors had been swirling that the LGBTQ community would be the next targeted, forced out of jobs, imprisoned in DetCens, even deported.

I carefully placed the frame back in the drawer, face down. My hands were shaking. I pressed them against my thighs, waited for them to still, then crept back outside.

It didn't change anything. Everyone had secrets. And I wouldn't tell anyone hers, not after what the government had done to my own family. Helsinger's secret was the type that could get her in a lot of trouble. It was why she had cultivated a relationship with Nancy Harker's law firm, Avett, Lucent, and Rogers. It was why she had been willing to do the favor in the first place. She couldn't investigate Anghen.

It was up to me.

Chapter 29

Mina

I SPENT THE rest of study hall searching the word *vampire*, but with each factoid I read, my thoughts became more muddled, as if my already too-complicated calculus problem had suddenly sprouted wings. I wandered, distracted, back to my room and didn't even look up until Lucy cleared her throat and announced, "Good night, Mina."

She was dressed in her one-of-a-kind flannel flamingo pajamas, her feet encased in fluffy red socks. She climbed into bed and pulled her thick comforter over her head.

"Already?" I said, though in truth, I had no idea how late it was.

"This medicine puts me out like the dinosaurs after that meteor," Lucy murmured, her eyes already closed.

"Let me get the light." It wasn't late, but I got ready

143

for bed too. I fastened the windows, locked the door, and activated my motion detector on Lucy's bedside lamp. An early night was exactly what we both needed.

***

It was quiet when I woke again. I tugged the blankets closer.

Did I screw up everything with Jonathan? The thought came unbidden.

I tossed to my other side, pulled at my blankets. It was freezing. Had the heat cut out? I closed my eyes. It was my imagination, just a chill, my life falling apart metaphorically.

No. It was FREEZING. I sat up. I didn't say anything for fear of disturbing Lucy. Thankfully, it was already light. I crossed the room to the old radiator. It was pumping out hot air. Then why—? I jerked up. The blackout curtains had been shoved aside, and the window was wide open. A gust of wind, flecked with ice, blew inside. I could see it clearly in the light. Light. My heart began to race. I turned to Lucy's bed. The bedside lamp, connected to my motion detector, was on. The blankets on Lucy's bed were shoved to one side. The bed was empty.

I leaned out into the still-dark night, skimmed the ground. Everything was wet, slimy, and muddy from a recent rain.

"Lucy?" I called hopefully. Nothing.

I leaned farther out, studied the ground. I could

make out faint footprints in the mud. Shit.

I got out socks, put on my boots. I didn't change from my cozy pants but threw a sweatshirt on, my coat over it. The door was still locked. I flipped the bolt and raced into the hallway.

I wouldn't wake anyone, not yet. I would find her, bring her back. No one would have to know. Not unless I couldn't find her or she was hurt or—

No, I wouldn't go down those paths. I would find her.

I followed the footprints across the commons, past Lovelace, toward town. The rain started up again, steady and icy cold. Lucy's path continued south, along Route 47, past rows of houses dark with blackout curtains. How far had she gone? How long had it taken me to wake up? Had it been that man at the window? Jonathan had mentioned people in the hospital too. Like that man I had seen. People watching him.

I pulled my hood closer, though it was already soaked. I continued over the bridge, across the Esk River, before finding a jumble of tracks in the slushy mud. I spun around, confused. But the footprints ended here. There was a rocky slope down to the abandoned Irving field house. The river current was strong, crashing against the rocks.

"Lucy?" I yelled.

The wind gusted, wet and raw on my skin.

"Lucy!" someone echoed.

I climbed down, carefully stepping over the wet

rocks, holding out my arms for balance. The water raced past, churning. In the distance, I could see Newholm Hospital's twinkling lights, but otherwise the island was dark.

"Lucy!" I screamed.

"Lucy!" someone echoed again.

I could barely make out a figure standing on a bench surrounded by weeds. He was wrapped in blankets, like he was sleeping rough. He was a black man, tall and skinny, all angles. A stranger.

"Have you seen her?" I called.

"She's been taken," the man answered.

Ice sliced through me. "What do you mean?" I yelled over the wind, the rain, the churning water.

"The king has come. I helped him find his counting house, just like I promised."

Okay, weird person.

I looked around again. There were no more footprints. Nothing but scrubby grass, tree roots, and trash. And the weird man standing on his park bench. He was swaying a little, like he was dancing. Or drunk.

The wind whipped across my face. I needed to find her. Maybe he had seen something; maybe there was some logic to his madness.

"Where's the counting house?" I yelled.

"There." He pointed to the old field house.

The windows were boarded up, the paint peeling. But its door hung lopsided, open. "Thank you!" I rushed toward it.

Plywood had been thrown aside, and a broken padlock lay in the doorway. The opening was dark.

"Lucy?" I called.

I cast my screen to flashlight mode and skimmed across the darkness. I could only make out a spiral staircase in the middle of the room. Above, I could hear scuffling. Mice? There was a musky, animal-like odor inside, but the rest of the building was dead silent. I climbed. Pale light sneaked in through cracks in the boards and higher windows that had been left untouched. I could make out my surroundings. I clicked off my xphone's light. I didn't dare make any noise. I didn't know what I'd find.

Then I saw socks waltzing across the floor: ridiculous, fluffy red socks. I hurried up the last few stairs. But I froze at the top. She wasn't alone.

She was posed like a dancer, her arms above her head, a man in a long black coat twirling her.

Dancing. Just like in her dreams.

The man looked up at me and I cowered back. His eyes were red. Like the man at our window. With eyes like an animal or a demon or...

He and Lucy turned once more. Suddenly the man was gone, and it was only Lucy in the middle of the room, arms raised.

Chapter 30

Mina

I CAUGHT LUCY as she fell and laid her gently on the wooden floor, then ran to the windows. The rain was falling harder now, but there were no footprints, no signs of the man in black.

I hurried back to Lucy, helped her sit up, leaned her against me. Her limbs were the consistency of pickles. I took off my coat, pulled it around her.

Lucy stared at me through a curtain of unruly blond hair. "Where am I?"

"The old field house."

Her eyes narrowed in confusion. "By the river? I dreamed I was dancing."

I couldn't find any shoes. Her fluffy red socks were wet and caked with mud.

"It was a ballroom with all sorts of elegant ladies and men in old-fashioned suits. I had such a big dress.

There was a band and waltzing. I was spinning in circles and— Oh."

Lucy took in her surroundings, the ragged curtains hanging from the windows, graffiti sprayed across the walls, dust caked thick on the floor. "How did I get here?"

"You were sleepwalking," I said, pulling her to her feet. "C'mon, we need to get you home."

"I'm fine," Lucy protested.

She was marginally better. But her eyes were flashing all about, and her teeth chattered. She leaned into me with each twist down the spiral stairs. By the bottom, my breathing was ragged, my legs beginning to shake.

"I'm sorry," I muttered. "I should have woken up when your light came on."

"But I took my medicine," Lucy argued.

Hell of a lot of good that had done. Her whole body was shaking.

We couldn't keep going like this. I cast my xphone screen, but I didn't know who to call. Mrs. Holmes? Knowing my luck, she'd expel me for sneaking out. Lucy's mom lived in Mayfield, out by Caine County Airport and the big detention center. Not too far away, but not exactly close. I wasn't sure any of my female friends could help. Would Jonathan even answer? I wished I had Arthur's contact, but I hated to bother him. I'd even call Dr. Helsinger, but she had set her info to automatically delete. Maybe a minibus? Except

I'd have to scan my ID, which of course I was missing once again.

I helped Lucy along the river, away from the weird man on the bench, and back toward campus. It was a slower route, but we wouldn't have to scale those rocks. The sky was beginning to lighten, the rain dying off. But as we crossed the bridge toward the rec center, the wind picked up, gusting into our faces, misting my glasses. I began to shiver along with Lucy. I clamped my teeth to stop them chattering.

"Mina?" I spun my head at the familiar voice and almost laughed out loud.

Quincey was running toward me. He was in his brigade gear, all tight and black, so he looked more like a shadow than a person. But he also looked like a knight in shining armor from one of those Dreamscape adventures Lucy loved.

"Quincey!" I cried. "Lucy sleepwalked, and I'm trying to get her back, but she's not feeling well."

"Hold on," he said, stripping off a layer. Then Quincey picked her up, nestling her in his arms like a precious package. "Trade you," he said, offering me his sweatshirt.

"What are you doing here?" I was suspicious I was hallucinating myself.

"Running. But I didn't realize how bad the weather was until I was already in it."

I zipped up his sweatshirt, warm with his body heat. A golden Omega pin twinkled from its breast. "Don't you already train with your brigade?"

"I have to be ready, Mina," Quincey said. "For whatever comes."

"You were," I admitted.

"Our hero," Lucy whispered from his arms.

Quincey rolled his eyes. But we kept talking, and together we walked back to Florence. In no time at all, we were home and Lucy was crawling back into bed. Safe.

But it was only the beginning.

Chapter 31

Mina

I WAS WOKEN by something at the window. My heart racing, I rolled over. Lucy was asleep. Light from under the door beamed from the hallway, reflected on her pale face, her closed eyes. What time was it? Something tapped at the window again. I swung around, carefully pulled aside the blackout curtains. There was a shadow peering against the glass. My heart leaped in my throat before I recognized the tan face, the specrays propped over his blond hair. I unlocked the window, pulled it open.

"Morning," Arthur said. "Is everything okay?"

I stared at him, wordless, exhausted, my fear rolling into fury.

"Sorry," Arthur added. "I didn't mean to scare you. Lucy didn't show up for breakfast again, and I started to get nervous since she's been sick…"

"So you're peeping in our window?" I demanded. "What time is it?" I grabbed my earpiece, cast my screen. Fifteen minutes to history. Shit.

"I'll go," Arthur murmured, backing away.

"No, I'll see if Lucy's up. It's just"—I checked my screen again—"we got back less than two hours ago. Lucy was sleepwalking, and she got outside, and if my friend Quincey hadn't found us—"

"Is she okay?"

Lucy was still asleep, her face pale. I didn't know what to tell Arthur. But an extra brain didn't seem like a bad thing at the moment, especially as I remembered Lucy saying he'd been working at Newholm's hospital and detention center.

"You might as well come in." I held out a hand as he scrambled through the window.

Arthur hurried straight to Lucy's bedside, reached for her wrist like a proper doctor.

Lucy shifted in her sleep, parted her lips, but her eyes didn't open. She must have been exhausted.

"She was cold," I told him. "Really cold, so I tried to bundle her up—"

Arthur pulled his specrays over his eyes, counted silently, frowned, then counted again. "Mina," he said, without taking his eyes from Lucy, "her heart rate is low. Really low. Has she lost any blood? Had any cuts or wounds?"

"There was a man," I said, my own heart beginning to race again. Unbidden, Jonathan's word, *vampire*,

153

whispered in my mind.

I hurried to his side. "Lucy," I murmured, touching her elbow, but she didn't open her eyes. I folded back her comforter.

"There don't seem to be any obvious injuries unless maybe they're internal," Arthur said to himself. "The sheets should be wet with blood, she should be... Did the man hurt her?" he demanded, turning to me, lifting his specrays back onto his head.

"I didn't think so. She didn't say anything like that. They danced..." I bit my lip, thinking. "What about period blood? Could that—?"

Arthur's face reddened. "No, I wouldn't think so."

"Lucy—?" I reached for her again but was interrupted by my xphone chiming. I cast my screen, saw Quincey's name. "Hello?"

"I'm out front. I wanted to check you were okay, getting Lucy to the clinic."

It was practically a party.

"You can come through the window," I told Quincey. "Arthur's already here."

"Lucy," I said, shaking her harder. "C'mon, wake up. There's a whole fan club of boys waiting for you."

That got her to open her eyes. "Mina? What time is it?"

"Lucy, you need to go to the clinic again," Arthur said.

"No, I'm fine," she protested. "Did you say—?" She glanced at me.

"Quincey's here too."

"Do I look okay?" Lucy whispered urgently.

"Stunning as always." In truth, she was very pale. We needed to get moving.

There was another knock at the window; then Quincey was climbing inside.

Arthur stared at him. Quincey stared back. But there wasn't time to sort out any of that.

"Arthur thinks she needs to go to the clinic," I said.

"Sounds like a plan," Quincey said, nodding at Arthur. "How can I help?"

I looked around the room, from Lucy in her bed, Arthur leaning over her, to Quincey locking my window. It was all happening too fast.

"Let me get my coat."

"No," Quincey said gently. "You're not even dressed. We got this."

Arthur was already pulling Lucy to her feet.

What if this man, this *vampire*, had attacked Lucy?

"You can't let her out of your sight," I said to Quincey. "She's been... Something may be attacking..." But I didn't have words for any of it.

"I won't take my eyes off her," Quincey promised. "Trust me."

They were out the door and down the hall before I could argue.

Instead, I grabbed some clothes and hurried to the bathroom.

***

I was at the clinic within ten minutes, but it was already too late. The receptionist insisted I go to class, as if I would be able to listen to anything my teachers said. I cranked the volume on my xphone up all the way so I wouldn't miss a thing. It seemed I had no choice but to trust Quincey and Arthur.

Neither messaged me until lunch, when I was already heading back to the clinic. But Arthur reported they had sent her to Newholm Hospital.

"Do they know what's going on?" I asked, casting my screen and switching to video.

"They gave her a blood transfusion and she's doing better, but they have to figure out where the blood loss came from. They're sending her to Newholm to get a scan, and they'll keep her overnight."

"So it's a medical problem?"

"The nurse certainly seemed to think so," Arthur said. "What else could it be?" His eyes met mine, wide, scared, not the confident, mini-me general I had expected.

I shook my head. At the hospital there would be doctors, nurses, machines. They would figure it out. It had nothing to do with Jonathan's Anghen, nothing to do with Dr. Helsinger's mysterious deaths. It was only a horrible coincidence.

"It will take me a bit to get down there—" I didn't have a car, and it was a long walk. I pulled up the minibus schedule.

But Arthur shook his head with a small grimace.

"Lucy insisted Quincey ride with her in the ambulance."

Great, next the boys would start performing feats of strength to try to impress Lucy. It was a play right out of that *Knights* Dreamscape. It would probably work. But I was thankful my roommate had so many people who cared about her. Besides, it also meant Quincey had kept his promise.

"Her mom's going to meet her there," Arthur continued. "You should get some sleep tonight. We both should."

***

After lights-out, our dorm room was so quiet. Usually Lucy and I would have been whispering about boys or school or finishing homework. Beside her bed, she'd left her purse, which I knew she'd miss—her travel makeup, her sunglasses, her lilac body spray, snacks. She carried just about everything in there.

"She'll be back tomorrow," I said aloud to fill the silence.

But it was worse when no one answered. What if it wasn't a medical problem? *Vampire.* She had been dancing with that man, just like in her dreams.

I should have gotten a good night's sleep: Lucy wouldn't disturb me, the window would stay closed all night. But it turned out I really didn't like being alone.

Instead, I turned on the lamp beside my bed and reached for the package security had handed me as I came into Florence. Jonathan's name was scrawled in

157

the top left corner. I hadn't heard from him since our argument—had that really been only yesterday?—but I wasn't surprised to see a small notebook inside.

I flipped it to the first page.

I think I'm in danger here, I read.

Chapter 32

Mina

I SPENT MOST of the night puzzling through Jonathan's spidery handwriting and strange story.

Whatever I had imagined, the notebook wasn't that. It was logical, detailed, and so very Jonathan. Except when it wasn't, except the parts where he was afraid, desperate, seeing things... I remembered his hands gripping the table as we talked, how his face had looked as if everything had fallen apart.

Whatever he had seen, Jonathan believed it. As I finished reading, I wasn't sure I did. I turned off the light next to me and let my eyes readjust to the darkness as I thought. But in that quiet moment, I sensed it.

The hairs on my arms stood up; a chill traveled down my spine. I looked at the door; it was closed, locked. I had locked the window above Lucy's bed too, closed the blackout curtains.

I stumbled to my feet, stepping on Lucy's purse. I absently picked it up as I pulled the curtains aside, leaned into the glass, looking out.

There was a woman on Florence's back terrace. She sat on the far stone wall, just visible in the orange glow of the outdoor light. She wore a full skirt with skirts underneath, all falling in pools around her feet. Her back was straight, and she had long, wavy dark hair.

"Stay away," I murmured.

But somehow she must have sensed me. Or maybe she had been waiting for me all along. She raised her head. Her eyes flashed red in the darkness. She smiled, rose to her feet.

The vampire woman! my brain insisted. That creature who'd threatened Jonathan, the one in the cardboard box. *She's here, now! Watching me.*

A fog must have rolled in. The dark outside felt heavy, dense. The window was dotted with mist.

I could only see glowing red in the darkness.

Lucy's purse shifted on my shoulder. I started digging inside. Lucy had to have something I could use, something to scare that monster away—mace or a whistle or... I scrambled, my fingers brushing object after object. I found her lilac body spray. I whipped it out, aimed for the creature's eyes on the other side of the glass.

A crack sounded in the silent night. I jolted back from the window, and the lilac spray fell to the floor. There was a shift, a swirl of gray, and then the window was clear. The monster was gone. Instead, a vaguely familiar car was idling in the parking lot, its old-time gas engine rumbling loudly. It must have backfired, my brain insisted. The rest was all my imagination.

My xphone chimed.

Mechanically I cast my screen.

"Are you awake?" said a gruff voice on the other end with no picture visible.

"I don't know." Could I be hallucinating like Jonathan? Or was this what a dream felt like?

"It's Dr. H," Dr. Helsinger continued, as if she didn't care if I was awake or not, let alone terrified. "I'm out back, in the parking lot behind the building. Is anyone else there with you?"

I looked around, suddenly afraid again, but I was alone. "No."

"Good. Have you invited anyone inside tonight?"

"No."

"Any strange dreams?"

"I don't usually remember my dreams."

"Useful, that," Dr. H said.

"But—" I swallowed. "There was a woman outside."

"No dream. She's gone for now."

"For now?"

"Do you know a Lucy?" Dr. H asked instead.

"She's my roommate."

"Of course. Always follow the coincidences."

Fear covered me like a blanket, consumed me.

161

"What happened? Is Lucy okay?"

"She's checked in to Newholm Hospital, correct?"

"Yes."

"And someone is with her now? A parent or a boyfriend or perhaps a sibling?"

"Yes," I said. "Her mom. But is she—?"

"Good, good," Dr. H muttered. "She should be safe for tonight."

"But what's happened?" Could it really be all Jonathan had feared? Could Lucy have been attacked?

"I will say no more over a digital connection," Dr. H said. "They have access to all our conversations. I'll meet you outside your dorm at four p.m. today. You'll be excused from your activity period, and I will transport you to the hospital myself."

"But they said they were just going to keep Lucy tonight for observation. She's supposed to come home tomorrow."

"Doubtful. If I were you, I'd bring an overnight bag for yourself as well as anything Lucy might need. Now, do you have all that?"

I didn't have any of it. I ran my fingers along the edge of Lucy's purse, bit my lip. I remembered Dr. H's illegal relationship, what she had said about understanding the pattern last time we had met.

"Why did you change your mind?" I asked. "Why help?"

"I was almost too late. And if that monster gets a toehold here—"

My eyes returned to the window.

"Am I in danger?" I didn't see the creature, but if Jonathan was right, she could be mist, a wolf, anything.

"Go to sleep. I'll keep watch on your room until dawn. You won't be disturbed."

That wasn't the slightest bit comforting.

Chapter 33

Mina

"IS SHE OKAY?" I demanded of Dr. Helsinger the following afternoon when she met me in front of Florence Hall in her antique driver-required car.

Dr. H shrugged. "We'll see when we get there. Come on."

Inside the car smelled strong, spicy enough to wrinkle my nose, and my stomach was already churning. I needed to see Lucy. I needed to figure out for myself exactly what was going on.

Dr. H dropped me off at the front lobby before driving to the parking garage. Most of it had been converted in the last pandemic to extra treatment space, but apparently there was parking on the bottom level. I checked in at the now-familiar front desk, gave them my name and Lucy's, answered their health questions, and let them scan my bag and Lucy's ridiculously full purse.

I hurried through the lobby, under the enormous cathedral ceiling, to the elevators, then on to her room.

"Mina?" Lucy whispered, her eyes instantly finding me.

Like Jonathan's, her room had three beds with curtains that could be pulled around them, but only Lucy's bed was occupied. She was ensconced in regulation white sheets and blankets, but she was wearing polka-dot flannels and had a dozen throw pillows of neon colors tucked around her. Her mom had definitely visited. But beside all the color, her face looked pale.

I sat in the chair beside her, leaned close. "How are you doing?"

"Okay. I finally got some sleep last night, so I'm sure that will help. Did you see my flowers?" She gestured at a vase full of roses on the windowsill. Hothouse flowers like that must have cost a fortune. "Arthur stopped by this morning to deliver them in person." She blushed as she said it.

More than a flower delivery must have occurred. I snorted. "Probably a little nervous after Quincey swept you away in the ambulance."

"I guess. But Mina?" The happy facade vanished. "Do I get to go back to school soon? The doctors keep coming and going, but no one's telling me anything. Is it the Bloodless Syndrome?"

"I don't think so. At least, Dr. Helsinger said it

wasn't." I told her about Dr. H, minus any compromising personal details, and how she'd probably be up shortly. "She seems to know things," I said, unsure how else to explain it.

"I don't feel right," Lucy admitted. "Like there's something else inside me. Someone."

"Someone?" I whispered, a chill flooding my body.

"I hear him," Lucy said. "He brags in my head about all his plans. Or maybe that's just a dream?"

Then Dr. Helsinger was beside me, clearing her throat behind her mask. "Let's switch spots."

I rose to my feet, my brain still humming, while she settled next to Lucy.

"Dr. Abigail Helsinger," she said, entrusting Lucy with her full name. "I teach religion and humanities at Irving, though I don't believe you've ever been in any of my classes either."

Lucy shook her head. "Sorry. Maybe next semester?"

"Never mind," Dr. H said. "I need you to tell me exactly what happened the night before last."

Lucy followed instructions, taking Dr. Helsinger through the night step by step, how she bundled up before bed, then dreamed of a party and dancing. "I had this red dress with lace across—" She stopped, realizing Dr. H had no interest in her dress. "There was a man there, and he was real nice and a looker too. So we were dancing—and then I woke up in that horrible field house."

"May I examine you?" Dr. H asked.

"Sure. But the nurses have been in and out all day, getting their numbers."

"All the same." Dr. H pulled gloves out of her pocket, then placed her hands on either side of Lucy's face, more gently than I would have expected. She pulled at the skin under Lucy's eyes, stared into each eye, then carefully pulled Lucy's hair from her neck.

She sucked in a breath. I bent closer, saw two small cuts midway down Lucy's neck.

"When did this happen?" Dr. H asked.

Lucy blushed. "I'm... not sure. I mean, maybe Arthur—"

"It was last week," I said, remembering the spot of blood. "I had just gotten back from seeing Jonathan in the hospital. You thought it was a pimple."

"Don't feel like you need to protect my innocence!" Lucy said with a half-hearted giggle.

Dr. H kept staring at the cuts. They weren't clean cuts but ragged, pricked with spots of blood. However, they were perfectly evenly spaced, like an animal had bitten her, or— Understanding flooded me. Like a vampire.

Dr. H stood abruptly, hurried to the window, and swiped the blinds tightly closed. "You've done very well. Now let Mina and I do some work for you. We've brought some greenery for you, and none too soon."

"Flowers?" Lucy said hopefully, though her eyes were heavy, as if she was already tired again.

"Not exactly," said Dr. H. "Mina?" She gestured toward two garbage bags she must have brought in with her. I opened one and reeled back. It was the smell from the car.

"Garlic," Dr. H announced. "All I could get. Thankfully, Whitby's Charleston Market is unusually well stocked." She lifted several stalks, each with white bulbs at the bottom.

"Garlic?" I repeated. This got more like a text-message novel than real life every second.

"Garlic is a traditional medicine; it was used by the Romans, the Chinese. It's an antiseptic. It boosts the immune system, soothes diarrhea, hypertension, counteracts cholesterol—"

"But none of those are Lucy's problem." I wanted her to say it.

"It's also a traditional folk medicine that may ward off evil spirits."

It didn't sound any better out in the open. I continued to argue with everything in front of me. "One of our classmates thought it could be something she was eating. An allergy or something. Or maybe she just needs a stronger dose of medication so she won't be walking around at night."

"The doctors will give her whatever they think best," Dr. H said. "But when dealing with something beyond our understanding, I have found the traditional treatments are the most reliable." Dr. H pointed at the bag. "Now string the plants around the room. You can weave them together, hang them from fixtures. Make sure you cover the window frame and the door handle."

I wondered what the nurses might think of this, but Dr. H had closed the door behind her.

"It smells clean," Lucy murmured from the bed. At least she thought so. I started weaving garlic plants together as Lucy fell asleep.

"You know, if your friends hadn't checked on her, Lucy might have died."

Dr. H's words slammed into me like a wave. "What?"

Dr. H placed a warm hand on my shoulder. I wouldn't have called her the reassuring type. Maybe she had to take a kindness class as part of her religious training or something. "I'm not blaming you, only making sure you understand what we're dealing with. I believe Jonathan's Anghen has indeed made his way to Whitby."

"And Lucy's illness, and the wolves, and the airport—it's all related?"

"I believe so."

"But why?" I asked. "Even if it is true, why Lucy? She doesn't know Anghen; she has nothing to do with Jonathan's mother's firm."

"Perhaps, being more open to dreams, she's more susceptible to attack?" Dr. H said. "That's one of the things I'd like to figure out. I'll reach out to some of my European contacts to see if Lucy's symptoms match up with anything they've experienced over there."

"But it's not the Bloodless Syndrome?"

"The Bloodless Syndrome may be a very different illness than we have been led to believe," Dr. H said cryptically. "It's possible we're dealing with multiple monsters, some who kill, some who have other uses for humans. I'll also need to speak to Jonathan. Can you share his contact details? He's no longer listed in school records."

I hesitated. I hadn't heard from him since the cafeteria. I wasn't sure he wanted to hear from me. Maybe anyone if he deleted his records.

"A lot hangs in the balance."

"Of course." I heard a ding from my xphone as she buzzed her personal contact info over. I whispered into my ear receiver and sent his information to her.

"Now," Dr. H said, "I'm not sure what plans there are for the evening, but Lucy must not go home. I will consult with her doctors and recommend that the mother get some sleep. Since you already know the situation and are clearly close, I would like you to stay with Lucy tonight. You may sleep too. The garlic will protect you both. But if you need anything, please make sure you contact me. Sooner rather than later." She gave me a stern look.

"Okay." I hadn't wanted to return to Florence's silence anyway.

"One final thing," Dr. H said, standing. "I'll instruct the nurses and other staff to announce their presence before entering. They'll need to check Lucy's vitals, deliver dinner, and so on. But once night falls, if someone knocks without announcing themselves, do not answer. Do not open the door, do not let Lucy leave, and do not leave yourself until you hear my voice again tomorrow morning. If I'm right about what this Anghen is, Lucy's safety depends on it."

I finally asked the question that had been preying on my mind. "Will she be okay? She won't turn into…?"

I couldn't say the word, but Dr. H understood. "Not if I can help it."

With that, she took off down the hallway.

***

"Mina?"

I turned from Lucy's closed door. She must have been awake after all and heard everything Dr. Helsinger had said. "What does she mean? Is there some creature inside me for real?"

"Not inside you," I murmured, "I don't think so. But it has attacked you and might try again."

"Is it a vampire?" Lucy said, putting all the pieces together for herself. "Mina Bird, be honest—am I going to die?"

"No," I promised. "I'm going to do everything I can to stop this vampire. We're going to figure it out, we're going to get you the best help, we're going to keep you so safe that no one can get to you."

"Good," Lucy said. "I have some serious plans for

our senior year." But her smile didn't quite reach her eyes.

I sat in the stiff chair at her bedside, prepared for a long night.

But Lucy kept talking, tried to sit upright. "You have to keep yourself safe too."

"Dr. Helsinger says we'll both be safe."

"It's you he wants to find," Lucy said. "My bed was just closer to the window. I'm the distraction."

"Distraction?" I echoed, my body growing frigid in the hospital's cool air.

"He told me," Lucy said, tapping at her head. "He could have just killed me. But now he's using me to keep you sidetracked from finding him. He's planned it all out."

"Go to sleep." I had no idea what more to say. I tried to put conviction in my voice. "You don't have to worry. We'll find him."

Chapter 34

Arthur

November 13, Newholm Detention Center

Patient 562:
    Age: 47
    Ethnicity: African American
    Gender: Male
    Condition: Stable
    Heart rate: 67
    Blood pressure: 120/72

THE DETENTION CENTER corridors were dim during the early-morning shift.

Arthur studied his glowing screen. "Your vital signs are all good," he said to Patient 562.

Mr. Renfield was sitting up in bed, watching him. "Of course they're good. I'm perfectly healthy.

173

Perfectly sane."

"Last time we talked, you were eating spiders in their webs." Arthur couldn't help himself. Earlier that evening he'd had the strangest conversation with Dr. H, his old historical religion teacher. She'd said she knew his mom, was even friends with her, though Arthur couldn't remember her ever being mentioned. And that wasn't even the strange part. His head was spinning. Why couldn't Mr. Renfield ever be asleep?

Mr. Renfield narrowed his eyes as if confused. "Eating spiders? I think you're mistaking me with another patient, Dr. Godalming."

"I'm not a doctor," Arthur said mechanically. Not to mention Mr. Renfield's entirely inappropriate use of Arthur's last name.

"Why not? You're young, ambitious. You should take charge. Clear my record."

This time Arthur didn't respond. He had enough people in his life waiting for him to take charge. Though Mr. Renfield did look better than he had in weeks. There was color in his cheeks, he was speaking in full sentences, carrying on logical conversation.

"What are you writing, Doctor?"

"I'm noting that you look better."

"Because you know this is a farce," Mr. Renfield said. "I insist on my lawyer."

"You have a lawyer?" Arthur asked, surprised.

"Fine. I'm not privileged like you and your friends. I don't have the right ID card, the right skin color, the right father."

"That has nothing to do with—"

"Of course it does," Mr. Renfield said. "Don't play dumb, Dr. Godalming."

"Until you're stable, the detention center can't let you go," Arthur said, falling back on the official line. "They need to trust that you won't hurt yourself or anyone else."

"But I helped your friends."

Arthur had no idea what Mr. Renfield was talking about. He ignored the conversation, returned to his notes.

Like Mr. Renfield, Lucy was stable. Better, even. Dr. H had said Mina was sitting up with her tonight, so Arthur knew she wasn't alone. But Dr. H had asked all these strange questions and provided no explanations, only insisting that she didn't talk over phone connections. He didn't blame her. His mom had taught him to be careful. You never knew who was listening, especially with his dad's military connections, his role in Europe. But Dr. H's obsession with security didn't make him feel any better. Something was going on with Lucy, and he couldn't make any sense of it.

"She's very pretty."

Arthur started. It was almost as if Mr. Renfield had heard his thoughts.

"Not so much the dark one. She's too intelligent with her all-seeing glasses. But I helped her find her friend. I told her about the king, about the counting house. The king won't mind. He has eyes everywhere. He's going to play his game, chase his prey. I see it all in my dreams." Mr. Renfield's mouth turned into a too-wide smile, full of teeth and menace. "And no wonder. Your Lucy is very pretty. She's young and full of the life ahead of her."

Arthur was standing directly over Renfield before he realized it. He was remembering past conversations, timing, trying to figure out what Mr. Renfield had seen or overhead. But Arthur hadn't said anything about Lucy, he was sure of it. He hadn't wanted to jinx anything between them. Then her illness had come on so quickly.

"How do you know about Lucy?"

"I told you. I helped her. Ask the goggled one." Mr. Renfield held his hands in front of his eyes like binoculars. Or glasses. *Mina, he means Mina, with her used glasses.*

Mr. Renfield was playing with him. He must have heard Lucy's and Mina's names somewhere and decided to use them as leverage.

Arthur took a deep breath. Renfield was a patient; he wasn't well. "Why do you think I'll help clear your record if you tell me stories about my friends and threaten to hurt them?"

"Not hurt them, help them."

"How could you have helped them? You live here."

Mr. Renfield was silent, studying Arthur. "You really believe that, don't you? Even after our discussion the other day. I told you, I only need my records cleared so I can be free for the rest of my long life. How could you believe this creaky old DetCen could hold me when you come and go as you please? When I lived on Dead Zone streets? When I know Whitby forward and backward, like the back of my hand?"

He raised his hand like a dancer, turning his palm one way, then the next. All down the back of his hand, his wrist, his lower arm, there were marks, crosshatches, twisting circles. No. Arthur stared in the dim light. Cuts. Miniature cuts everywhere, like the patient had drawn a whole map on his arm.

"All of Whitby and the surrounding area. Especially Newholm, Irving Academy, the river," Mr. Renfield whispered, tracing a meandering scar with his finger. "All for him. I'm going to be one of his special friends too."

"Nurse!" Arthur called, jamming the call button. "Nurse!" Then he cast his screen between them like a shield and captured the image.

Chapter 35

Mina

IT DIDN'T TAKE long for Lucy to sleep. But I refused to let my guard down for even a moment, for both our sakes. Instead, I returned to the beginning of Jonathan's notebook, this time whispering while my xphone transposed my voice to text. There were faster ways to get a typed, searchable copy. But it was like Dr. Helsinger had said: I needed to understand the pattern. So I reread the whole thing, aloud this time.

As the night went on, no one knocked or tried to enter, and Lucy's sleep was apparently dreamless. By the time I finished the final page, I could no longer keep my eyes open. I set my xphone alarm to beep every thirty minutes, then curled into the stiff hospital chair and fell asleep.

But every half hour when I checked, Lucy was sleeping. She was curled under the hospital blanket, her

178

lips slightly parted, her cheeks pink, like a sneaky Sleeping Beauty. *Maybe the garlic worked some magic after all*, I thought as the early-morning sunlight began to stream in and I fell back to sleep.

I was jolted awake by a knock.

A voice announced, "This is Dr. H of Irving Academy."

I swung the door open.

Dr. H's face was inches from mine. "Are you safe? Is Lucy human?"

I stared at her, then back at Lucy, before finally mustering a yes.

Dr. H exhaled. "My garlic must have worked. Let me get the mom from the waiting room."

***

When I returned that afternoon, Lucy's room was still festooned with garlic. Her poor roses had mostly withered. They had never stood a chance.

"One of the nurses tried to open a window," a familiar voice chimed in behind me. "That teacher of yours nearly bit his head off."

"It was close," Lucy added, laughing. "When that doctor tried to set up a 'contagion zone,' Dr. H told him he was a professional hack. But Mina, look who's here!"

It was reassuring to see Quincey in a chair at Lucy's bedside. It made me feel less alone.

"Quincey is like penicillin," Lucy announced. "But

179

in a miracle-cure way, not in a moldy one. I'm feeling so much better."

I nodded, hoped it would be true. Lucy was always an optimist. But we needed a more concrete plan.

Another face appeared in the doorway.

"Me again," Arthur said. "Can I see how she's doing?"

"The more the merrier!" Lucy insisted.

It seemed both boys were determined to make their presence known.

Arthur checked the screen above Lucy's bed. "Nothing's changed," he murmured.

"Dr. H says I'll need to stay another night," Lucy said.

"Why is Dr. H—?" Arthur started to ask.

"Quincey says he can watch over me," Lucy added.

Arthur abruptly took in Quincey sitting beside Lucy. He frowned but covered it by introducing himself: "Arthur Godalming. I know we met the other morning, but—"

"It was a little chaotic," Quincey answered, reciprocating with his full name: "Quincey Jordan."

Then silence. I was trying to figure out some inane, friendly thing to say when Jonathan rushed into the room.

"I've been trying to find you," he huffed at me. "Dr. H called. She says the monster attacked Lucy. Are you okay?" His whole body was trembling.

"Monster?" Quincey asked, looking from Jonathan

to Arthur, back to me.

"I'm fine. For now. But I know what's wrong with Lucy," I announced, taking them all in, all eager to do something. Everyone needed to be on the same page. "It's surreal, but the pieces fit together. And I'm going to need your help."

"I've been going over every possibility," Arthur started, ticking off diagnoses on his fingers. "Of course, the doctors suspect the Bloodless Syndrome, but—"

"You haven't gone over everything," I said. "With Jonathan's permission, I'd like to send you each a copy of the notebook he kept this past fall."

Jonathan shook his head, his hands clenching into fists, as if Anghen might suddenly appear in our midst.

"It's the only way," I mouthed back. Otherwise they would never have a chance of understanding. "I should've believed you from the beginning."

Jonathan closed his eyes as if it were too much. But then he reached for my hand, offered a tense nod. Arthur opened up sharing on his specrays, and I buzzed the file to all of them.

Lucy's earpiece chirped and she blinked open a screen. Quincey's screen also flared to life. Arthur pulled his specrays over his eyes.

"You digitized it?" Jonathan said as he squeezed my hand.

"I wanted everyone to be able to read it."

I passed the notebook back to Jonathan. He automatically took it, jammed it deep into his pocket.

My hand ached when he let go.

"We should keep talking," I said, pushing the others. It would take them hours to read everything, and we had more to do. "I'm also sending you a rough timeline of what happened when. While Jonathan was in England, Lucy's dreams began."

"And the man in my dreams, you think he's Jonathan's guy?" Lucy asked.

"What does he look like?" Jonathan jerked his head upright.

Lucy's description matched Jonathan's description of Anghen exactly. Jonathan closed his eyes. But I kept talking through Lucy's dreams and the rest of my timeline, the airport deaths, the wolf attacks, the field house. I told them about the creature in my window a few nights ago.

"He brought her with him, and now she's watching you," Jonathan said, his jaw clenched.

"There's something else," Arthur said from the chair he had settled into by the window. "One of the patients I've been monitoring at the DetCen. It's confidential, so I really can't give any details, but—" Arthur cracked each of his knuckles as he told us what his patient had said about me, Lucy, his rhyme about the king in the counting house. "He's tall, skinny, black."

"Cheekbones?" I asked, drawing a high, almost modelesque face over mine.

Arthur nodded.

"He was the man on the park bench, the one I thought was homeless. Anghen must be his king."

"He must have told Anghen about the area, even made a map out of his own skin. He says he has terrible dreams. Just like Lucy."

I didn't realize I was biting my lip again until I tasted blood.

"It sounds like he needs help instead of just being locked up," Quincey muttered.

Arthur frowned. He must have heard the edge in Quincey's voice. "He's got doctors. That's why DetCens are almost always housed alongside hospitals."

"So much for the three-day rule," Quincey said.

Quincey was right. DetCens weren't supposed to hold anyone longer than three days. Only enough to get them help, or barring that, transfer them elsewhere. But lately there had been rumors that people were detained longer or even disappeared.

"We're taking care of him," Arthur protested. "We're trying to make him better."

"Did he eat flies before he was locked up?" I heard the other questions in Quincey's voice. Was there anything else on this patient's record? Or was it just an excuse to lock up another person of color?

"It's a hospital room!" Arthur snapped, rising to his feet. "He's a patient—we're taking care of him!"

Quincey didn't reply, but he stood as well. Arthur glared back at him as an awkward silence fell over the room. Maybe we should have done this meeting remotely rather than face-to-face. The boys hardly knew each other; I hardly knew Arthur. What did we have in common except Lucy? And even that was turning into a competition. I understood now how Jonathan had felt when he first confessed everything to me. Why would any of them believe this mess of a story?

Quincey spoke up. "It's wild, but all the parts about this Anghen track." He lowered himself back into the seat by Lucy's bedside as if signaling he was willing to work with us, regardless, for Lucy's sake.

Arthur frowned. "But what if there is some medical explanation? What if we can solve this another way?"

"The doctors can keep working on that," I said. "Lucy can stay in the hospital. She's safest here anyway."

"But what about you?" Lucy asked. "Where will you go?"

"You're not safe in Florence," Jonathan reminded me.

I remembered that woman at my window, her red eyes watching me. I was tempted to turn to Jonathan, to let him take care of me, to hide out in his suburban condo. But what about Lucy? What about Dr. H and Arthur and his patient? If there really were vampires, we needed to do something.

"There's no fighting him," Jonathan said, as if he could read my mind.

"But we have to try," I argued.

"You could stay with me," Arthur piped up. "If

Jonathan doesn't mind. Dad arranged a suite for me, so I've got a spare bedroom."

I caught Quincey rolling his eyes, but Arthur continued. "You'd still be on campus, close to Lucy, but this monster won't know where you are and we can watch out for each other."

Relief flooded through me. I hadn't wanted to return to Florence. "Okay."

"So what's the rest of the plan?" Quincey said.

"We need to find Anghen," I said. "He's the one who caused Lucy's illness and may be the only one who can stop it. We can report him to the police, the hospital, whatever it takes."

"Will the police believe any of this?" Quincey asked.

"Dr. H thinks the Bloodless Syndrome in Europe may be connected to the recent deaths at Caine County Airport. And it may not even be a disease but rather a symptom of attack. If Anghen is the missing link, I think they'd have to at least investigate it."

Arthur nodded. "My dad's stationed in France. He probably can't share any information from his end, but if there's a connection, he could take it to the top."

I exhaled. Maybe this whole wild thing was possible after all.

"Jonathan," I continued, "can you compile a list of everything you know about Anghen's powers? Maybe you can cross-reference it with what is known generally but highlight the things you specifically observed?"

Jonathan nodded.

"You should also see if your mom has any information on whether he purchased a house in the area. In the meantime—" I bit my lip. The next part was going to sound senseless, but I knew I was right. "We need to find him. Now."

While we had talked, the evening had grown later. The sky outside was hazy, even darker through the film of the hospital windows.

"If I'm following all this correctly," Quincey said, "he's at his highest powers right now. But if we wait a few hours—"

"It's insane!" Jonathan said. "You haven't met him; you don't know what he's capable of. Even during the daylight— No, I promised Mom I wouldn't get involved, that I'd stay out of it."

My eyes met his. "Then go."

Jonathan jerked to his feet, spun in a slow circle. But he didn't leave.

"We can be there at dawn," I said, casting my screen to check the time. "That will give us some time to get ready."

"Where?" Arthur asked, cracking his knuckles, already preparing for action.

"The field house," I said. Renfield had been there, Lucy, Anghen. Everything connected to it. We needed to return.

Chapter 36

Mina

WE GATHERED OUTSIDE the hospital again at dawn. Arthur pulled up in his driverless red car. It pinged with some sensor or alert—it looked like it had all the latest technology.

Quincey returned from the government blockade at the edge of Whitby with a hammer and bag of wooden stakes he had borrowed from somewhere. Jonathan fingered the Star of David around his neck but said nothing. He hadn't said anything for hours. We slid into the back seat.

While Arthur's car drove to the rec center, he explained his plan. "We can park in the back lot, closest to the bridge to the island. Across the bridge is the trail through the forest. We'll follow that to the field house."

"You're a regular GI Joe," Quincey muttered.

"I scouted it out," Arthur admitted. "My dad has

187

sent me to leadership camp every summer since I was six."

The expression on Quincey's face changed with Arthur's unexpected honesty. "Good," Quincey said, this time without any snark. "Let's save Lucy."

Arthur continued. "We can circle around the back, make sure we cover the perimeter. Mina and Jonathan will take the west side, Quincey and I will take the east. We'll meet at the front door if we don't meet anything else first."

We talked through every step. If we encountered anyone, Quincey and Jonathan would hold them, Arthur would drive the stake. If we were lucky, Anghen would be asleep, just like Jonathan had found him.

"The plan is to kill him?" Quincey asked.

"We have to," Jonathan finally said, his voice gruff with disuse. "He's not human—he's a monster. I've spent all night looking at the research. It says destroying him is the only way to save Lucy."

Arthur nodded in agreement, grim like a man headed into battle. "We can report the death anonymously to the police."

Quincey looked like he didn't believe anything to do with the police would be anonymous, but he didn't argue with Arthur. Instead, Quincey folded his arms around himself as if trying to hold everything together. We were just kids. But what had the media, the school, the government itself done to protect us?

The sky was gray and hazy in the early-morning

light as we crossed the river and started single file along the forested trail. I turned as the trees closed off the light behind us. I imagined all the horrible things that came out in the darkness. All the things that were watching us. But nothing moved.

I continued after the boys. The river water was more black than blue. It was shallow but running quickly with the recent rain.

Quincey stilled in front of me. "Did you see——?" he whispered, slowly raising a hand to point ahead of us.

Maybe I hadn't been imagining things.

Arthur nodded. "I'm not surprised. Renfield said Anghen has friends. As long as they're only watching…" He reached for his waistband and pulled out a gun.

Quincey stepped back. "I suppose you know how to use that thing?"

"What do you think?" Arthur cracked his knuckles, his face grim.

"I think leadership camp sounds like a terrible place," Quincey muttered.

"You have no idea." Arthur continued down the trail, deeper into the undergrowth. The rest of us followed.

The field house loomed in front of us, shadowed. Jonathan took my shoulder, continued close behind me as we kept moving west. Just like that horrible night, the windows were boarded up. But this time the door was closed.

Arthur and Quincey appeared from the other side. Quincey reached for the handle.

The door wouldn't open.

He leaned forward, pushed against the handle. Arthur joined him.

The door flew open. The boys stumbled into the darkness. Arthur raised his gun.

We had lost the element of surprise. But inside, no one moved.

Arthur turned his specrays to light mode and scanned the perimeter. It was silent. I could make out the graffiti on the walls, the spiral staircase. I remembered the stench, as if there was a mouse infestation or an animal had died. Or... maybe that meant Anghen was here after all.

Arthur climbed upstairs, Jonathan behind him, Quincey keeping watch with me below. They returned only minutes later, Arthur shaking his head.

"Look at this," Quincey said instead, gesturing. In the floor was a thin line, a rectangular indentation of a door. It reminded me of what Jonathan had written about the basement at Bram Manor, the coffins.

Quincey must have had the same thought. He knelt on the dusty floor, ran his fingers along the sides of the door. He dug deeper, wedged his fingers inside, and pulled.

The door swung open with a crack against the floor. Arthur aimed his gun.

Nothing.

I joined Quincey's side, peered down. It wasn't a
full basement, only a crawl space with a dirt floor.
Quincey slid feetfirst, dropping below. It was deeper
than I had expected; Quincey stood almost full height.
He held out a hand for me.

"Mina!" Jonathan hissed. "Let me go first."

Quincey helped him down. Jonathan wrapped his
arms around my legs, lowering me until my feet
touched the floor. I turned, taking in my surroundings.
The space must have been used for storage—I could
faintly make out a row of canoes, a weathered wooden
board hung with life jackets, a tarp hanging from the far
end. And just in front of the tarp, two long cardboard
boxes.

"They've been here," Quincey whispered.

"Might be here still," Arthur said, joining us below.

Jonathan moved toward the boxes, ducking his
head under the low ceiling. Suddenly he cried out, his
voice part scream, part gasp. Arthur ran his light along
the edge of the boxes. Beside the boxes was a body,
then another. It was just like the pictures in the news
from Europe. Their skin was taut over their skeletons,
their frames emaciated. The Bloodless Syndrome.

"I'm calling the police," Arthur announced. But
even with the specrays' advanced technology, we could
hear the hum of a missing signal. Arthur retreated to
the base of the trapdoor. The hum continued. Arthur
reached for the main floor, pulled himself up slowly.
His specrays beeped with life.

A laugh burst out behind me. Someone grabbed my hand, pulled my body into theirs.

It was the woman—the creature—who had been at my window! I stared at her mouth, twisted in a red smile, her hair lost to shadows.

I struggled in the creature's arms. I hadn't thought she'd have power, but she was stronger than me, holding me tight. It was so dark inside—maybe daylight didn't reach this place.

The boys stared, helpless. Quincey dropped to a fighting stance. From above, Arthur aimed his specrays into the gloom. The creature's white skin glowed in the light.

"Got you!" she whispered in my ear, taunting me.

Her breath at the back of my neck was rancid. She raised a hand to my face. Her nails were long, twisted. The creature ran one along my cheek. It stung, and I could feel a pinprick of blood well up. The vampire licked her lips.

"Let her go!" Jonathan demanded, abruptly rushing forward.

"It's you," the creature purred, eying Jonathan from head to toe.

Her face turned back to me, her frigid skin inches from my own. "Too bad the king's saving you, dear," she whispered.

The creature threw me forward, tossing me into Jonathan's arms.

The room echoed with gunshot from above. The

vampire stumbled back, held a hand to her shoulder.

"She's vulnerable!" Arthur shouted.

Quincey slammed into the creature's side, knocking both of them to the dirt floor.

"Get the stakes!" he yelled.

Arthur vaulted back downstairs, ran to Quincey's side. But even as Quincey tried to hold the creature down, she fought back, twisting and turning under him. She leaned into his face, hissed.

Quincey started, and the monster leaped to her feet.

Even with her injured shoulder, she moved like an animal, springing to the door above us, hauling herself up, slipping away in the light.

Arthur charged after her, rushing up through the trapdoor.

"He's not going to catch her," I cursed, starting up. The daylight was growing, casting even the dark crawl space in gray morning light.

"But someone else might still be here," Jonathan whispered, gesturing at the boxes in the still-dark corner. They were cardboard, encrusted with rich dirt, thick with several layers of brown packing tape.

My heart skipped. Jonathan grabbed an oar from the wall beside him. He thrust the oar downward, hacking through the cardboard, deep inside. I held my breath.

Jonathan frowned. He slashed the oar to the side, creating a wide gash in the box. Black earth spilled out. Nothing else.

He turned on the other one.

Quincey had an oar in his hand as well and worked alongside Jonathan, shredding the cardboard.

"He's not here," Jonathan groaned.

"What about—?" I pointed to the hanging tarp.

"But we were right," Quincey said. "They're more vulnerable during the day. Arthur *shot* her."

"Wish I had silver bullets," Arthur said, peering down at us. "Isn't that what the stories say?"

Whatever I was going to ask about the tarp left my mind. We all looked up, expectantly, but Arthur shook his head. "She was too fast. But we had her!"

"We had her," Quincey echoed. "We can destroy them."

"And we can keep them from using this space ever again," Jonathan said, kneeling. From his bag, he pulled several bulbs of garlic. He buried them deep within what was left of the cardboard's earth. "These are the first two boxes," he said. "Anghen left with eight. Now he's down to six."

Arthur moved to the bodies. "The police should be here soon," he said, kneeling. "They'll figure out who these people are, get notification to their families. And look—"

He slipped on gloves from his pocket, then reached for the closest body, gently cradling its head as he tilted back the neck. For a moment he didn't look so much like the general, more like someone who could be a doctor. In Arthur's light, I saw a pair of gaping wounds.

"Let's tell Lucy," Quincey said, rising to his feet.

Chapter 37

Mina

I LET THE boys recount their adventures at Lucy's bedside and instead spent most of the rest of the day at school. When I returned that afternoon, Lucy's eyes were closed. Dr. Helsinger must have refreshed the garlic; combined with the hospital's bleach, it smelled like a very clean Italian restaurant. I set a white carrier box on the chair beside Lucy's bed and cast my screen to take a picture of her latest data.

"I look like the model of success, don't I?" Lucy whispered, stretching as a smile beamed across her face.

"You do." Her blond hair fanned out over her pillow, her eyes were bright, even her eyelashes... "Are you wearing mascara?"

"There're all these boys in and out, Mina Bird. I have to keep up my appearance!" She cackled, sitting up. "Have you seen the hot brigaders manning the door? They're not those scary Alphas but from something called the Omega Brigade. Quincey says they're the good guys."

There was no point arguing about the brigade again. Lucy's mom had been exhausted staying up with her. Lucy's brother was nearby too, but he worked remotely for one of the tech towns and could somehow never manage to get time off work. So Quincey had persuaded his brigade friends to help out. The two guarding the door were slightly older, black, with the same sparkling Omega pin that Quincey wore. It was enough for now that Quincey trusted them. Someone needed to keep an eye on Lucy twenty-four seven.

"Speaking of triceratops," I muttered. But I couldn't help smiling even in the midst of my exhaustion. Lucy was getting better. We would find Anghen. She could beat this thing.

"Mom's going to see if I can go home soon. She thinks it will be better for me away from the hospital—quieter without all the nurses and boys and brigaders. Though really, I think she's just sick of garlic. She hates it!" Lucy laughed.

While Lucy chatted, I cast my screen, pulled up our file. I had already crossed the field house off the list of Anghen's possible locations. Jonathan's mom had insisted she couldn't help us find Anghen's castle, but maybe she still thought Jonathan was only delusional. Regardless, the next step had to be talking to some contacts in Whitby. Maybe Quincey's brigade would prove useful in that regard as well. We needed to find out which houses had been moved into recently. We needed to check any suburban hotels too. I added it to my list.

"What about school, Mina?" Lucy asked suddenly.

I wondered if she had noticed the dark circles under my eyes, but I kept my voice light. "Dr. H has permanently excused me from activity period."

"But when did you last sleep?" Lucy protested. She had definitely noticed my eyes. "Have you moved into Arthur's yet? That's the most important thing, otherwise we're right back where we started. Besides, Mom's been here all day. Quincey's supposed to come soon. The hot brigaders are just outside. The point is: you should go back to school and get settled in his suite. Then you can do some homework and sleep without having to worry."

I shrugged. "I'm still on track to make valedictorian." We had about a month left of the semester, but that last history test had helped tremendously. Calculus was less complicated than my own life at the moment. I only needed a seventy percent or higher on the final to ace physics. I'd done this enough years in a row I knew the drill.

"You're a professional!" Lucy said. "Straight As for four years at Irving. No college would dream of turning you down!"

I bit my lip, not sure how to put what I'd been feeling lately into words. "What if I want to do something else instead?"

"But you're the smartest person I know. College needs you. The world needs you!"

That was just it. I'd been focused so long on being perfect, no matter how many laws they passed against people of color. But what if it wasn't enough? Or what if I didn't want to play their games anymore? I knew Lucy would listen to whatever I had to say, but I wasn't sure what that was.

Lucy continued. "Actually, being stuck in this hospital has got me thinking. I want to be just like you. Except in my own Lucy way. I'm going to do all the things, leave my mark, change the world."

"Whatever you do will be amazing," I said. "But for the moment, I need to focus on finding Anghen, destroying him."

"*We* need to find him," Lucy said. "I'm not some invalid, remember? I can do my part. Besides, I'll be out of here soon. Then everything will go back to normal, you'll see." Lucy propped herself up higher, started to say something else, then pointed at the bedside chair. "Wait—" She squealed. "Is that a carrier box from Fortilly's?"

Fortilly's was a fancy dress shop out in Mayfield.

"You're going to Midwinter Ball?" I handed her the box.

"I didn't *mean* to buy it." Lucy swiped her code, then pulled it open. "But it was perfect, and quite reasonable, and— Look."

She pulled the dress from the tissue paper it was wrapped in and held it out. It was a shimmery blue with extra fabric wrapped around the shoulders to make a kind of halter. The bottom was a full skirt sparkling with sequins.

"Remember how we were supposed to have the best senior year ever? I still want to do everything, Mina Bird," Lucy continued.

"So who's the lucky boy?"

"Arthur. I've known him forever, and we always have so much to talk about. Plus I think this doctor thing suits him, you know? He's branching out." She frowned. "But I don't want him to get too serious. Maybe I should just tag along with you and Jonathan?"

Jonathan and I hadn't even talked about it yet, and I certainly hadn't ordered a dress. But I'd figure it out if that's what Lucy wanted. "Sure."

She folded the dress, then carefully slid it back into the narrow box. She begrudgingly handed the package to me.

"You should keep it," I said.

"Where?" Lucy gestured around her hospital room.

"There's a coatrack." It even had an ancient plastic hanger on it. "That way it can stretch out a bit. And give you something happy to look at."

"Like sunshine in a cave." Her voice was suddenly quiet, sad, as if she didn't have the energy to pretend anymore.

I strapped the dress on the hanger and positioned it

so it was facing her, but she offered only a tight smile.

"I wish Quincey had asked," Lucy murmured.

I sat back, surprised, but Lucy kept talking. "Ever since that night when he saved me at the field house, I've been wondering if there could be something between us. It's stupid, and I know he's more your friend than mine, but I thought... I thought something else might be going on. Before everything fell apart."

"There's time," I said. "Pretty soon things won't be falling apart and you can ask him or whomever you want."

I snuggled into bed next to her, and for a moment I forgot everything else: the hospital, vampires, the feeling of being in a dark, cold cave. It was like we were back in our dorm room in Florence, gossiping about boys.

"He's so serious," Lucy whispered. "But serious in a good way. He knows things, and he wants to make the world a better place. And did you know he reads poetry?"

"Poetry?" I snorted, teasing. "Didn't you say Quincey was coming?"

"Yes," said a voice behind us.

We both turned.

Quincey was leaning against the doorway. "Sorry, I didn't want to interrupt, but I wanted to let you know I'm here."

"You're just in time for dinner," Lucy said without missing a beat. "I'll tell the cafeteria we need an extra."

She clapped her hands like he was the best thing that had happened all day. And Quincey smiled like a hospital dinner was his idea of a perfect evening.

I needed to get going. "I'll see you both around."

"See you, Mimi," Quincey said while Lucy waved, already whispering her dinner order into her xphone receiver.

I lingered in the hallway, staying within earshot. I told myself Lucy would have done the exact same snooping if our roles were reversed.

"I've wanted to ask you out." From my position in the hallway, Quincey's voice sounded husky, tentative in a way I'd never heard before. "But you and Arthur are so close, and I wasn't sure—"

A smile crept over my face.

"You wanted to ask me to Midwinter Ball?" I heard Lucy ask in that same quiet, careful tone—as if afraid she'd miss a step if she rushed ahead.

"Yes," Quincey said. "That. And just dinner. And movies. And whatever—I want to do it all with you."

"Yes," Lucy echoed. "I would've said yes. To all of it."

"You'll go out with me?"

"Yes," Lucy repeated, as if she couldn't stop saying it.

I did a little dance in the hallway.

"I'll be all better soon, you'll see," Lucy promised. "By the time Midwinter Ball rolls around, I'll dance all night with you."

Now it was really time to go, yet my feet still slowed on the walk to the elevator.

"Quincey," Lucy said, "what's your middle name?"

"Morris. It was my grandma's family name."

"C'mere, Quincey Morris Jordan," Lucy said, her voice sounding breathy but no longer sick. "I want to do everything with you."

I hurried down the hall before I heard any more, a wide smile on my face. Lucy was going to be just fine.

Chapter 38

Mina

AFTER STUDY HALL, I stayed up, working at the small desk in my Florence dorm room. Dusk turned to darkness, but I was making progress. The latest calculus problem set had clicked in my mind like a puzzle piece. There were still several calculations, but I knew where I was going, how to get there. I kept shuffling the numbers on my screen, moving steadily from step to step, almost done.

My xphone sounded with a message from Lucy. It played through the speaker in my ear: "Are you still at Florence?" Lucy's voice said with a side of exasperation.

I rolled my eyes. She knew me too well. I started to whisper text, to explain that I just had a few more steps to finish my calculus for the night, when another message came in.

"I can see the building. He must have his spies circling around. Or he's already there himself."

A chill shuddered down my spine. I sat upright, startled, unsure what to do.

"Get out!" The next message echoed in my ear. "Go through the window like the boys. Go to Arthur's. I'll get his passcode ASAP. Now!"

My heart raced as I stumbled to my feet, knocked my chair backward. My eyes rose to the window. I didn't see anything, but Lucy's words reverberated in my brain. "Get out! Get out!"

I got out. I grabbed my sweatshirt, threw aside the curtains, opened the window, and jumped to the patio below. No one was there. Yet. I ran through the dark night. I could come back tomorrow for my things, my toiletries, a change of clothes. I didn't stop running until I was across campus, in front of Sheridan, Arthur's fancy new dorm. Lucy had already sent the passcode, so I showed myself up to his empty, enormous suite.

Safe.

It wasn't until later that night, only as I was drifting to sleep in Arthur's unfamiliar spare bed, that I thought again about Lucy's messages. She hadn't known I was in Florence. She had *seen* the building through Anghen's eyes.

Chapter 39

Jonathan

Sunday, November 18

THERE'S MORE TO say.

I never thought I'd open this notebook again. But I need to write more. It's the only way to hold on.

For the past several days, I haven't spotted the men trailing me. Either they're getting stealthier or they've given up, deciding I'm as powerless as I feel. Whatever Anghen's plan, it seems as if I no longer factor in it.

So I planned to join Mina tonight—I'd stop by the hospital first, in case she was still there, then I'd check Arthur's. I wanted to be sure she was safe, had moved to his suite like she promised. Regardless of how she feels about me, for the first time in a long time, it felt like we were winning and I wanted to be by her side, whatever that entailed.

206

I went through security, got to the lobby. It had a high, cathedral ceiling and plants everywhere. I couldn't remember which floor Lucy was on. I bent to study the map. An elevator door opened, footsteps passed, and I glanced at the person over my shoulder: big, dark-haired, pale-skinned. *Anghen?*

It's a good thing the map was in front of me. I stumbled forward, banged my head against the screen. But I didn't let go. The screen held me up.

I heard the automatic door behind me swish open and shut. Whoever it was had left the hospital.

It felt as if one of those English trains were rushing through my body. The sound reverberated in my head. My hands shook with the momentum. I couldn't catch my breath. I replayed the image over in my head: the tall frame, broad shoulders, dark hair, again touched with gray. Except he had been dressed as an American, in a suit and tie under a trench coat.

"Young man?" someone called. "Young man?"

I pushed myself up from the map. There was no one else in the lobby. If it had been Anghen, he was gone.

The woman in the security booth was staring through the glass at me. "Are you sick? Should I call someone?" Panicked visions of the Bloodless Syndrome probably rushed through her mind.

"I'm fine." The pulsing in my ears had died slightly. But I couldn't stay silent. "There's a patient here, Lucy Westin. Please send a nurse to check on her. That man may have—" I couldn't finish my sentence.

"Bathroom?" I murmured.

She pointed and I ran, barely making it into the stall before I threw up.

Afterward I flushed, then moved to a different stall. I sat, buried my head in my hands. They were still shaking.

My xphone chimed, and I answered automatically.

"Where are you?" Mom demanded.

I couldn't find a voice to answer.

"Jon?"

"I'm at the hospital," I whispered. "I was going to visit Mina."

I had known Anghen was in Whitby. He had attacked Lucy. We had just fought the other monster. It wouldn't be surprising if I saw him. If anything, I should have chased after him. But my mind was reeling with memories, that horrible animal smell, and my old, paralyzing fear.

I knew I couldn't see Mina. I couldn't call a shuttle home. I was too afraid to leave the bathroom.

"Jonathan Kirsch Harker, you listen to me. Whatever's going on, I need you to come home right now. Your mind can't handle this pressure. Not to mention, there's something funny going on with your Mr. Anghen—they won't let me access any of the files, and whenever I ask— Regardless, I don't want you wrapped up in any of it."

Mom was right. I didn't know how I'd make it

home. But I couldn't stay here. I should have known better. There was no winning against this monster.

Chapter 40

Arthur

November 18, Newholm Detention Center

Patient 562:
    Age: 47
    Ethnicity: African American
    Gender: Male
    Condition: Stable. Left hand and forearm bandaged
    from self-injury. Infection cleared, swelling down.
    Heart rate: 71
    Blood pressure: 124/73

"GOOD EVENING, DR. Godalming," Renfield said as Arthur examined his hand.

The map that had caused so much trouble, that had led Anghen to Lucy, had faded into a crosshatch of faint cuts. Arthur wrapped it in a clean bandage without responding to Renfield's taunt.

He was supposed to be in a good mood. Lucy had been overjoyed when they shared the news that morning. They had found one of the monsters. It was vulnerable in daylight. It *was* good news. But Arthur had seen the way Quincey watched Lucy, the way she had smiled at him. She had messaged earlier that evening, but it was only to get his dorm room passcode for Mina. He had known Lucy longer than anyone. This time he had thought this thing between them might stick. But it was clear after today that he was only standing in her way.

He wished it didn't hurt so damn much. He turned his focus back to Renfield.

He'd been skimming through Renfield's record, Quincey's words gnawing at him about that too. Surely Renfield had always been unstable. There was addiction in his past; typical for Dead Zone residents. That must have been why he was picked up for the DetCen in the first place. But the record didn't exactly say that.

"How are you feeling?" Arthur asked, looking up.

"I want a cat," Renfield said.

"What?" Arthur felt as if he had missed a step in the conversation. There were a few feral cats around Newholm, and sometimes people fed them and took them in, though plenty of people also killed them, either for their meat or just because they were dirty animals.

"You don't understand, Doctor. I'm a sane man,

211

imprisoned in an insane asylum, without any of the comforts of home. And the nights get so cold."

Honestly, the air was a little cold. Arthur stared at the heating duct above Renfield's bed as if he could see what was wrong. "I'll ask an orderly to bring you an extra blanket. No animals."

"Really? But the rooms are full of animals—flies, spiders, silverfish," Renfield said. "A cat would do the trick. Clean up your little infestation in a jiffy."

"I thought you were doing that." Arthur couldn't help taunting back. He was in that kind of mood.

Renfield smiled. "I was. But I saw the reaction I got. I guess it's okay for the richies to put cricket powder in their smoothies, but we poor people can't eat a spider. Even for immortality. I've invited the king to join us inside Newholm's hospital and detention center. I've done his favors, and in return he's promised to take care of me properly, make sure I get my long life."

Arthur froze. Could Renfield still be in communication with Anghen?

"He's dangerous," he told Renfield. "No matter what he tells you."

But Renfield wasn't listening. "He's going to be in charge someday, you know? I know it's only a small DetCen here, but it's just the beginning. First the DetCen, then the government. He's already visited Dr. Eisley and taken control from him. The king is nice, and he has bags of money, so he usually doesn't hurt people. But sometimes people won't do what he wants.

Like your friends."

Dr. Eisley was the executive director of the hospital and detention center. Was he in on something with Anghen?

"Anghen's a monster."

"He's already helped your Lucy. In my dreams, I see her dancing in that pretty blue dress." Renfield raised his eyebrows suggestively. It made Arthur's stomach churn.

"What?"

But Renfield kept talking. "Soon he'll run everything; he'll start his war. And I'll be by his side. But in the meantime, there must be another way to take care of myself. Perhaps a proxy. A cat would eat the bugs, even mice and rats, and I would gain all their lives inside me."

"If you know where he's living, you could help stop him," Arthur said. "You could tell me. We'll keep you safe."

Renfield shook his head. "No, Doctor. You can't give me what I need. You have enough problems of your own."

"What do you mean?" Arthur said, desperately trying to make sense of it all. When Renfield said Anghen would take charge, that he had already visited Dr. Eisley, what if he meant—

"If I were you, I'd check on your Lucy."

Arthur flew to his feet. "What?"

"I've seen that in my dreams too. He's very angry

213

with her. She shouldn't have resisted the king."

Arthur stared at the tablet in his hand. He had all his data. He tucked it under his arm, then rushed out of Renfield's room, sealing the door behind him before he took off down the hallway, into the lobby, and crossed over to the hospital elevator. His breath was unsteady, too fast.

The door to Lucy's room was open. The brigaders who had been seated at either side were gone. Only Lucy's mom remained, curled into the far chair by the door, apparently asleep. No. There was a sea of blood in her lap. Arthur reached for her. Her throat had been ripped out.

Arthur spun—there were no nurses, no orderlies. Had Lucy's mom sent everyone away? There was a pile of garlic stalks at the door, crushed, wilting. He raced into the room—the rest of the garlic was gone.

And Lucy—

"Help!" he screamed.

Chapter 41

Mina

WHEN ARTHUR MESSAGED me that morning, I dropped everything to rush to the hospital. As I rounded the doorway into Lucy's room, I saw Arthur and Dr. Helsinger sitting on the nearby empty bed, facing Lucy.

"I came as quickly as I could. What's—"

The words died in my throat. Arthur's head was in his hands.

Something must have happened. Something horrible! I kept moving, though I couldn't move fast enough. Lucy!

She was sunken in the bed, dwarfed by all her colorful pillows. In contrast, her skin was carrier-box white. Her wrist, propped up on the armrest of the bed with an IV needle in it, looked so thin that if I touched it, it might shatter. Her eyes were deep, surrounded by shadows. Her lips had gone from lipstick red to pale blue.

"Is she breathing?" I whispered.

"Not well. They're giving her oxygen periodically to help her," Arthur said, joining my side while Dr. H gave us some space. "They did a blood transfusion last night—after I found her—but she's not stabilizing like she did before." Arthur cracked his knuckles. His face looked as if it had been chiseled out of rock, like there was no emotion left. Whatever moment I had caught him in when I first arrived, he had shoved it deep inside. "They've got her on the same medication regimen they do for organ transplant recipients," Arthur continued. "Plus some morphine to help her sleep."

"Do they think—?" I didn't know how to finish my question, how to find the words.

"They don't think she can outlast it." Despite his best effort, his voice broke. He swallowed, cleared his throat. "Look." Arthur flicked his specrays over his eyes, snapped a picture of Lucy, then projected it onto the blank wall in front of us. I studied the image, the uncomfortable chair, the window, the bed with its rumpled sheets. But Lucy was nowhere to be seen.

I fell into the chair next to her bed, my legs failing beneath me. "I don't understand."

"I took a picture when I got here." Arthur's words tumbled over themselves. "I wanted to record everything. Then I took another, and another, and another. She wasn't in any of them."

"She's turning." I remembered how Anghen hadn't appeared in Jonathan's video; Jonathan had included it in his list of Anghen's traits and powers.

"What happened?" I asked, desperate to understand.

"Renfield said something." Arthur shook his head. "He must have had some sense things weren't right. I rushed over here, but I was too late. The brigaders were gone, her mom—her throat was ripped out. And Lucy—" Arthur shoved his fingers against his eyes as if to keep back tears.

"She fought back," I realized. She had sent me that message, warned me to move. So Anghen had attacked her instead and murdered her mom.

"Her mom must have sent the brigaders home, then removed the garlic," Arthur continued. "That's all I can figure. It was mostly gone when I arrived."

"Lucy said her mom hated the smell." I only then noticed the odor was gone, replaced by a sterile antiseptic. Something was pressing on my chest, making it hard to think, hard to even breathe. "How could she?" I hissed. "We explained about the garlic! Dr. H, me. Lucy even liked it!"

"She didn't understand," Arthur said. "And she's certainly paid the price."

"It's the vampire's fault," Dr. Helsinger said, joining us at Lucy's bedside. She wasn't wearing her typical mask, as if even she found breathing difficult at the moment. "Don't ever forget that. He's the monster."

I couldn't forget any of it. I bit into my lip, tried to swallow the gunk in my throat.

Arthur pushed ahead. "I'm sorry I didn't call earlier. I couldn't— I didn't know what to say. I thought Dr. H might know what to do. Then I wanted to make sure Lucy was stable."

"Does she?" I spat out, taking them both in with my glance.

Arthur's eyes met mine, confused. "Does she what?"

"Does Dr. H know what to do?" I snapped. Then, without waiting for an answer, I kept talking, practically shouting as I stood beside Lucy's bed. "I mean, what the hell are you both doing just sitting here? Has anyone called Quincey? What about his brigade? Or even the police? Surely we have enough evidence now. If time's running out, we need to stop Anghen, kill him. None of this was supposed to happen!"

"The doctors are going to put her in a medically induced coma," Dr. H answered. "They can put her on a respirator if need be, continue on morphine. She can keep fighting the infection without fighting for her life too."

I sank back into the chair at Lucy's beside. "Will it work?"

Dr. Helsinger shook her head. "Hopefully it will keep her alive. The blood transfusion and medication should expunge the contamination. But the only way to be certain is to destroy Anghen."

"I haven't told Quincey yet." Arthur's eyes were dark, his back bowed.

Dr. H put her hand on his shoulder. When had the two of them gotten so close?

Never mind. They were both listening to me, trying to answer.

"I'll call him," I offered.

**

Quincey arrived panting, as if he had run the whole way. He dashed into the room, right to Lucy's bedside. Her eyes were closed. He dropped a bag at his feet; apparently he had packed in anticipation of this horrible moment.

He took her hand. "Lucy," he whispered.

It was the most devastating voice I had ever heard.

I busied myself hanging my jacket and bag to the side of Lucy's blue dress, tried to give them some space.

"I have to tell you. Anghen. His plans," Lucy whispered, her breathing labored.

"We'll find him," Quincey promised. "Stop him."

Lucy shook her head. "He's too powerful. So many connections. He already took Mom. He'll keep destroying everyone I love. Even you."

"I won't let him," Quincey swore. "I'll fight back." Then: "Tell me something else. What do you need? Is there anything I can do to make you more comfortable?"

"Hungry," she murmured. "So hungry."

"I'll order food," Quincey said, eager to have something to do. "What do you want?"

"It won't help."

Was she already losing the will to fight?

"Think about Midwinter Ball," Quincey urged, his voice husky with tears. "I ordered a blue bow tie to match your dress."

My own body was wracked with a sob as I ran my fingers along the shimmery fabric of Lucy's dress.

"Lucy?" Quincey whispered.

Then I heard a low, deep growl.

Quincey was sitting on her bed, his arm around her shoulders. But Lucy had jerked upright. Her teeth were bared. Her eyes flashed red in the dim light. She turned for him.

"Lucy!" I screamed.

Quincey reacted faster. He levered his arm under her chin, pushed her back onto the bed.

Lucy had always hated exercise. She came down with a stomach bug anytime we had to run in PE. But now Quincey couldn't stop her. She pressed up, arched her back, somehow fighting against his weight.

"Don't let go!" I yelled. "She's turning. The monster is taking over."

Quincey shook his head. But tears ran down his face.

"So hungry," she pleaded, tears leaking from her own eyes. "It won't hurt." Her voice was raw and desperate, so different from Lucy's. "It will feel like a kiss. I will feed. But then we will never lose each other. We can dance every night together. We will never have to say goodbye."

I ran to the door, screamed for the brigade, nurses, doctors, anyone.

"I want to be with you forever, Quincey Morris Jordan!"

In her mouth, his name sounded wrong, all sharp angles.

"Do *not* say his name!" I said.

"Mina!" she hissed. "This is your fault. You were supposed to be the smart one. You were supposed to save me!"

It was a gut punch. "I tried," I gasped out, my voice catching in my own throat.

Quincey shifted, his eyes locked with hers.

"No!" I cried, rushing for them. "No no nononono!"

But no one was listening to me anymore. Not Quincey, not the brigade, the nurses. No one was coming to help.

Not-Lucy licked her lips, leaned into Quincey.

Quincey closed his eyes.

"Yes," the thing inside Lucy urged. "Don't fight it."

But she wasn't headed for his lips. Her mouth opened. The long teeth caught in the light, tilted directly toward his exposed neck.

"No!" I screamed.

I barreled into Quincey. He lost his balance, fell to

the floor.

Lucy jumped to her feet on top of the bed, screamed.

But then Dr. Helsinger was there and two brigaders and more nurses. It took all of them to bring her back to bed. A nurse strapped her down.

"Quincey Jordan." Not-Lucy spat out his full name, like it left a nasty taste in her mouth. "Mina Muto. You have both made your choice."

There were no other options. We had to destroy him. For Lucy.

Quincey hadn't moved from the floor. He covered his face with his hand.

I forced myself to look at Lucy again. Her eyes were open, watching. It might have been the lights, or the machines surrounding her bedside. But I saw a red glow in her pupils.

I could not leave her side.

***

Later that day there were more visitors. Lucy's aunt, a wispy-haired grandmother, and Lucy's brother, whose xphone kept quietly beeping with messages. To his credit, he ignored them that day.

At some point Jonathan appeared. His hair was a mess of curls, as if wherever he had been, whatever he had been doing, he hadn't slept in ages. I could relate.

"Arthur called me," Jonathan said, wrapping an arm around me. "How is she?"

I couldn't find breath to speak. It was happening too quickly. We hadn't had a moment to find Anghen, to stop him, and now—

Lucy was hooked up to even more machines; they beeped and whirred. The nurse added something to an IV. Minutes later, Lucy settled into her body, closed her eyes.

"She's gone," I whispered.

"Not gone," Arthur protested. "She's just no longer conscious—"

Quincey didn't buy it either. "Goodbye." He choked on his tears.

Jonathan closed his eyes, maybe in prayer, as he held his grandmother's Star of David tightly in his fist.

We stood in silence for minutes, maybe hours. It was Lucy I had always talked to, and there was so much left unsaid: about Jonathan, how lately I wasn't sure how I felt about him anymore, about how Quincey looked at her like she was pure gold, about school and college. I didn't know how to deal with any of it without her. I didn't know how to live without her. My whole body was shaking.

"Go home," the raspy voice of Dr. Helsinger said from behind me. "All of you. If you believe in it, say a prayer for her. I will stay with her tonight, ensure she continues to be safe."

But I didn't move. "We need to destroy him," I said. "Now."

Then her voice was right next to me, hissing in my

ear. "You will and I'll help you. But not now. He's at full strength. He just fed. Go home."

I closed my eyes, shook my head. "I can't."

Lucy was gone. I was on my own. I couldn't begin to imagine any of it.

But in the end, I had no choice. Jonathan carried me to the elevator.

Chapter 42

WHIT News

BLOODLESS SYNDROME IS HERE
Nov 15, 2---

WHILE RUMORS HAVE been spreading for months regarding the Bloodless Syndrome infiltrating American soil, tonight brought the first recorded cases. After an anonymous call led to an abandoned field house on the campus of Irving Academy for Gifted and Talented Students in Newholm, police investigators found two dead. Upon further investigation, after clearing out a tarp and boat supplies, a cache of six more bodies was discovered. All remains showed evidence of severe exsanguination. Further autopsies will be performed, but researchers say the deaths are consistent with the effects of the Bloodless Syndrome.

Newholm is the government seat for the Dead Zone in nearby Whitby. There is no indication of how these individuals came to be on Irving's campus nor of what they might have in common. The Bloodless Syndrome has been described as a disease carried and spread among people of color, but several of these victims are white. Further investigation will be forthcoming.

However, this is the first acknowledgment from the public health department that the Bloodless Syndrome has indeed made its way to American shores. Experts have expressed concern over whether Americans have the fortitude to fight another global health pandemic, but it appears we might have no choice.

Chapter 43

Arthur

November 19, Newholm Detention Center

Patient 562:
Age: 47
Ethnicity: African American
Gender: Male
Condition: Not recorded
Heart rate: Not recorded
Blood pressure: Not recorded

ARTHUR RETURNED TO work late that night. He had made the mistake of telling his mom about Lucy. Mom had called three more times since. She wanted him to take time away from school and fly home to DC. Instead, as soon as Mina had fallen asleep, he sneaked away from his dorm room and back to the hospital. For the past twenty-four hours, his brain had been a nonstop recording of Renfield's words, sprinting to Lucy's room, the blood everywhere, her mom murdered, and Lucy's face… Dr. H had been so kind to him. But if he had put the pieces together sooner, kept a better eye on Lucy, she would still be safe. She wouldn't be trapped in this deadly waiting game.

If he really wanted to be a doctor, if he really wanted to save people, he needed to become inured to the blood. But he couldn't. The horrific events had infiltrated his brain. He couldn't sleep. He couldn't cry. He couldn't imagine going home. He tried to think about Anghen, still out there somewhere, only growing stronger and more powerful. But Arthur couldn't focus. He could only watch that horrible movie in his mind.

So he returned to work, donning a mask and gloves as part of the new protocol. Maybe the work would steady him. The next morning he could talk to Mina; they could form a real plan.

Arthur knocked, then used his xphone to enter Renfield's room.

Renfield stood opposite the door and smiled as Arthur appeared. "Dr. Godalming," he said. His face, hands, and shirt were covered with blood. He licked his lips.

Arthur stumbled back. He could hardly breathe through the face mask.

At Renfield's feet was a disemboweled cat.

"It's delicious, Doctor."

Of course Arthur had seen blood before. Earlier that year he had been taught to draw blood, had a chance to practice neat, even stitches. But the movie in his head had changed everything.

"It's life." Renfield held out a blood-soaked hand with some part of the cat resting in his palm as an offering to Arthur. "Doctor?"

Arthur swallowed. He knew now that he could never be a doctor. He stared at the tufts of fur, the curling tail, the blood so bright, vibrant on the pristine white floor.

"No, thank you," he whispered, trying to hold it together. Something rose up in his throat. He swallowed again, tried to breathe.

Renfield laughed. "Aren't you going to ask where I got it?"

Arthur urged himself to action. There had to be protocol. Renfield needed to get cleaned up and changed. They needed to dispose of what was left of the animal, give the room a thorough cleaning. Who knew where he had gotten it, what diseases it might be carrying. But Arthur couldn't think what he was supposed to do first, what he was supposed to say. Instead, he pushed the emergency call button.

Renfield's room was flooded with orderlies, nurses, a doctor, all in the same masks and gloves. Some of them hurried the patient to a containment ward, others disposed of the cat, still others were down on their knees, cleaning the blood.

Arthur stepped away, his nose thick with the smell of cat and bleach. His legs trembled beneath him. He walked the perimeter of Renfield's room once, a second time, as if somehow he could pull himself together. Each time he passed the heating vent, the air felt colder. Arthur held his hand up to the metal tubing that dropped from the ceiling. It was freezing. He took the chair in Renfield's room and climbed up. He curled his fingers around the grate. The panel came loose in his hands. Arthur peered into the tube. There was a small platform a few inches up—low enough that someone strong could prop themselves up inside. The tube followed the ceiling, continuing into the darkness. A cold wind blew against his cheek.

When Arthur pulled his head out, the people below were staring at him.

"I think I found out how he's escaping."

One of the orderlies helped him to wedge the grate back into place. Custodial appeared minutes later with replacement screws.

Arthur stared at the tube, the wall it traveled through. He wondered if Renfield had crawled the length of the building to some hidden exit, all to help Anghen. Regardless, he'd be stuck now.

"Arthur? Arthur?"

Arthur realized someone was repeating his name. He shook his head. "I can't."

"No," the orderly said, gesturing at the xphone

behind his ear. "The hospital's paging you. Apparently they've been trying to get a hold of you for a while."

Arthur pulled his specrays over his eyes. There were three new missed calls and one message.

He couldn't take any more.

But it was too late. His dad was dead.

Chapter 44

Mina

IN THE DARK, early-Tuesday morning, my receiver chimed with a message from Arthur: "Are you awake? I need to talk to someone."

I must have been asleep, but I was awake now. I stared at the blinking light, then at my unfamiliar surroundings. *Arthur's suite,* I remembered. *I'm in Arthur's suite.* But where was Arthur? In a rush I remembered more: *Lucy.* I sat upright in bed, my hands shaking as I called him.

"My dad died late last night," he explained in a rush. "I only heard. I uploaded the photo to the digital folder."

"What photo——?"

Arthur pressed ahead, as if he had to talk, as if he was afraid to stop. "I'll do whatever it takes. We need to find Anghen. For Lucy's sake. For Dad's."

"Arthur—" I tried to keep up. Arthur's dad and Lucy had nothing in common, right? "Is Lucy okay?"

"Lucy's fine; she hasn't been disturbed. The brigaders are keeping watch."

But that didn't explain anything. "What happened to your dad? Where was he?"

"Europe. Southern France. I knew he was in the thick of it, but I never imagined... What if there're multiple vampires, all trying to expand their territory, and Anghen..." His voice momentarily trailed off, and then he sprang back into action. "Show everyone the photo. I'm flying home to help Mom, but I'll be back in town as soon as I can. I'll do whatever needs to be done. But in the meantime, stay safe. He's still out there somewhere."

I glanced at the dark window. Red eyes met my own.

I jumped. "Arthur?"

He must have already disconnected.

When I dared to look at the window again, the eyes were gone.

***

There was no going back to sleep.

Instead, I tried to plot our next move. But my brain, my whole body, felt encased in lead. Or it was as if I were drowning. As if I'd been swallowed by a whole ocean of grief. We could lose Lucy forever. And now Arthur's dad...

One problem at a time. I cast my screen, asked my xphone to search the name Godalming. Colonel Anthony Godalming's death was already all over, along with several brief mentions of his life before. He had been on active duty with the US Army in France. His troops were tasked to quell the unrest in Europe. But when it came to his death, sources were light on details.

The Post read: "The night before his death, Colonel Godalming waited with his troops outside the ancient Roman amphitheater in Arles, France. It had been rumored that Sphinx Army terrorists were using the ring as a meeting place as well as a storage facility, hiding hundreds of assault rifles. The American forces stormed the amphitheater, took everyone inside prisoner, and regained the suspected weapons with no casualties. Of course, Godalming was right beside his soldiers."

"Colonel Anthony Godalming started his career at West Point. Fresh out of high school, he was already determined to serve his country."

I skimmed to the end, trying to figure out exactly what happened. Had he died at the amphitheater?

"When his soldiers discovered his death that morning, they still reported for duty, continued with their mission. It's what the colonel would have expected."

They had discovered his body in the morning? It must have been a heart attack or something, something out of the blue that killed him.

I backtracked, searched Arles, France, and found this:

"The Arles Amphitheater, built in 90 AD, stands in the city center. It is predominately used for festivals, performances, and bullfighting. However, lately the amphitheater has found new purpose in the European uprisings. The Sphinx Army reportedly uses the building as a base. They hope its ancient walls will protect the traditions they would like to uphold: namely anti-immigrant policies and a celebration of France's white ancestors."

I was lost in my thoughts, trying to understand Arthur's links between France, England, and Lucy. Only then did I remember Arthur's photo. It was good I was already sitting down.

It was an unrecognizable body—pale, skeletal, collapsed on itself. Just like the other Bloodless Syndrome deaths in Switzerland and England but also like the baggage handlers at Caine County Airport and those bodies from the field house. Arthur was right. It was all connected and so much bigger than Lucy.

No, it wasn't just connected. Arthur's dad had died only hours after Anghen attacked Lucy.

It was just as Lucy had warned. It was coordinated.

Chapter 45

Mina

THAT AFTERNOON, THE sky filled with dark clouds and steady rain. Of course Arthur wasn't back yet, and neither Jonathan nor Quincey had returned my messages, but that didn't surprise me—I was sick of me too, sick of everything. If only I could think straight, but all my thoughts felt oatmeal-thick.

I found Arthur's gun in his desk drawer, beside a small carrier package of silver bullets. He had gotten them after all. I picked up the gun, ran my fingers along the dark, cold metal. I ejected the magazine in its base, loaded the bullets. My family had always had a few guns, and my brothers had taught me how to shoot. Out in the country anything could happen, whether wild dogs or brigade raids. Or monsters. I hid the gun in my coat pocket and slipped outside.

I pulled my hood up as I walked through the

pouring rain. I reviewed the past weeks in my mind: Jonathan's journal, the group's notes. But it was an exercise in frustration. We hadn't had enough time for a systematic search. Jonathan had been so pleased when we destroyed those first two boxes. But there were still six out there. We had so much more to do: get information from local hotels, a list of Whitby newcomers. Something dark and terrible welled up inside me. Perhaps Lucy had been right all along about being a distraction. And then there was Lucy's mom and now Arthur's dad. By all counts, Anghen was winning.

I passed Thornley, remembered when I first met Lucy my freshman year in our tiny dorm room. Back then we had acted like it took hours to get to and from classes, but it seemed as if my feet had taken me there in no time at all. I circled around the theater—Lucy had talked about trying out for the musical that spring. I passed Rickman, remembered meeting Jonathan that first time. I felt decades older, sadder. Both Lucy and I had had so many plans for our senior year.

Now I wasn't sure what this year held for me except endless rain, inside and out.

I remembered telling Lucy, before everything fell apart, that I had begun to doubt my college plans. I couldn't imagine it at all now. I didn't belong on some fancy campus, surrounded by rich white people, everyone desperately trying to find answers in old books or screencasts. What was the point? I wanted to be out in the world, doing something that mattered.

Mom had pinned all her hopes on my future. But neither of my brothers had gone to college. Stephen had a steady, business-y job. Along with his wife's job, it was enough to support their family. Jackson had started his own repair company, having inherited Dad's obsession with taking everything apart—but he seemed to be doing okay too.

My eyes filled with tears. I couldn't imagine ever doing okay again. I kept walking. I needed to focus, figure out where Anghen might be hiding.

As I passed Slains, I saw a light in Dr. Helsinger's office and discovered the front door to Slains was open. I hurried inside. Helsinger would have a plan. The basement heater was still broken, but it felt good, like the tropics. I was soaking wet, freezing. I unbuttoned my coat and raised my hand to knock when I heard her voice.

"They won't reauthorize your ID."

IDs were usually automatically renewed unless something had changed, there had been an arrest, a criminal charge, or something else out of the ordinary.

There was a pause; then Dr. H kept talking. Someone else must have been on the other end of an xphone connection. It was so unlike her to broadcast anything personal. "No, that's not it. The paperwork's all correct. Avett, Lucent, and Rogers checked everything. The government has decided not to reauthorize."

There was another pause. Then: "None of it matters if they won't reauthorize! They must know about us."

I wondered if she was referring to her relationship, perhaps speaking to that woman in the framed picture. It wasn't illegal yet, but the government also didn't have to provide any rationale for identity determinations.

Her voice broke. "No, I don't know what else to do."

The floor shifted, as if she had sat down or collapsed. I wasn't sure which, but besides compromising personal information, I'd also never heard Dr. Helsinger sound so sad.

"I can't do that," she whispered.

I crept away from the door. Clearly she had her own problems to worry about.

Chasing this first thought, I wondered if this was part of Anghen's coordination: Jonathan, Lucy, Arthur, now Dr. Helsinger. Could he have already risen so fast in the government bureaucracy?

It was still early, but outside was fully dark, the rain relentless. I knew I should go back to Arthur's. But I didn't have any homework to do. For the first time ever, I had skipped class today. I certainly couldn't make myself care about food or even curfew. And if Anghen found me? There would be no hesitation. This time I'd destroy him.

I was shaking, whether from cold or not eating or anxiety, who knew. All of the above? I sank to a nearby bench, wrapped my arms around myself, tucking my hands deep in my coat sleeves.

It wasn't yet pitch-black. A fog had settled over the distant river.

I'd get up in a minute. Then, when I got back to Arthur's suite, I'd call Quincey and Jonathan. I'd tell them about Arthur's dad, my theory on how everything was connected. Then we'd make a concrete plan, divvy up responsibilities. Even if the police and the government refused to do anything, we'd find him, stop him.

I tried to think of something else, something happy. I thought about the end of the quarter, winter break, New Year's. Dad was obsessed with creating the perfect fried chicken. He had repurposed a metal trash can and added a candy thermometer to track the fryer's temperature. It made the whole house smell like a carnival. Mom would serve all the real meat along with a smorgasbord of other foods, imitation meatballs, a green bean casserole that only my brother Stephen really loved. I hadn't seen my nieces since summer. I wondered if they still played hide-and-seek every chance they got.

As I stared into the night, wishing I was far away from all this, the mist thickened. The clouds must have been moving, shifting. The stars were suddenly visible, like a string of lights twinkling through the gloom. It reminded me of Lucy's party, how she had danced with the guests. Such a Lucy dream.

Is this a dream? I usually never remembered my dreams, had always suspected I didn't dream, but this was weird. With all the industry around the area, the stars were hardly ever visible. And the mist continued to swirl, forming a shape. The lights twirled around, all different colors. Except for two glowing red eyes.

My heart quickened. It was him. I recognized him from that night when Lucy danced with him. But I had also seen those eyes again since.

He towered over me in a black suit. His hair was edged with gray but carefully trimmed. He reached out a single hand, as if inviting me to dance. His hands were covered in dark hair, the nails filed to a point.

Get up, I screamed in my head. *Fight back! Shoot him!* But for all my bravado, I was frozen in place.

Anghen pulled me to my feet.

My legs felt like useless things, floppy, imitation string cheese. He drew me close. His breath was hot, rancid.

This is a dream, I told myself. *A nightmare. You can wake up.*

I could see other dancers spinning around us. Men in workers' jumpsuits, little kids in hospital gowns. A man in a suit with skin so pale it looked like wax. That female vampire with long, dark hair. My eyes drew back to Anghen. He smiled. His white teeth glistened in the light. They were pointed at the tips. He smiled wider, wider.

No. I lifted my gun, aimed for his horrible mouth.

But then his hand was on my wrist, pinching me like the vise in my dad's tool shop. Pain shot up my hand. I dropped the gun.

I woke with a start. Everything was dark. No one else was there. Rain had soaked through my coat to my clothes, my skin. I pulled my hood tighter, but my right hand ached. My vision spun. I grabbed for the bench before I fell. *I need to get back to Arthur's. Now.*

I pocketed the gun, then stepped carefully through the mud to the path. I was so tired. My determination had evaporated into the fog. I forced myself to keep moving. I was lucky it had only been a dream. I had to get back to Arthur's before something really bad happened, before I hurt myself, before my only hope was that Quincey might magically run by.

Somehow I made it back. Only then did I cast my screen, check the time. It wasn't even ten. I locked Arthur's door behind me and stumbled into my room. I made sure all the windows were solidly shut, the blackout curtains pulled tight, then I fell into bed. Sleep took me completely.

Chapter 46

Quincey

IT WAS RAINING as Quincey walked to the hospital. He didn't mind. He pulled up his hood. The wet and cold, the dark clouds, it all suited his mood. The farther he walked from Irving, the quieter the night became. No conversations or laughter or music… only rain.

Hold fast to dreams, Quincey thought, remembering the Langston Hughes poem. *For when dreams go / Life is a barren field / Frozen with snow.*

It wasn't that cold, but otherwise it seemed accurate as Quincey turned through the automatic double doors into the bright light of Newholm's hospital and detention center. He had wanted so much more. Whenever he was with Lucy, he always felt as if he could do anything, go anywhere. Except now.

"Course, Lucy would hate a night like this," he said into the silence of the elevator. It was the wrong

243

weather for dancing.

He nodded to the pair of brigaders still watching over the doorway to Lucy's room. He would talk to them before he left for the night. He had already wasted too much time today. They needed a list of everyone who had moved into Whitby recently, where they were living. The Omegas' network was vast; surely they could uncover the monster.

Quincey settled in the chair beside Lucy's bed. He had just wanted to see her once more before getting swept up in everything again.

"I hope you're dancing tons," he whispered, taking in her closed eyes. "I'm not religious like Jon," he continued, "or medically trained like Arthur. But I hope wherever your mind is, there's unlimited handsome partners, a band..." He started crying again and gave up trying to make sense.

She would be okay. She would have to be. They would figure this out.

Someone had restrung the room with garlic. He ran his fingers along one of the green stalks, murmuring, "Watch over her." He wasn't sure if he was talking to the garlic, God, or something else entirely. But whatever was out there owed Lucy big-time.

Quincey lost himself in memories. He remembered Lucy's laugh, her soft skin, her kisses. He closed his eyes tightly, as if yesterday had never happened, as if he could wish it all away and her eyes would open and she would be the same Lucy she had always been.

But when he opened his eyes, Lucy's were still closed, even in the glaring light of the hospital. His screen showed it was an hour before curfew.

"I have to go back," Quincey said even as he wondered if anyone would notice if he stayed there all night. He closed his eyes again.

But that wasn't an option. He had to talk to the brigaders. He had to call Mina. They needed a plan.

The Omegas at the door were all business. One cast his screen, put in a call to HQ. Apparently a list had already been started. They promised they'd check with a few others and get Quincey the full list later that night.

He made it downstairs in the elevator, then through the glass atrium and out the double doors into the street. It was pouring. Quincey was going to get wet. He pulled his hood over his head, stepped out into the night.

Then he saw the truck.

There weren't that many vehicles, especially in walkable Newholm. The headlights cut through the rain and fog as the dark-colored electric truck quietly drove along Lyceum Road. Then, right opposite him, it stopped.

Quincey bowed his head, kept walking. He didn't feel like talking to anyone. It was probably just a coincidence. Something had happened, someone had an accident, and they were looking for the hospital's entrance in the dark. Nevertheless, an uneasy feeling prickled at the base of Quincey's neck.

The truck's door slammed, then another car door from somewhere behind him. Two vehicles. At least.

Quincey cast his screen, set it to mirror. A man was coming up behind him: big, white, with dark body armor, the triangular A patch on his chest. Alpha Brigade.

Quincey performed a quick status check: he didn't have anything to fight with, only his ID in his back pocket and his xphone behind his ear. He checked the time. It was well before curfew. He flicked off his screen, pulled his hood off his head, let his hands hang loose at his sides, and kept walking. No threat here.

"Hey!" someone yelled in the night.

"He's there!" someone else yelled.

A siren sounded.

Quincey's heart raced ahead. His eyes swept over Lyceum Road, the pharmacy, the McDonald's. But no one else was outside. These Alphas were looking for him.

"Record," he whispered into his xphone.

"Put your hands up," a voice directly behind him growled.

Quincey did as commanded, lifting his hands inch by inch, like a dancer in slow motion. Someone pressed something hard in the small of his back.

"Don't move," said another, different voice.

While Quincey froze, he counted bodies out of the corners of his eyes. There were two men on either side of the blazing light. The man behind him. Three more to his left, giant guns raised and trained on him. Another two to the right. They were all Alpha Brigade with second-skin body armor, military grade, giant guns in their hands. All white men. The Alphas had money, and they didn't mess around. No high school students or renegades. This was the real deal—and they had a whole squadron. For him? He trembled.

An agent in a silver uniform stepped in front of him, flashed his badge: CMS. Citizen & Migrant Security.

Quincey had never heard of a brigade working side by side with CMS beyond doing their dirty work for profit. His heart dropped in his chest.

"No funny business," the man behind him growled.

"No, sir," Quincey answered, completely honest. He was still standing, but it felt as if the wind had been knocked out of him.

"Quincey Jordan?" the officer asked.

This wasn't accidental or random racist harassment. They knew his full name.

"Answer him," the man behind him ordered.

"Yes, sir. Quincey Jordan, sir." He'd learned from his grandmother. Respect authority. Especially if they had a gun. He forced himself to breathe, to hold himself together.

The person behind him stepped away, two other brigade members grabbed him, practically hauled him off his feet. Quincey kept his body limp, harmless. *Inhale… exhale*, he thought. All he had done was visit

Lucy. It was before curfew. He was a student at Irving Academy. No crime had been committed.

"Search him," the CMS agent said.

One of the Alphas held him while another patted him down. Nothing personal, but intense—between the legs, under the arms, his waistband. He was bathed in sweat.

The Alpha pocketed Quincey's earpiece, his ID. "He's clean."

The CMS officer nodded, unclipped handcuffs from his belt.

Quincey knew he shouldn't speak. But it happened out of the blue, so fast he wasn't ready. "Are you arresting me?"

An Alpha leered at Quincey, jammed an elbow into his side. As Quincey doubled over, the officer slipped the first cuff on his wrist.

"You're not under arrest," the officer growled. "Just detention."

Quincey had never worn handcuffs before. They were already digging into his skin, heavy, not just with symbolism.

"Stop recording!" he yelled to make sure the microphone would catch before it was too late. "Send to Arthur!" Someone had to know what was happening. Someone with pull. He knew Arthur would do whatever he could.

The Alphas marched him back from where he had come, past the hospital's entrance, around the side of the building. As he passed the bright lights and once again was plunged into darkness, his heart started really racing. From when he was small, his family had practiced the whole charade: be polite, soft-spoken, don't question an officer... But now that he had been apprehended, he didn't know the rules anymore. What would happen next? Would they kill him? Leave him someplace on a deserted road? It all seemed plausible. Or were they telling the truth, which at the moment seemed almost as bad? He was right outside Newholm's hospital and detention center.

Chapter 47

Quincey

THEY ISSUED QUINCEY a pale blue jumpsuit and a detention room probably identical to Renfield's. There was dingy linoleum, a metal bed frame, a chair where someone like Arthur would sit, demanding him to be sane. At least he had a window, though of course no curtains. He watched the sun rise, filling the sky with gray light.

He paced, counted his footsteps. Six by twelve, by six again. Only long enough for the bed. Quincey tried to lie down. But even though he had been up the entire night, the second he stopped moving, his mind raced ahead. Had Arthur gotten his recording? Was he even now plotting a jailbreak? Quincey smiled, imagining Arthur scaling the building, clenching a knife in his teeth. No, he was probably calling every one of his dad's contacts. Quincey found himself strangely grateful for leadership camp. And Arthur.

Quincey wondered if they would let him make any phone calls. He didn't want to notify his family. With any luck, the three-day rule would hold and he would be out before his parents could get themselves involved. Irving would have more clout, but he couldn't imagine they'd go too out of their way for him. He could call Mina. She'd be practical, reassuring, probably have a whole plan she could lay out for him. Yeah, that wasn't a bad idea at all. Assuming he got a phone call.

You just need to wait, he told himself. But his mind buzzed ahead.

It was like being in the hospital all over again, watching Lucy fall into that coma and feeling so helpless. The terrible weight of waiting. Quincey repeated the phrase. It could make a good poem. But the words wouldn't stick in his head.

Instead, he kept thinking about Lucy. While he was stuck in here, she was still waiting to be saved, waiting for them to stop Anghen. He trusted those brigaders were keeping a tight watch on her. But what if he never saw her alive again?

He sank to the bed, his eyes wet, his legs trembling underneath him.

A sickening crack sounded; then someone screamed from the other side of the wall. Quincey jumped to his feet before he realized nothing was happening in his own room.

He was being naïve, hoping for a phone call, the

three-day rule. They'd never let him go. He thought about Renfield, the others who had been vanishing from the streets, now him. *I should have fought back*, he thought. *I should've at least landed a punch.* What had all his training been for if not that? But it hadn't even occurred to him. He had followed the rules, like always. Stupid rules.

He was rusty anyway. When had he last run? What was the point? The brigade training had been a childish belief in strength, in weapons, nothing more. It wasn't a true resistance. How could you resist systemic racism, hatred, monsters?

Whatever had happened next door, it had stopped. Now there was only a steady, low murmur. It was vaguely familiar, maybe some sort of prayer? "God of our weary years, God of our silent tears. God of our weary years, God of our silent tears." Over and over again.

Quincey sighed. Yeah, no way he was going to get any sleep now that the lunatics were starting in.

Soon you'll be one of them, he told himself. After all, Renfield couldn't have always eaten flies.

It was just like Lucy had warned: Anghen was coming for him. For all of them. Everyone they loved.

Quincey paced around the room, checking the corners. There weren't any flies, no spiderwebs to gorge himself on. That was a relief.

On his next circuit, Quincey looked up at the heating duct. It was a human-sized tube of sheet metal running upward, then lengthwise across the room, through a hole in the cinderblock wall. Quincey wondered if it would hold his weight. *Fight or flight*, he thought. After all, Renfield had found a way out.

He held his hands up beneath the grate. It was shockingly cold.

The prayer next door grew into a cry. "God of our weary years, God of our silent tears!"

Quincey covered his ears, leaned his head against the wall.

He heard something else, something from outside. A rhythmic beat, marching feet. He looked out the window.

Outside the detention center, below him on the street, people were gathering, chanting. There was even a tinny drumbeat from someone's phone, calling the others to action. It was a brigade. His brigade, the Omegas.

Chapter 48

WHIT News

HOSPITAL'S NEW HEAD HAS CLEAR VISION
Nov 20, 2---

DR. WILHELM ANGHEN has been appointed as the executive director at Newholm Hospital and Detention Center. At a press conference today, Dr. Andrew Eisley, the Newholm group's former director, announced his abrupt retirement while anointing Dr. Anghen as his successor. Anghen, a relative newcomer both to the hospital field as well as the United States itself, has a background in hematology, but he's always seen his role as more of a caretaker's than a doctor's. As he explained, "I've always been interested in people, not science. Solving problems, promoting problem solvers, and helping organizations maintain community, both inside and outside hospital walls."

Until this past summer, Dr. Anghen resided in England. However, he spoke regarding his long fascination with the United States. His move was apparently carefully planned and a long time coming. "I'm a believer in the American Dream," Dr. Anghen said at the press conference. "I love this country's faith, work ethic, and strong shoulders. I love that even someone like me, an immigrant, can be welcomed here and be able to contribute to this melting pot. It seems I have always been an American in my heart."

Dr. Andrew Eisley, Newholm's former director, offered only enthusiasm for Dr. Anghen. "He intends to make an example of Newholm, not only to the rest of the country but also to the world."

The field of medicine is complex at this time, given the Bloodless Syndrome's increasing surge in Europe and Asia, and the recent emergence of more than a dozen cases in the United States. Dr. Anghen laughed when one reporter asked about rumors of monsters. "I'm a firm believer in science, not science fiction," the new director quipped—notably without mask or gloves even as the hospital has returned to pandemic protocol in the past week.

Dr. Anghen believes the current lack of reliable

information offers an opportunity for Newholm Hospital to orient itself in a new direction. "We need to be at the forefront of medicine. We're already a bedrock in Newholm and the surrounding area with our hospital and detention facilities. We'll become a premier destination for research into the Bloodless Syndrome, and our detention center will continue to expand as we make America into the country it was always meant to be."

Chapter 49

Arthur

November 21, Newholm Detention Center

Patient 562:
Age: 47
Ethnicity: African American
Gender: Male
Condition: Stable; broken arm (in sling)
Heart rate: 109
Blood pressure: 141/93

WHEN ARTHUR AND Mina arrived at the hospital, the entire block was surrounded by Quincey's Omega Brigade. They must have sneaked from Whitby's Dead Zone across the Newholm checkpoint in waves throughout the day. They wore their black uniforms, a handful with weapons at their sides, while they marched in a tight formation to the drumbeat booming from their xphones.

"Justice for Quincey!" they yelled. "Black is not a crime!"

Their signs read: DETENTION WITHOUT CAUSE = INJUSTICE, WE WILL NOT BE SILENCED, and many more said JUSTICE FOR QUINCEY.

They must have all seen the video. Arthur had sent it to Quincey's family but also to WHIT News, several racial justice organizations including the Omegas, and Citizen & Migrant Security itself.

Hours later, it seemed everyone in the world had seen that video, which had been dubbed the "Quincey Jordan, Sir Video" after Quincey's respectful attitude had made no difference. Quincey had been detained with no accusations of substance abuse, no violence, and no public disruption. And now Anghen was the executive director of the hospital and detention center.

But Arthur pushed his fears deep inside, alongside his dad's death and Lucy's coma, and zipped it all closed. For the first time since his late-night flight back to Whitby—if he could hold everything together—there was a plan. At midnight, together with the Omegas, they would get both Lucy and Quincey out.

Arthur flashed his specray's access code at the hospital's front desk, asking, "Is it okay if I bring someone with me to observe my rounds today? She's interested in the field." He gestured toward Mina at his side. "I can have her sign in."

"ID?" the man behind the desk grumbled, holding out his hand.

Mina handed it over. The man studied her from head to toe, then her ID, and frowned. "It's not protocol."

"I got permission. Dr. Anghen himself. You can call to double-check if you want." Arthur kept a slight smile on his face even as his mind raced. *Please don't let him double-check.*

The man's frown deepened. "No need," he murmured as he waved them both through the scanner and handed back Mina's card.

Arthur led Mina down the side hall toward the older detention center facilities. Mina was bundled in a heavy coat, a scarf wrapped around her neck. Fall was giving way to winter. But it wasn't just the thick layers that made her feel distant. Mina had been quiet most of the way over. Arthur guessed the news about Quincey, then Anghen, on top of everything with Lucy, had overwhelmed her. As director, Anghen would have free rein over the detention center. Mina must have suspected he had coordinated everything.

They followed a behind-the-scenes route back into the hospital, up to Lucy's room. Two Omegas were stationed at either side, as Quincey had promised, though they had already changed into street clothes.

"You're civilians now," Arthur said. "Family friends. Nothing else is safe."

"We're in touch with the others," one of the

Omegas answered, tapping the xphone behind his ear. "We'll make sure she's out tonight."

"Thank you," Mina said, though her voice was barely a whisper.

She and Arthur headed back down the hallway, into the detention center facility. Arthur stopped at the intake desk. "Any information about the new patient brought in last night?"

The guard shrugged. "Six of them."

"Six?" Arthur repeated.

"Wild, huh?" the guard said. "Bumper night."

Arthur looked to Mina. She was pale.

He turned back. "What was the reason?"

"Three drunk and disorderly. Must have been some party. Two out after hours, looking suspicious. One, get this, sneaking around our own facility. Some CMS agents were on-site and brought him in."

"Where is he?" Arthur asked.

"Room 312."

Arthur froze. "312?" he repeated. The DetCen intakes were usually stored on the first floor for their admission and temporary quarters.

"312," the guard repeated. "Must be a real looney, huh? I think CMS was looking for him."

"Upstairs," Arthur said to Mina, heading for the elevators. "They've put him next door to Renfield." It had Anghen's hands all over it. He must have been the one to call in Citizen & Migrant Security. Arthur jammed his finger against the third-floor button once, twice, again.

There was a CMS agent, decked in the government's silver uniform, outside Quincey's room. It was a level of security Arthur had never seen.

Arthur repeated his lie about Mina's interest in the field, said he was showing her around. "Can we take a look at the latest intake?"

"Permission is not granted," the agent barked.

"Oh, sorry." Arthur displayed his access code.

The agent didn't even look at it. "Permission is not granted," he repeated. "This unit is under twenty-four-hour surveillance. No visitors, no phone calls in or out."

"I didn't know they could do that."

The man didn't bother answering.

Arthur exhaled, tried to calm himself. He'd always known the DetCens made up the rules as they went. But between CMS and the DetCen, they were doing everything possible to make Quincey disappear. Something was churning up inside Arthur, threatening to overflow. He breathed again, tried to calm down. It wasn't working.

"Can I at least confirm a name?"

The man shook his head.

Arthur slammed his fist into the wall.

The CMS agent crouched into a fighting stance. The gun strapped to his back was in his hands in an instant.

"Backup to unit D-4," he snapped into his earpiece.

At least someone was taking Arthur seriously. But he held up his hands, stepped back. "Sorry." Losing his temper wasn't going to solve anything. "It's been a long day. I won't bother you anymore."

Arthur abruptly turned back to the elevator, Mina following silently behind him. Thankfully CMS let him be—he must have reverted to looking harmless again. He pulled his specrays over his eyes to pull up Quincey's file, but it was missing. As if it had never existed.

"No record," he murmured aloud.

If the DetCens kept people without records, without even a database of names, there was no documentation of what happened to them, how long they stayed. It made the whole system meaningless. Rotten to the core. Maybe people really were disappearing. It was exactly what Quincey had argued when Arthur first met him, while Arthur was still oblivious, playing doctor. And Quincey had been proven right in the worst way possible.

On top of everything else, Arthur's hand was throbbing.

"I should finish my rounds," he murmured. He had to keep up the illusion of normalcy tonight.

Mina pressed the button for the elevator. "I'll go back to the main waiting room," she said with a shiver, as if she was cold even under all her layers. "From there I can work on the security system."

Her voice was soft, her face turned from his.

He glanced toward her. "You okay?"

Mina shook her head. "I just can't think straight. It's almost like—" She stopped herself. "Never mind. I haven't been sleeping well. That's it." She shook out her wrist like it was bothering her.

"There'll be plenty of people there, so you don't have to be afraid," Arthur said. "I'll stop and check on you between each patient."

"I'll be fine," Mina insisted. But Arthur noticed tears in her eyes too.

He walked her downstairs, promised himself as soon as he checked on Renfield, he'd be right back.

***

Arthur knocked before he entered Renfield's room.

"Dr. Godalming?" a fragile voice called out. It was Renfield, but not as Arthur had ever heard him before. Arthur hurried inside. Renfield sat on the floor in the corner of his room. His legs were pulled to his chest, one arm wrapped around them. The other was tied in a sling. His face was ragged, his eyes sunken.

"Dr. Godalming?" he repeated. His voice wavered.

"I'm here," Arthur said, not bothering to correct him. "Are you okay?" He crouched at Renfield's side.

Renfield smiled. "It's almost like you care, Doctor."

"I do," Arthur said.

Renfield grabbed Arthur's arm, dug in his nails like they were claws. "Then listen. The king is in charge now. Running the whole show along with his female vampire, the others."

"I know," Arthur said.

"You don't know anything. He's only toying with you and your friends. Soon he'll go all the way to the top, be in charge of the whole country. I should never have invited him here. And with that vent screwed shut, I have no way out. You must let me go."

Arthur shook his head. "You know I don't have that authority." Even with the brigade, he couldn't free every patient.

Renfield kept clutching at his arm, met his eyes. "But I'm not insane, Doctor."

Indeed, the eyes that looked into Arthur's were serious as death, without a tremble or hesitation.

"The king isn't who I thought he was," Renfield continued. "If he doesn't get what he wants, the Bloodless Syndrome will be everywhere. You must let me go." Renfield squeezed Arthur's hand so hard he feared something would crack. "I'm begging you. Before he finds me again." He gestured at his arm wrapped in a sling. "Before he uses me!"

Arthur stood. "I'm sorry."

"Please!" Renfield begged. "Please, Arthur!"

Arthur couldn't remember Renfield ever using his given name. What if he really was in danger?

"Tonight," Arthur promised under his breath. "I'll come find you tonight."

Renfield nodded, closed his eyes, sank back to the floor as if spent.

"God of our weary years, God of our silent tears," Renfield murmured under his breath, almost like a prayer.

This time Arthur would do the right thing for his patient.

Chapter 50

Mina

I CURLED INTO a sagging, stuffed chair in the detention center's main waiting room. I listened to the whispered conversations around me, the tears, the calls to family, the constant hum of the newscasts. The noise itself wasn't comforting but the people were. I didn't want to be alone. I closed my eyes. I was probably coming down with something. I was still wearing my coat, my scarf. I couldn't warm up. And I felt as if I could sleep for days.

You're scared for Quincey, I told myself. Not to mention the lack of sleep, food.

I had work to do. I stood up, stretched my arms over my head, turned from the security cameras at opposite ends of the room, and recast my screen. First I checked the Omega app, but there were no new messages. Then back to the hospital's system. I had already broken in. I just needed to find a backdoor into staff permissions. I would give Arthur access to every door.

But instead, my mind wandered. I thought about the press conference Jonathan, Arthur, and I had watched via newscast. What I hadn't told Jonathan or Arthur was that I recognized the former hospital director. He was pale like wax, sweating in a too big suit. He had worn that same suit as he danced in my dreams.

My head felt heavy, my arms so weighted I sank back to my chair. It was such a strange sensation. Was I asleep? Dreaming? The overhead light had dimmed. In the darkness, I saw those red eyes. Watching me. Not again.

I tried to pry my eyes open, but my body was like lead.

No. I jolted to my feet, forced myself awake. What the hell was the matter with me? I looked around the room at all the other families, mothers, loved ones— except they were all asleep. My heart began to race. I spun in a slow circle. The nurses, guards… everyone was asleep.

I cast my screen again, but there were no new messages. Jonathan was supposed to join the Omegas in their attack at midnight. But what if Anghen was here, now? What if, even as we planned to save Quincey and Lucy, Anghen launched an attack first?

I recast my screen. Amid the streams of data, I saw

the backdoor. I could automatically open all hospital doors. With a click, I heard the locks deactivate. Another step and the security cameras switched off.

But I didn't stop to message Jonathan and Arthur. Before I could change my mind, I was already heading for the elevators to find Anghen before he found us.

Chapter 51

Quincey

A SCREAM CUT the night. Quincey sat upright, tried to make sense of his surroundings.

He was in the DetCen. It was dark. It must have been late. He couldn't hear the faint music from the nurses' station, laughter, footsteps in the hallway, or even his brigaders chanting. Everything was strangely quiet, as if the entire hospital were trapped in a thick mist. So who screamed? *Lucy!* He knew the brigaders would do everything possible to keep her safe. But what if something had happened? Quincey rose to his window. The sky was dark, heavy with clouds.

Quincey climbed back into bed. Probably a dream or an ambulance, something unimportant.

"God of our weary years!" a high-pitched voice screamed. "God of our silent tears! God of our weary years, God of our silent tears!"

Quincey jumped out of bed and ran to the door. Something was wrong. The voice thundered in his ears, through the wall, desperate, terrified. He imagined Renfield. Whoever was next door, he needed help.

"Close your pathetic mouth!" a different voice hissed.

Quincey heard an explosive CRACK.

Quincey waited for an orderly like Arthur to charge inside.

There was only silence. Then a groan. Another crack and the sound of something heavy smacking the floor.

Quincey heard nothing from outside. He had to do something. He jumped onto his bed and reached for the heating duct. There was a metal grate covering it, but otherwise it would fit a person. Maybe. It rattled against his hand, already loose with time and rust. Quincey used his fingernail to pry at one of the screws holding the grate in place.

"Please," the original voice called. "God of our weary years—"

Quincey kept turning. One screw spun loose into his hand. He dropped it to the floor, started on the next.

The man next door cried out. Quincey let another screw fall. He jerked at the grate. No, it wasn't loose enough. He started on the third screw.

"You thought you would defy me," the other voice said. "You thought you would play with the devil himself. But no one outwits me."

Another crack, as if bone were breaking, shattering.

The third screw fell to the ground. Quincey yanked the grate from the tube. He looked up. There was a platform only a few inches above him. With a jump from the bed, Quincey got his fingers up, then an elbow. He wedged his body inside, pulled his butt up onto the ledge. The metal plating dipped, shuddering with his weight. Quincey froze, let it still.

The man started wildly, wordlessly screaming.

The tunnel would hold. Or it wouldn't. Quincey couldn't let himself think about it. The duct continued in either direction. His brigade training took over; he was more machine than living, breathing person. Carefully he flattened out, pulled himself forward.

He could see faint light ahead, glowing upward through the tunnel. He kept crawling. The duct shivered under him, bowing with his weight. Just a few more feet. There. The light was below him.

Quincey waited a moment longer, listening. The man was still being beaten. He was groaning, gasping. His voice had become faint.

"You will never cross me again!" the other voice hissed. "I will make sure of this." There was a final, thundering crash, a scream, then echoing, horrible silence. Quincey jumped down the tunnel, threw all his weight on the grate. It shuddered and broke loose, and he dropped, tumbling to the bed below. His legs rocked and he fell to the side.

271

Quincey stuck up his head. There was only one man in the room now, lying prone on the floor, face down. Renfield. It had to be him. He was just as Arthur had described: tall, skinny, black. But around his head was a puddle of blood.

Quincey crawled to the body, put a hand on his shoulder. "Renfield," he whispered, as if he was asleep instead of the other, terrible alternative. But no, his body was still warm. "Renfield," Quincey said louder.

Renfield groaned. But his eyes were open, watching, shifting, as if he were carefully sorting something out.

"It's Quincey. You don't know me, but I'm friends with Arthur. They imprisoned me here too. Next door. I heard you and came to help." He spoke in short sentences, as if Renfield were slow, not bleeding. His brain couldn't adjust. "I'm going to roll you over. See how bad the wound is."

Renfield weakly stuck up a hand. "No time," he said. "Dying."

"I should call someone," Quincey said. He was in a hospital after all. He got to his knees, but Renfield raised his hand again. "Mina?"

"Yes," Quincey said, "I'm friends with Mina too."

Renfield shook his head, barely a fraction of an inch. "Mina," he said again. "I couldn't save her." His voice was ragged, faint, even though they were only inches apart.

"Save her?" Quincey repeated, his heart beating even faster. "Mina's in danger?"

272

"From him," Renfield said. "He runs the whole show here now."

Quincey's body went cold. There could only be one him.

He heard Lucy's voice echoing in his head: *He'll destroy everyone I love.*

Renfield kept talking. "I tried to stop him. To save her. Please tell Dr. Godalming I tried."

"We need help," Quincey said. Once again the brigade training was there, making him move before he was thinking. Quincey jammed his thumb against the call button, then rattled the door in its frame. He beat at it with his fists. "Help!" he screamed. "HELP!"

Renfield was still talking, as if the few words he had uttered had whet his lips and now he couldn't stop himself. "He's been sucking her dry. He basically told me. He promised strength to me, and life, double my own, but now he's given it all to her."

"Mina?" Quincey asked.

"Yes. She's his prisoner now. But he doesn't keep his deals. He promises so much, but he never keeps his deals."

Where the hell was the staff? Quincey jammed his thumb against the call button again. His heart was racing. His feet needed to be racing too, running. Mina was in danger. He could feel it, taste it. He needed to get to her. Quincey peered into the duct. Could he escape to another room, get someone's attention?

The door flew open and he spun around.

273

"There's been an attack," Quincey announced to a white woman in nurse scrubs whom he didn't know. The door slammed behind her. "Renfield is dying. But someone needs to—"

She interrupted with a scream, running to Renfield, taking in his blood, his face. They both watched his eyes slowly close. The nurse whirled, pointed at Quincey. "How did you get here?" She pressed the call button herself. "What did you do?"

"I didn't do anything," Quincey protested.

"You're under arrest," she said. "They'll put you away for a long time. Murderer!"

Quincey's body froze. "I didn't touch him," he insisted. "My room's next door—"

But the nurse had cast her screen, was speaking into it. "Security needed at room 314. Patient dead. Black male suspect at large."

Quincey looked wildly around the room, his heart racing. He had to get to Mina.

The nurse was still talking to someone. "I don't know what happened. I was on duty. I was in my chair, waiting, but suddenly I was asleep. Then I heard—"

The door clicked unlocked. Quincey ducked behind a faux wood cabinet, anticipating all sorts of armed guards, even silver CMS agents, but no one appeared in the doorway. Quincey dashed forward.

"Stop! Murderer!" the nurse screamed behind him.

Quincey flung the door open. Nestled at the base of it was Arthur. Quincey's heart dropped. He bent down,

nudged Arthur. Arthur blinked. He was only sleeping!
Then Quincey was already on his feet, running.

Over his shoulder he yelled, "Anghen has Mina!"

Chapter 52

Mina

I RETURNED TO the front lobby. The information desk was there along with a giant map. I wanted a plan.

The building was strangely empty, heavy with muffled silence. Through the reinforced windows of the guard station, all I could see of the outside looked dark. It must have been late. I studied the floor list: emergency room, pediatrics, pulmonary... There. On the top floor was the director's office. The elevator dinged and opened empty. I hurried inside, pressed ten.

As the elevator climbed, I crossed my arms, pressed my trembling hands into my armpits. I went over my cover story, how I was shadowing my friend Arthur and we got separated, so I was looking for him. I hadn't realized he wouldn't be on the same floor as the director.

Okay, it was stupid. The doors slid open, my stupid

276

story on the tip of my tongue. Except no one was there.

The carpeted hallway held a row of offices. I followed the numbered doors, assuming Anghen's would be at one end. 1001, 1003, 1005... The numbers climbed. Shoot. I hadn't noticed any room numbers downstairs. But no one was here. The cameras were still dark. I hurried down the hall, trying not to look too out of place.

At the end of the hallway was a gold-colored plaque reading EXECUTIVE DIRECTOR.

I reached for the handle, and sure enough it started to turn... My hacking had worked even here. Feeling a small burst of pride, I threw open the door. But the room was dark, seemingly empty. As my eyes adjusted, the shadows coalesced into chairs, a long, L-shaped desk, a row of bookshelves, an oriental rug. A coffee machine made the whole room smell rich, important. Nothing obviously connected the suite to Anghen, but I hadn't expected a coffin in the middle of the room. The blackout curtains across the way were open; the sky was dark.

Anghen wasn't there.

I needed to search the whole hospital, top to bottom. Or would it be better to message Arthur, let him know what I suspected? I tapped a finger against my head. Why couldn't I think straight?

"I knew you would find me."

I gasped, spun around. No one was at the door. But I could feel eyes on me. I kept turning, rotating 360 degrees back to the desk. Anghen sat in the desk chair, hidden in shadows, his fingers steepled in front of his eyes.

A cold dread settled over me.

His lips crept into a smile, wide and toothy. My body started to shake.

He gestured toward a chair opposite his desk. "Have a seat, let us talk."

I should have attacked him. I should have at least screamed. But it felt as if my whole body was made of imitation cheese. I sank into the chair.

"You know I've been watching you for some time," Anghen said, his voice quiet and horribly calm. "But everything came together for tonight: my promotion, the detention of your friend, your so-called plan, this bustling hospital." He gestured, taking in the building.

But it wasn't bustling. It was quiet. So quiet I could hear the whoosh of the air. I only realized then how weird it had been. Not only the sleepy waiting room but the empty lobby, the elevator, the hallway... especially with all the doors open! Somehow he must have put everyone to sleep.

"I'm a very powerful man, Mina Muto," Anghen said, reveling in knowing my full name even as he seemed to read my mind. "All done on your behalf, of course."

"You didn't need to," I said, as if this were some formal English movie and I was performing a role, following a script I had no control over.

Anghen was like an actor too, familiar from all the different roles I'd seen him in: on the newsfeed, with Lucy in the field house, through Jonathan's descriptions. His voice sounded more polished than I had remembered; his accent charming, easy to understand. But it was more than that: the dark hair streaked with gray, the sunken cheeks, the smell of animal, the red eyes studying my own. I knew him, I remembered him. I had thought it had only been a dream.

"I've been watching since I first arrived," Anghen said. "Your roommate was easy prey—friendly, a dreamer of dreams. A perfect, blond-haired and blue-eyed prize." His mouth twisted, spat out the next words. "Until she was taken from me."

My whole body shook. *Get up*, I thought to myself. *Run!* But it was as if I were at the bottom of one of those aquariums with thousands of gallons of water above, pressing down on me.

"Then I realized Mr. Harker had been right. The real prize was you all along. I made you mine."

It had been no dream. I vaguely lifted my fingers under my thick scarf to my neck. I felt two spots of dried blood. My heart fell. It was too late. I was too late. My hands squeezed the armrests. But still I couldn't move. Anghen had me under his control.

"You're surprisingly clever. No wonder Mr. Harker trusted you. All the boys do. They let you sit in on their planning, take their notes, even lead their meetings. I assume the deactivated security system is your doing too. It's unfortunate your education has fallen to the wayside."

"I graduate in less than five months," I snapped without thinking.

"Strong too," Anghen added appreciatively. "You see, we're not so different, you and me. Both immigrants. But when Americans see me, they see the American Dream. They see my white skin, my money. My accent has even improved, thanks to your Mr. Harker. In me, they see potential. But you—" Anghen shook his head. "Your skin is too dark, isn't it? A RAT, your countrymen call you."

"Enough!" I said, raising my voice over his. "I'm calling Arthur—he'll call hospital security."

"I love this country," Anghen said, smiling widely to show his feral teeth. "So honest, so hopeful."

"Call Arthur," I whisper-texted into my xphone.

Anghen sat back in his chair, patiently watched. He could probably hear the line buzzing, over and over again, with no answer. My heart raced ahead.

"You have no other options," Anghen said. "I really must insist we have this conversation. Turn it off."

The sound died just like that. Had it been him? Or me?

"You see," Anghen continued, "I realize you are in a difficult spot in your fledgling life. Your grades have suffered as of late. Lucy mentioned you were losing interest in college. Unfortunately, your only job experience is in your high school office part time, and you have absolutely no money to your name."

He knew it all. I looked at the windows, the pitch-black outside. Everything had fallen apart. I couldn't stop him.

"However, I might have an idea for you," Anghen continued. "I would like you to work for me."

My heart doubled, tripled its beat. I tried to pull away, but somehow my hands felt stiff, my fingers still tightly wrapped around his desk. I wasn't strong enough. I had never been strong enough.

"You're not listening, dear," he continued, leaning closer. "I would not harm you. In fact, I quite respect you. Further, this would be no internship, as I believe Mr. Harker called his temporary position. You would be an administrator, a manager. You see, my plan is only in its infancy. With time, my position in this country will rise. I'll have press releases, interviews, and rather complicated travel. Of course, there will be room for your promotion as well. An eternity of room. I could make you so powerful. You would never want for anything."

I couldn't move. I felt like a balloon, empty, lifeless. His words bounced back and forth in my head. *You would never want for anything, you would never want for anything.*

"I could never work for you!" I spat out.

Anghen raised his eyebrows, smiled. "Feisty, I believe is the term."

281

Then the tide overcame me. I tried to stare up at him, contradict him, even to form the word no, but my eyes were so heavy.

I slumped across his desk, and everything went dark.

Chapter 53

Jonathan

Wednesday, November 21

AT MIDNIGHT I joined the Omegas as they streamed inside Newholm Hospital. We swarmed through the double doors, past security, through the body scanner, everything open, just as Mina had promised.

Even better, the security guard had her head nestled in her hands, her eyes tightly closed, sound asleep.

We rushed into an empty front lobby. Quincey's Uncle Leon posted himself at the door along with a guy who couldn't be any older than me.

"My team will secure the front and the back receiving door," Leon called out, pulling his gun from his side holster. "I'll have them message you when they're ready for the girl."

Gabriel, the intense young man who led us, nodded

283

and gestured at a handful of other brigaders to join him. They all carried guns strapped to their backs. I led them down the hallway into the detention center elevator. Gabriel pressed the button for the third floor: Quincey.

The Omegas had everything in hand. Soon we'd walk out with Lucy and Quincey safe. But I cast my screen, scanned my messages again. There was still nothing from Mina.

My stomach twisted. I had failed her over and over again. Back in Yorkshire, Anghen had escaped my pathetic attempts at stopping him. I had seen him in the hospital but been too afraid to even check on Lucy. And Lucy was attacked again, trapped in this coma, and if we didn't do something, she might never wake up. My mom had never needed a man to protect her. But I had wanted to be everything to Mina. Partners.

And now? As the elevator climbed upward, my heart began to race. I ran my hand along Mom's gun at my side. All my bravado had disintegrated. *Where was Mina?*

Chapter 54

Arthur

November 21, Newholm Detention Center

ARTHUR WOKE.

He remembered Quincey yelling something at him, something important. He rubbed his eyes. How the hell had he ended up asleep on the floor? He pushed himself up. He was right outside Renfield's room. The door was wide open.

A body was inside. Renfield, still, motionless. Blood pooled around his skull.

No! It couldn't be true. Renfield was supposed to be full of life. He had swallowed all those bugs, then that bloody cat. Renfield had taunted Arthur since day one, scratched a map into his own arm, been able to move freely. He couldn't be dead.

Arthur crawled closer, held his hand to Renfield's

285

wrist, waited for his pulse. Nothing.

Arthur wasn't paying close enough attention. He tried again. He pulled his specrays over his eyes, but he couldn't see his screencast—his eyes were flooding with tears. Below Renfield's head, the blood was thickening, congealing, matting into his hair.

Arthur pressed deeper into Renfield's skin, but the patient remained motionless. Arthur thumped Renfield's chest, breathed into his mouth. Renfield gave no response.

But Arthur had promised him! He'd told him he'd help him escape. But he had also had Custodial screw the vent shut again. Arthur had sealed him inside. Left him to his death.

Arthur's heart was thrumming in his ears. Anghen. This had to have been Anghen's work. Where was he?

Arthur looked around for clues, reports, staff. Where the hell was everyone? A nurse was stretched out on the floor beyond Renfield. Arthur rushed to her side, touched her shoulder. She jerked awake.

"Renfield is dead," Arthur snapped. "What happened?"

"There was a murderer." Her eyes grew wide. "I tried to stop him. I yelled for help—"

She stared around Renfield's room as if she had never seen it before.

"And?" Arthur cracked his knuckles so he wouldn't hit something.

"But I was ordered to sleep," she finally said. "By

someone important, someone up top. I remember thinking it was ridiculous, but I couldn't disobey an order, and I was so tired."

"Arthur?" It was Jonathan, flanked by a handful of Omegas. "Have you seen Mina?"

Arthur shook his head. Hadn't she been in the waiting room? But how long ago had that been? Jonathan raced ahead, the brigaders following him. Arthur could hear other doors being opened, them yelling to each other. Something about Quincey.

But Arthur's mind was running in a different direction. "Someone important told you to sleep?" he repeated to the nurse.

"Yes, that new man. I think. Sorry, it's all foggy. I wanted to make a good impression, but—"

Arthur was already standing. The new man. The new director. Anghen.

"Arthur!" Jonathan bellowed from down the hall. "She's not here, not in the hallway, not in the waiting room. We need to find her!"

"Quincey's missing as well!" the lead brigader behind him announced.

"This way!" Arthur called from over his shoulder as he raced for the elevator. He prayed to everything he believed in—medicine, science, that damn leadership camp, Mina, Lucy, Lucy, Lucy—that they weren't too late.

Chapter 55

Quincey

QUINCEY SPRINTED ALONG the empty tenth floor. He passed a custodian's cart, but the hallway itself was empty. Just like downstairs. He ran for the door at the end of the hall. When he skidded to a stop in front of it, Quincey heard a now-familiar male voice, the same voice he had heard in Renfield's room. Anghen's, he was sure of it. No response from Mina.

Quincey looked wildly around. He ran back to the custodian's cart, grabbed a mop. Quincey hefted the stick in his hands, thinking. He unscrewed the mop end. It wasn't great. But if it came to it, he could at least do some damage.

He returned to the door, his feet silent on the carpet, but he no longer heard any voices. He tested the door. The handle pressed smoothly down, unlocked. Quincey slowly opened the door.

It was a fancy office with plush carpet, a table, chairs, and a big wooden desk. Wide windows, their blackout curtains pooled at either side, overlooked the dark night, glimmering with the hospital lights below. It was through the faint light that Quincey could make out the horrible scene in front of him.

He recognized Anghen from Jonathan's writing, his dark hair streaked with gray, the scar where Jonathan had attacked him. He was on top of the desk, squatting over something like a dog with a prize. He started as the door opened, looked up. His face was smeared with blood.

Only then did Quincey see Mina. She was still in her coat but face down against the desk, arms askew, as if she had passed out. Quincey raised the mop pole and charged.

Anghen's red eyes flashed in the darkness. He threw aside Mina's body. She tumbled onto the carpet. Quincey swung the pole, aiming for Anghen's head. Anghen leaped over the desk.

Quincey turned, moving and swinging with one motion. Anghen ducked, rushed for the door.

Quincey threw the stick spear-style after him.

But Anghen was only mist, already vanishing into the air.

Quincey hesitated for an instant, watching the mist dissipate down the hall, escaping. But he turned back to Mina.

She was curled on the floor, her neck smeared with

blood. "Mimi." He brushed hair from her face. "Mimi, are you okay? Are you awake?"

Her eyes fluttered open. "Quincey? You're free?" she whispered, always quicker and smarter than anyone else in the room.

He nodded. "I guess so. Are you hurt?"

For all her intelligence, she hadn't thought of herself yet. She looked at her hands, ran her fingers down her neck. Her eyes shot back to Quincey's.

He reached for her, trying somehow to stop the horror in her face. "We'll find him, we'll—"

"Get away from me!" she shrieked, crab-walking backward, stumbling over her own feet. "I'm not safe!"

Then more people rushed inside. The light flashed on. Quincey spun, raised his hands before he recognized Gabriel, the leader of the Omegas, and several more Omegas alongside Arthur and Jonathan. They must have come for him. Jonathan ran for Mina, scooped her into his arms.

"No," she protested. "No."

But he cradled her against him. Mina buried her face in his chest.

Quincey turned away, gave them a moment even as his own eyes filled with tears.

"He got me," Mina murmured.

"You're so cold," Jonathan said. "We should take you downstairs, get you checked out."

"No," Mina protested.

"No," Arthur echoed. "Not here. It's not safe."

Arthur crossed the room, reached for Mina's wrist, and quietly counted. "Your pulse is solid. I don't think you need a transfusion. Probably just lots of water, food."

Mina shook her head. "We need to stop him. He's probably still here—" She pulled away from Jonathan and Arthur, grabbed her scarf and knotted it over her wound.

"Quincey?" It was Gabriel, yelling from the hallway, his finger pointing at his earpiece, then over his lips.

The group went silent as a voice crackled out: "They're here. Half a dozen—" The voice abruptly stopped. All they could hear were screams.

"The lobby," Gabriel commanded, the Omegas already charging for the stairs, another set for the elevators. Gabriel unholstered his gun.

Arthur followed after them but called over his shoulder. "Jonathan, you can take her out through the receiving door of the morgue. Use the service elevator to avoid everyone. The other brigaders are already there with Lucy. Quincey—"

He wanted to follow Jonathan. He wanted to check on Lucy, hold her once more in his arms. But he couldn't.

"I'm coming with you," Quincey said, racing after the others for the elevator. "That was my uncle."

Chapter 56

Quincey

THE ELEVATOR DINGED as it opened to the lobby. A shot rang out. Arthur shoved Quincey back against the elevator wall, then drew his gun. Quincey jammed his finger against the Door Open button as they peered around the door.

Quincey saw blood, a mess of bodies: Omegas, Alphas, even patients. The air was thick with the smell of something burned, something metallic. Someone screamed.

Quincey's head darted up with another shot, and the Omega by the front door exploded with blood. There was a prone figure on the other side of the door: his uncle. A woman in black with long dark hair knelt over him.

"Stop!" Quincey yelled.

"Stand back!" Arthur raised his gun.

The glass doorway shattered. The dark woman disappeared in a flash of mist. Arthur charged after her, stepped over the glass outside. Quincey rushed to his uncle's side. There might have been another shot, but he could only pay attention to Uncle Leon.

A jagged cut ran across his face. He was covered with blood.

Quincey knelt at his side. "Leon?" he whispered. Quincey tentatively reached for his shoulder. He wished Arthur were there to check his pulse, to tell him everything was okay.

"For God's sake, son, it's only a bloody nose."

Quincey sat back on his heels as his uncle's eyes opened.

"Don't waste your time on me," Uncle Leon ordered. "Check Mikey. I think—" His words died as a howl cut across the building.

Quincey jerked around as a figure materialized out of mist in the middle of the lobby, then raised his head to the high ceiling, howled again. His hands were hairy, his nails pointed, his hair thick black.

Anghen. Where was Arthur?

Another howl answered from outside, then another. Alphas around the room gathered close, surrounding Anghen with their guns, protecting him. Then Anghen vanished in a cloud of mist. The Alphas raced for the door, for Quincey.

Quincey braced himself over Leon, buried his head. But the howl must have been some type of cue. In seconds, the room was still, quiet.

Quincey rushed to the Omega who had been stationed on the other side of the doorway, a boy his own age. Mikey. He was motionless, sprawled across the floor, blood everywhere. Quincey held a hand to Mikey's wrist, as he had seen Arthur do, but there was no life in him. Quincey looked back at his uncle, shook his head. Uncle Leon cursed.

Quincey took in the rest of the lobby. Another Omega, one he didn't know, was down, alongside two Alphas. There were also bodies in hospital gowns, including a motionless little girl. Nearby was a dead man in a suit. His arms were thrust out as if he had tried to stop the horror, but it had come anyway.

"Dr. Eisley," he heard Arthur murmur from behind him. "The hospital's executive director. Until Anghen."

"They surprised us," Uncle Leon said, rising to his feet, hand on his gun. "Must have been a dozen of those Alphas and monsters."

"I tried to get that vampire woman again," Arthur muttered, shaking his head, his voice heavy with emotion. "But I couldn't. I wasn't fast enough. She turned into a wolf, howled, turned into mist, and then she was gone."

"Anghen left too," Quincey spat out.

Arthur took in the rest of the bodies and knelt beside the girl in the hospital gown. The Omegas were already tending to their own.

"Does me good to see you free," Leon continued to

Quincey, leaning on his shoulder. "Now get out of here."

"What?" Quincey shook his head. "But you're hurt. And the monsters won't have gone far; they could be back—"

Leon shook his head. "But the cops will be here soon. We've already lost at least two. Your mom will kill me if anything happens to you. Get."

"He's right," Arthur said. "There're plenty of other Omegas here. I can check your uncle over. But if they see you..." Arthur frowned. "Besides, we need you to check on Lucy, make sure she gets back to my room, that she's still stable." His eyes pleaded with Quincey's.

Lucy.

Quincey nodded, then stepped through the door with its shattered glass. Outside was still pitch-black, as if the night would never end, as if the rest of his life would be only darkness. But first he would ensure Lucy was safe. He slipped outside, into the shadow of the building, and ran around the perimeter until he found the receiving door and the morgue.

Chapter 57

WHIT News

BRIGADE KILLS 7 AT LOCAL HOSPITAL
Nov 22, 2---

PROTESTERS SURROUNDED NEWHOLM Hospital and
Detention Center Tuesday night in response to a viral
video some have dubbed "Quincey Jordan, Sir." But
those protests turned violent less than twenty-four
hours later as on Wednesday night, members of the
Omega Brigade stormed hospital facilities. The security
and surveillance system was hacked and the glass
entryway shattered. At least seven have been reported
dead, including three patients and Dr. Andrew Eisley,
the hospital and detention center's former executive
director. Several detainees have also apparently escaped.
No suspects are yet in custody. "I was afraid for my
life," security guard Maycie Deloitte reported. "There
were gunshots everywhere and blood and bodies—I

didn't know what was happening."

Officials are also investigating the sudden nature of the attack. Victims reported being overwhelmed by exhaustion prior to the raid, pointing to the possibility of chemical warfare.

It is not the first instance of a rogue brigade group employing violence on unarmed civilians. As police and government departments increasingly rely on brigades made up of private citizens and other individuals, some worry about the lack of oversight. There is no security footage of Newholm Hospital's attack, but based on injuries sustained and individual reports, Omega brigaders carried firearms as well as knives and perhaps other unauthorized weapons. Newholm Hospital serves several of its nearby suburbs as well as Whitby, which is now a designated Dead Zone and allegedly the home base of the Omega Brigade.

However, members of the initial protest point to Quincey Jordan to highlight perceived irregularities in the arrest and detention of individuals. Common practice requires detainees to be held for only seventy-two hours, enough time for health, drug, and psychological testing before a patient is either required to enroll at the detention center or is free to go. While Jordan was detained for less than twenty-four hours before the attack, friends and families have claimed some patients at Newholm have been held for extended time—for multiple weeks, even months. Destiny Summers, at the entrance of the institution early this morning, claimed, "My boy has been held in there for twenty-seven days. Twenty-seven! That's not right. He hasn't done anything wrong and now he's lost his job, he can't see his own family, and people are getting murdered."

It is not yet clear why Dr. Andrew Eisley, the Newholm Hospital and Detention Center's previous executive director, was present at the hospital. The hospital is also rapidly trying to account for all their staff, patients, and detainees and secure anyone missing.

Dr. Wilhelm Anghen, the executive director who only days ago advanced to his position, called an impromptu press conference. "What happened today, in my hospital and detention center, is a tragedy. Lives were lost, including our beloved former director, Dr. Andrew Eisley, and patients, whom we had a duty to protect. It is with heavy hearts that we start this new day. But these are the moments where leaders are required to show the way forward. I have already enlisted the help of Citizen & Migrant Security, and I promise swift action in our investigation. I swear to you, all perpetrators of this mob violence on Newholm's hospital and detention center will be brought to justice."

Dr. Anghen argued that detention centers play an essential role in the US. "This country is home of the brave. Anyone who does not have our best interests at heart is not welcome. Citizens who don't hold American ideals, who don't love and respect this country—these people fall prey to crime, drugs, or even perpetuate falsehoods about their great nation. I like to think of this as America's 'patriot problem.' We need to keep a close eye on such people before they become dangerous to society, as these rogue brigaders have tonight. This is the mission of our detention centers. Its inmates will not be harmed or arrested. But if they don't fit into their communities, their country, we must find another place for them."

Dr. Anghen concluded his speech with a call for hope. "Now is not the time to lose heart. If the United States is to fulfill its destiny as a city on the hill, to continue as this great nation your forefathers created, we must move forward in action. As an immigrant myself, I have not always been privileged enough to be part of this great nation, but it is because of this that I see clearly. You must live to your country's full potential. We must rise."

Chapter 58

Jonathan

Thursday, November 22

WHILE MINA DISAPPEARED into the suite's bathroom, the Omega brigaders carefully placed Lucy on one of the beds in Arthur's suite—probably Arthur's since it had been neatly made, very military. They checked Lucy over before leaving, using Arthur's tools: blood pressure, temperature, heart rate. While she was pale and unbelievably motionless, she was stable and ticked all the correct boxes on Arthur's chart. They offered to stay or send replacements, but I turned them down. They needed to check on the rest of their brigade, help in whatever way they could. And it wasn't like I was going to bed anytime soon. I mindlessly fingered the Star of David around my neck before knocking on the bathroom door.

300

"Give me a minute," Mina snapped from the other side.

Right. I needed to keep myself busy, find a way to be useful. I made sure the blackout curtains were firmly in place, the doors locked. My gun was ready. Then I cast my screen, checked the time: it was so late it was already Thursday.

Finally Mina opened the suite's bathroom door, still wearing her jeans but changed into a too-large T-shirt that must have belonged to Arthur. I went to her, desperately trying to distract myself from the picture in my head of her neck, the blood, and what Anghen must have done to her. I took her hand. Her skin was warmer, clean from the showerless absorbing gel, but she was still so pale.

"You should sleep," I said.

She shook her head. "Is Lucy okay?"

I gestured to the side bedroom. "They put her in there."

Mina hurried to Lucy. She touched her cheek, presumably feeling its warmth, before settling down in the chair next to her. Only then did she meet my eyes as I leaned against the doorway. "Don't you dare call my mom."

"Why would I—?"

Mina kept talking before I could get another word in. "The monster already got Lucy's mom, Colonel Godalming; Anghen stopped Dr. Helsinger's partner from renewing her ID; they arrested Quincey." Mina

301

shook her head again, violently, as a shudder ran through her. "I don't want my family involved. Besides, this time we're going to fight him head-on; this time we're going to stop him. We have no other choice."

"Okay, but—"

Mina continued as if I hadn't interrupted. "Did you know Anghen can put people to sleep? I suppose that's what the vampires did to you that night in the tower, but we've never listed that in our notes. I think they can interfere with people's minds even on a mass scale." She chewed at her lip, which was already bitten raw. "Tonight I felt like I was underwater, like I could hear him talking to me but inside my head too. Just like Lucy said. I tried to resist him this time. I wanted to stop him from interfering, from attacking you and Arthur and the Omegas, but I wasn't strong enough."

This time. A horrible cold covered me. "Has this happened before?"

"Maybe," she whispered.

I jumped upright, hurried to her side. "Maybe? Do you know or not?"

I was standing over her. My voice echoed in the silence. Mina had her fingers under her glasses, massaging her eyes. Was she crying?

I sat down on the sofa opposite the bed. "Sorry."

Mina didn't respond, only continued her story. "It was Tuesday night. I thought it was just a dream, maybe triggered by everything. But I've never had dreams before. Look at my neck."

Mina tucked her hair behind her ear and pulled aside the collar of Arthur's shirt. There were marks there, just like Lucy's. Raw, red with blood. My whole body shook with fear, exhaustion, rage.

"I saw them in the bathroom," she said. "And earlier tonight, after Anghen..."

His name echoed in the quiet.

"But you knew," I said. "You knew Anghen was out there, you knew how dangerous he was. You saw how he manipulated Renfield, wormed his way into the hospital. And after he attacked Lucy that second time, she was too weak to recover. Nothing worked—not the garlic or the blood transfusions, not even all those Omegas watching over her. You saw. She was turning into a monster!"

"Jonathan—"

But it was my turn to keep talking, growing louder with each word. "Or we can go back even further, to Bram Manor. Do you remember the wolves? How he called to them? How they ripped apart that mother, just as the monsters devoured her child? He has superhuman strength. Remember how I couldn't even open my window, but he whipped it up like it was nothing? I wrote my whole notebook to tell you, to warn you. And now here you are—" I threw up my hands, out of words.

"No." She didn't yell. Her voice was so quiet I could barely hear, but she looked me in the eye. "That's not the whole story, Jonathan Harker. You attacked him with a shovel while he was completely asleep, but you *missed*. You were attacked by those three women and only saved because he wanted to protect you. Don't you see? I'm his victim. He wants me, and I need to stop him before it's too late." Mina's hands trembled; she clutched them tightly together in her lap.

Tears clouded my vision. "I know all that. I've been trying so hard to keep you safe. But it wasn't enough."

"I'm not some princess in a tower. We're supposed to be a team."

"I've been looking for him," I told her. "Tuesday before everything happened, I talked to one of the Omegas. Later that night they sent me and Quincey a list of all known new residents or unexpected squatting activity in the past month. There's less than a dozen. I'll spend today on the minibus through the Dead Zone, knocking on doors, talking to people. We'll figure out exactly where his lair is."

Mina pushed up her glasses. "Really?"

"I had to do something," I said. "I never told you…" My voice faltered, but I swallowed, plowed ahead. "That night in the hospital, when Lucy was attacked, I was there. I was looking for you, but I thought I saw him instead. I had a panic attack. I called Mom, and she told me to come home."

"You saw him in the hospital?" Her voice was brittle like glass.

"I wasn't sure. I didn't know if I was seeing things again or—"

The look in Mina's eyes silenced me.

"He was leaving," I said. "So whatever he'd done must have already happened. I sent a nurse to her room. Or at least I requested one."

"It was probably too late," Mina said, her voice barely above a whisper. "But what if it wasn't?"

"I know." It was like a broken movie in my head, playing on repeat, over and over. "I couldn't bear to tell you."

But Mina wasn't listening to me. "Afterward I couldn't stop thinking of all the things I could have done, should have done, to save Lucy. I had to let her go into that coma, not knowing if I'd ever see my best friend awake again. But you—"

Her voice broke, filled with tears.

She was right. But I couldn't bear to have Mina give up on me, not now. "I've failed you so many times. But I'm not afraid anymore. I'll do whatever it takes. I won't lose you."

"It's not just about me anymore."

She was still listening! I would never forgive myself for what had happened, but there was still a chance. "I know. This time we'll destroy him. I promise."

"But will it be enough?" Mina bit her lip. "There are other monsters out there. The ones you met at the castle, and Arthur thinks that's what happened to his dad. Dr. Helsinger suspects they're working throughout Europe and Japan. Plus there could be hundreds of cases like Lucy's that we don't even know about."

"And it isn't just the monsters," I continued, my brain whirring ahead. "The system has supported them. You heard Anghen on the news talking about expanding detention centers. The ID system allows the government to track everyone, to target people of color like you and Quincey."

"It was CMS who brought Quincey in," Mina said. "The whole government could be in on it, supplying weapons here and abroad. So it's not just one monster. We need a whole revolution."

"Yes!" I echoed.

"No." Mina shook her head. "It's too big. I don't even know how to start, if we're even capable—"

"We start with Anghen," I said. "Together."

Mina raised her eyes to mine. They were red, rimmed with tears. I couldn't stand it. I got up, reached for her.

Mina froze under my arms.

I couldn't forget. Everything had changed.

Chapter 59

Mina

WHEN I WOKE, it was dark again. Jonathan was on the floor by my bed, his screencast in front of him, paging through columns of text. I rolled over, closed my eyes, as if I might relax for a moment longer. I had no idea what time it was. The blackout curtains were tightly sealed, the room dark. But it was too late. I recognized the unfamiliar sheets, Arthur's suite. I remembered what had happened.

"Mina?" Jonathan was at my side, ran a cool hand along my hair, brushing it from my face. "How are you feeling?"

It didn't matter. "What time is it?" I asked instead. "Is Quincey okay?"

"I'm here."

I sat up in bed as Quincey appeared in the doorway. His hair was ragged, his nails bitten down, and he was still wearing the pale blue jumpsuit of detainees. His whole body was twitching.

"Sorry," he said, as if I minded him bursting in, as if I weren't already awake. "It's morning, probably too early. I got in late last night. Jonathan let me take the couch, but I can't sit still."

"You saved me." I had to tell him while I still remembered, while I could still thank him, before I became whatever Anghen had planned for me.

But Quincey shook his head. "It was Renfield. He told me about you, then—" Quincey's face blanched.

"What happened?"

"Renfield—he didn't make it."

As I clutched the bedsheets to me, Quincey told me about Renfield, beaten to death, another victim in Anghen's plan. Not just Anghen—the whole government system. After all, he had been detained long before Anghen arrived on the scene.

"And Arthur?" I couldn't imagine what he would be feeling, losing his patient, not to mention his dad, possibly Lucy.

"He's okay, should be here soon." But then Quincey described the attack in the lobby, the monsters, the death. "I ran here," Quincey said. "Arthur suggested it. But I have to keep moving. They'll look for me eventually. They've got my xphone. They must know where I live, my friends, my parents, the other Omegas."

"Did you see the news?" Jonathan asked.

"Yes." Quincey's frown deepened.

Jonathan cast his screen for me.

"He's not just trying to pin the blame on us," Quincey said as my eyes skimmed through the text. "He's single-handedly ruining the Omegas' reputation. My full name's already out there, but once they release Omega names, all other brigaders as well as CMS will be hounding our every move."

"We'll make sure they don't find you," I promised.

Quincey shrugged even as his voice was full of quiet determination. "I won't go back."

My xphone chirped beside me. I tucked it over my ear, cast my screen. "It's Arthur."

"You should get more sleep—" Jonathan protested.

But then Arthur's picture appeared before me from just outside the dorm. "Are you okay?" he asked in a rush. "Did Lucy make it okay? Is Quincey there?"

"Yes," Quincey called from behind me. "On all counts."

Arthur exhaled. "Good. I'm coming up," he said, quickly disconnecting.

When Arthur arrived at the suite, he reached for his back pocket. "I figured you'd need this," he said, passing Quincey his ID.

Quincey took the ID, ran it through his fingers. "That makes life a bit easier. Thanks."

"Your file doesn't exist in the system. I don't know if they told you. With any luck, it means there's nothing on your record."

"Luck," Quincey murmured, like he didn't believe in it anymore. But he pocketed the ID.

Arthur checked over Lucy first, measured everything. "She's stable," he announced as he returned to my bedroom in the suite. "None the worse for wear."

But then he sat by my side, still holding his medical bag close. "What about you, Mina? I know I'm not qualified, but when Lucy was sick, Dr. H and I compiled a list of symptoms from both here and abroad."

"Symptoms?" My voice didn't reach above a whisper.

"Pointed canines, pallor, a red tint to the eyes in certain light, uncontrollable urges, sleeplessness—"

As Arthur's list grew longer, my heart grew heavy. They were all Lucy's symptoms. But some of them had become familiar.

Jonathan must have been thinking the same thing. He slumped onto my bed. He looked so tired with heavy shadows under his eyes. He must have watched over me the whole time I slept.

"You better check me out," I said to Arthur.

Arthur opened his bag, his face stony. It was as if both sides of him—doctor and commander—had found an uneasy balance. He placed a small black device on the inside of my wrist to measure my blood pressure. I watched his face, hoping to see some hint of my health as he moved to my temperature, then told me to take deep breaths while he listened to my heart. But he gave no sign, caught only in grim determination. He carried on, checking my teeth, looking into my eyes.

When he started to put his tools away, I couldn't take it anymore. "How far gone do you think I am?"

Jonathan opened his mouth as if to argue, but there was no point.

"It's not as if I'm an expert in vampires," Arthur said, with an uncomfortable laugh. "I probably don't even have a job anymore. I already called Dr. H— hopefully she'll get back to me. I asked if she could get her hands on any more garlic—"

"Arthur." Jonathan raised his voice.

"Your teeth are coming to a faint point," Arthur said. "I don't think they were before."

He waited, as if he thought I was going to whip out my dental records, but I only shook my head. I had never thought of my teeth as pointy before.

Arthur continued, "Your body temperature is 96.3 degrees, blood pressure ninety-eight over sixty-four. It's low but not life threatening. Not beyond normal range."

"Runners have low blood pressure," Jonathan said.

Something heavy settled in my throat. I remembered Lucy and I running on Halloween from the guy who had demanded to see our IDs. That seemed lifetimes ago. Obviously, I was no athlete.

Arthur's eyes met mine. They were deep, brown, suddenly heavy with tears. "It's not too late," he whispered.

"We need to destroy Anghen," Jonathan said, his hand on the gun at his side. "It's the only way."

The others nodded in agreement.

"As soon as possible," I echoed. "Whether it's day, night, in the middle of the hospital, at his house, wherever."

"He's a public figure now," Quincey added. "He can't hide forever."

"I'm sorry," Arthur abruptly said, turning to Quincey. "You told me about the DetCens, ages ago, and I didn't take it seriously— I didn't know—"

"It's okay," Quincey murmured, but Arthur met his eyes.

"No, it's not. I should have known, I should have opened my eyes long before. Did you see that mess of a news story? I tried to tell the police the truth. I told them about Renfield—" Arthur squared his jaw, closed his eyes, as if everything might flood over him. "He was my responsibility."

"Anghen's got all the power on his side," Quincey said. "The whole system. Just like Lucy warned."

"And it's coordinated," I said. "He's picking us off one by one."

"But we know things too," Jonathan said. "I've narrowed it down. The castle can only be one of a dozen houses. We know he's weaker during the day, and he has to sleep sometime. If we can find him—"

"We'll have the whole power of the Omegas behind

us," Quincey promised. "This is their fight now too."

"If we check each house—" Jonathan said.

"We could find him today," Arthur finished.

The others were already on their feet when Jonathan added, "I'd like to try one other thing. Just in case." Jonathan reached around his neck, unfastened his Star of David. "There may not be any science that can explain it, but it should keep you safe until we destroy him."

Jonathan pulled my hair to one side. He leaned forward, reached around my neck with the clasp. The Star fell to my chest.

I screamed. The pain burrowed into my body, seared my skin. My whole body was red-hot fire. I jerked away while Jonathan stumbled backward. The Star fell on the bed between us.

I put my head in my hands, held my body tight, and waited for the pain to stop.

"Mina, Mina," Jonathan cried, reaching for me.

"Mina?" Arthur echoed.

But I pulled away from them, across the bed. Tears blurred my vision. "Don't touch me."

"Are you okay?" Jonathan pleaded. "Did I hurt you?"

"Look!" I demanded. I pulled down my shirt's collar and held my head high, baring my chest for them to see what I already felt. The Star had branded itself into my skin.

Jonathan gasped.

I cast my screen, reflected my image. Only the top of the Star had touched my skin, but it had left a blistering red A. Like Hester Prynne. I had been branded like old-time livestock. A monster. Tears kept coming, blinding me. I squeezed my knees, buried my head.

"You can see your reflection," Quincey whispered.

"That's something," Jonathan said.

But I couldn't see any silver lining. The teeth, my temperature, it had all been scary, but nothing like this. I was no longer one of God's children. Not that I was even sure I believed in a god. But whatever Jonathan was, I wasn't that anymore. I was a creature, like Anghen, like his female vampires. Like Lucy threatened.

"If I become a monster, I want you to destroy me."

Quincey fell back against the window with a thud.

Jonathan settled at my side. "No, no, no. We'll take you to the hospital. Like Lucy. We'll put you in a coma—" He reached for me.

I held up my hand. "Don't touch me. You don't know when it will start, how quickly I'll change!"

I massaged my eyes under my glasses, which had never fit quite right. I tried to keep the tears from falling, but when I spoke, my voice was gravelly. "I don't want to hurt anyone. Please—" I couldn't finish. Tears ran down my cheeks.

"But Lucy should be safe," Arthur said. "We'll take care of you too."

None of them were thinking. "What if there's not

314

time?" I demanded. "What if we're searching for this monster and I get attacked again? Or what if I transform tonight, completely, and we're nowhere near the hospital?"

The boys didn't say anything to that.

It was Quincey who came to me, wrapped his arm around me. "I won't let you become a monster."

It wasn't enough. I looked at the others, insisting on their commitments.

"We'll do whatever we need to," Arthur said, his voice grim.

My eyes finally settled on Jonathan, next to me on the bed.

"Don't ask that of me," he pleaded.

"Would you rather I become a monster?"

He shook his head. His eyes were filled with tears. "No, please don't ask—"

"We'll watch out for you, Mimi," Quincey said. "We'll make sure—"

"No." I slammed my fist into the mattress. "I want Jonathan to promise. If he loves me—"

"Of course I love you!" Jonathan snapped. "That's why—"

A knock sounded on the door.

Chapter 60

Mina

THE BOYS MOVED to the door as a group, like silent guards. Jonathan's gun was in his hand. Arthur pulled down his specrays to check the outside camera. Then he unlocked and opened the door. Dr. Helsinger stood in the hallway, her arms clutched around her body, her boots muddy, a garbage bag at her feet.

"Sorry for not coming sooner. I brought garlic."

As Arthur let her in, she thrust the bag at Jonathan. I had never liked garlic's acrid, sharp smell before, but there was something clean about it, something comforting.

"Can we get you anything?" Arthur offered. "I have real coffee."

"No, there's not time." She turned, took in all of us with her glance. "I need to explain the other reason I'm here."

316

It was the serious tone of her voice. No one interrupted. Jonathan stood protectively beside me.

"Anghen visited my house today." She said it matter-of-factly, like a teacher's prepared lecture. But her arms were wrapped across her chest.

My eyes traveled to her neck. She had a ridiculous wide-collared shirt, and her pale neck poked out like that white bird, a swan. Clean.

I bit my lip as I touched my own neck. Infected.

"I'd never met him before," Dr. H continued. "Not in person. My— No one else was home. I recognized him from Jonathan's description. And... you've seen him on the news?" She must have seen by our expressions that we had. "I didn't expect him to be so... human. His manners, his accent—"

"He didn't hurt you?" Arthur asked, his voice heavy, urgent.

"No, no. Only—" She pushed ahead. "He thanked me for my help in connecting him with Jonathan. He wanted to let me know that he'd be out of town for the next week. The president pro tempore has invited him to the White House for a summit with CMS leadership. Anyway—" She swallowed.

I continued to press my teeth into my bottom lip. Helsinger was practically shaking, her voice wavering— and it wasn't that cold out. It meant something.

"He's going all the way to the top," Arthur said.

"Bet the government's interested in his techniques," Quincey said. "They want him to scale up his business."

"His business?" Jonathan interjected. "Killing people? Creating monsters?"

"He's going to take care of the 'patriot problem' once and for all," Quincey said, his voice cold.

"Does the government know what he is?" Jonathan demanded.

"They know," Quincey said, his voice hard. "The cities have been given permission to round up petty criminals, addicts, activists, anyone who might cause a disturbance. They don't care what happens to them."

"If they use Anghen, they can make the bodies disappear," Jonathan said.

"Or make an army," Arthur added. "It's like Mina's been saying—it's all coordinated: this whole business in Europe, the Filipino terrorists in Japan, fighting that doesn't stop, colonels who go missing in the dead of night. Lately there've been rumors about the people who disappear at DetCens and what happens to them. People say the government is creating an army. What if they could make an army of creatures like him?"

"He must already have armies positioned across the globe," Quincey said.

"And with the White House backing him, he's got all the political connections he needs," Arthur said.

"He'll start the war Lucy dreamed about," Jonathan murmured. "The one where everyone dies."

As the boys talked, I watched Dr. H. She was so quiet. She was many strange things, but I had never known her to be quiet. I wondered why she'd come at all. Was it only because Arthur had asked her to bring the garlic? Or had she wanted to tell us about Anghen? But there was no way Anghen would have let her escape if he didn't want her to be here.

"There's more." Dr. H's voice was empty, as if she were reciting memorized lines. "He said he's leaving tonight and he intends to take Mina with him."

Jonathan's "No!" was too loud for Arthur's quiet suite. "We'll keep Mina safe," he insisted. "He'll never find her. The doors are already locked, we can finish stringing the garlic everywhere—"

"They share a connection now," Dr. H said. "Just like Anghen had with Lucy. He said he'd find her in her dreams."

"We can't hide," Arthur argued. "We need to fight him."

Dr. H ignored them, instead turning to me. "You once told me you never dream. Is that still true?"

"Why?" I was struggling to keep up with my own brain. I remembered when all this began, how Dr. H had said one thing but told me something very different.

"It's unfortunate, that's all."

Before I could even process her words, she was standing up.

"Wait!" Arthur called. "We need to find his house, to try to stop him. Do you know—?"

"I have no idea where his home is," Dr. H said, already at the door, showing herself out. "I'm sorry I

319

can't help any more."

"But—" Jonathan tried to interrupt.

The slamming door cut him off.

The others were quiet. Jonathan reached for my hand, but I shook him off. "Didn't you think she was weird?"

"She seemed scared," Quincey said.

"Anghen visited her house," Jonathan said.

"So why didn't she call someone?" I said. "Maybe not the police, but school security, or us, or—I don't know! We've been trying to find him, to stop him, and he was right there."

Arthur shrugged. "She said she was all alone. But as soon as she was free, she came right here, told us about it."

"What if he asked her to come?" I could tell the boys weren't following me, but the pieces were coming together in my mind. "What if Anghen threatened her? Dr. Helsinger's a lesbian, you know. That's how she got involved in all this in the first place. Jonathan's mom's firm has done some legal favors for her, just in case the government ever changes the rules or decides to get in her way, so in return she agreed to write a recommendation for Jonathan's internship. Anghen could expose her, threaten her family."

Jonathan stared at me, open-mouthed.

Arthur's eyes blazed. "You shouldn't out her," Arthur snapped. "Ever."

"I'm not—" I started. I hadn't meant to out her. I

knew what it was like to be the "other," to always worry about where my ID card was, what bigoted rule the government would implement next. I understood her fear. But I also wanted to understand exactly what Dr. H knew, what she was trying to tell us.

"She helped us," Arthur said. "From the very beginning."

"She believed me," Jonathan added.

"She protected you, she protected Lucy. She even brought us garlic! How can you think she's not on our side?" Arthur argued.

I shook my head. "I'm not saying that. Just that her information might not be one hundred percent reliable. Anghen might—"

"What about you?" Arthur argued. "You're not the most reliable witness right now either."

"Hey, hey," Quincey said, holding out his hands like a referee.

But Arthur was right. Why had I blurted out Dr. H's personal life like that? Even her full name? I had put her in danger. Not that my friends would do anything, but I knew better. I should have known better. The realization spread over me again, as if I had suddenly plummeted into the ocean. I was becoming a monster. What if I couldn't even trust my own brain anymore? And then I remembered the other thing Dr. H had said: Anghen and I shared a connection. And she had asked about my dreams.

I turned to Jonathan. "In Judaism, are there any

sorts of trances or meditations?"

He stared at me.

"I want you to hypnotize me. You heard Dr. H. He's leaving tonight. With me. But what if we find him before he finds me? What if we can fight?"

Chapter 61

Mina

JONATHAN REPEATED THE string of Hebrew words a second time, a third.

My family had gone to church once when I was a little girl, before most people had given up on it. A few of my friends had been religious, and I had always wanted to be part of it too. I enjoyed it at first—the candles, the robes, everything solemn and quiet. Then I got bored. I remembered the priest singing on and on, the words blending together, becoming meaningless. That's what Jonathan sounded like.

"Repeat it," he whispered.

I shook my head. "I can't understand it." I was nestled into my bed in Arthur's suite, flanked by Jonathan and the other boys, as if at any moment I might turn into a monster. "What if it's like the Star? What if—?"

"They're only words," Jonathan said. "You're praising... Actually, it doesn't matter. You're not supposed to understand it—you're just supposed to get lost in it."

I wondered if he was second-guessing himself, but then he chanted again, "Barukh ata Adonai Eloheinu..."

I'd never been afraid of words before. "Barukh ata Adonai Eloheinu..." I repeated.

Jonathan shook his head. "Eloheinu. There's an *H*."

"Do you want me to repeat it or practice for my bar mitzvah?" I snapped. I wished the boys weren't all around me. I wished it didn't feel like a calculus test that everyone knew I was going to fail.

Jonathan surprised me by smiling. "Right. Repeat it. Barukh ata Adonai Eloheinu..."

I said it over and over again. The words masked the sound of the rain falling outside. Jonathan closed his eyes. I closed mine.

Like in church all those years ago, I let the words wash over me, totally and utterly meaningless. But somehow powerful all the same. Maybe it was the dignity Jonathan gave them. Like they were special. I kept repeating until I forgot about failure, about the boys watching me, until I could no longer hear the rain. I repeated until I knew the words by heart, like a pattern. I repeated until I didn't think, until it was only the mechanics of my mouth moving.

The air changed, musty and moldy. I looked from

one side to the other. A wooden box surrounded me. "I see something," I murmured between lines.

Jonathan kept chanting.

I heard Arthur whisper, "Can you look around? Without disturbing him?"

I continued to chant, let my words find their rhythm again, my mouth its patterns. I let my head empty until all I saw was wood on either side. His coffin. I raised my hands above me. The top opened. I looked down at Anghen's body, motionless. Quietly, slowly, I stood in the coffin, stepped out. I pressed the lid back into place. Everything around me was dark and cold.

Focus, I told myself. *Keep moving. Figure out where you are.*

I repeated the words as I crept forward. Ahead I saw light, a staircase. I started to climb.

It grew lighter. The light was refracted, sparkling in shadows on the wall.

Something growled in the darkness behind me. Suddenly I was back in the suite's bed, my voice quiet, three pairs of eyes staring at me.

"Mina." Jonathan squeezed my hand. "Are you okay? Did you see him? Did he hurt you?"

I reached for my arms, felt my own flesh and bone. I pinched myself to make sure. It hurt.

"Mimi?" Quincey pressed.

"I think I'm okay." I tried to explain what had happened, what I had seen. The light must have been

325

from a prism of some sort. Maybe a chandelier?

"But what woke you?" Quincey said. "You were doing so well, chanting up a storm. Your pronunciation even got better." He winked at me.

"I heard something. I don't know what it was..." I didn't say any more. It was Anghen. I was sure of it. He had felt me inside his mind, his body. But the boys were so pleased. Arthur got me a cold rehydration drink; Jonathan held my hand. I felt like a hero. I didn't want to ruin the mood.

"You must have been in a basement—" Arthur started.

"Not many of the newer houses have them," Quincey said. "Maybe somewhere on campus?"

"You've already narrowed the castle down to a dozen houses in Whitby," I said. The way they went back and forth, we'd be stuck here another year. And when I closed my eyes, I felt as if I were still trapped in that coffin. With *him*. "He was in his box. Chances are it's stored at the castle, his headquarters. I would get old real estate information, pictures, floor plans if you can." Irving's data subscription service was top line. My fingers itched to be searching myself, but if there was something to find, the boys would find it.

Arthur's specrays were already over his eyes. As Jonathan recited addresses, Arthur cast image after image for us to see, rotating between them.

"That one," I said. "The castle is 1624 Blandois."

"You sure?" Arthur said, flipping back to a previous

picture. "I thought this one looked—"

"No," I insisted. "Only eight of them have basements, and of those only the Blandois one has that picture of a chandelier."

"Okay then," Arthur said. "That's why she's valedictorian."

I rubbed my eyes. Was it unusual for me to be this tired? "We need to get there. Now. Before he leaves."

"He'll have all his strength," Quincey said, pointing at the time on Arthur's screen. Already there was hardly any daylight left. It was November, counting down to the darkest day of the year.

"Can we call your brigade?" Arthur said to Quincey. "They need to be ready. We could have some of them come out here too, to keep an eye on Lucy. Just in case."

Quincey nodded as Jonathan said, "I'll do it." His screencast with the Omega app was already pulled up.

Arthur pulled his specrays over his eyes. "I'm contacting school security too," he said. "I'll tell them we've seen people sneaking around outside the building. That should guarantee they keep an eye on things on this end."

I remembered Anghen behind me in the darkness, growling. I was sure Lucy was safe for the moment. "He knows we're coming," I said. It was why he had sent Dr. Helsinger to us. I didn't hold anything against Dr. Helsinger. She had probably done what she needed to do to protect herself, her family. "Anghen's flushing

327

us out. We're probably walking right into a trap. But we don't have any other choice."

At least, thanks to Jonathan and Dr. Helsinger, I had one other trick up my sleeve. We were going to need it.

Chapter 62

Quincey

ARTHUR DEACTIVATED HIS car's self-driving mode to go twenty above the speed limit through Newholm, into the north end of Whitby. The roads in the Dead Zone were rutted with potholes, lined with abandoned clothes, carrier boxes, and other detritus. The car turned onto Blandois Avenue, right next to a house that had been gutted by fire. Down the street, Quincey thought he saw another car pulling away.

Arthur parked along the street, perpendicular to a crumbling brick wall alongside an open field—maybe at one time it had been a garden? The castle itself was almost entirely hidden from the street by a large willow. It had to be an old, tough tree—it was one of the few that remained from pollution and the riots that had rocked the Dead Zone over the years.

From the car window, Quincey glanced down the

street in either direction. No one else seemed to be around. Every window that wasn't boarded up or burned out held blackout curtains. Whatever happened, good or bad, brigade or CMS, no neighbors would dare get involved.

Quincey ran his thumb along the stolen cafeteria meat knife at his side. The blade couldn't be very sharp, but it was all he had.

"It's quiet," Arthur said.

Quincey rolled his window down a few inches. It *was* quiet. The rain had stopped. If Anghen was there, he was lying in wait.

"Here's the plan," Arthur said, turning in his front seat. "Quincey will throw open the front door, I'll jump in with the gun. We'll secure the perimeter and then make a decision based on that. Now let's go."

"What if the door's locked?" Jonathan asked as they cautiously climbed from the car.

"We can always call the police," Arthur said, heading up the front walk, aiming his gun from left to right. "I can be concerned about my mom—she's not answering her xphone, and she lives all by herself—"

It was a good lie. The police didn't come to Whitby anymore, but with Arthur's connections, he could probably convince them of anything. They wouldn't know his mom was safe in DC. Except Anghen had plenty of government connections too.

"We agreed," Quincey said, "police are too dangerous. Maybe—" He reached for the doorknob. It was old, rusted, and wouldn't turn. But there was no resistance either. He pushed, and the door swung open into a dark hallway.

He sprang back, shocked. Arthur leaped inside, swept his gun from left to right.

"Quincey, follow behind!" he snapped.

The others followed closely into the shadowy front entrance.

"Monsters don't need to lock their doors," Jonathan muttered darkly, Mina by his side.

Of course he was right. Especially if it was all a trap.

The entry hall was octagonal with tall windows and a wide staircase. The space should have been grand. But black shades were drawn over each window. Cobwebs hung from the corners. A spider scurried across Quincey's path. Mina looked up as the chandelier swayed, its glass tinkling with their sudden entrance. Her body shuddered. But they didn't see anyone.

"Let's search bottom to top," Arthur announced. "That way there shouldn't be any surprises."

Mina's description had sounded like a basement, and after all, in Bram Manor Anghen had slept on the lowest level as well—assuming they were lucky, assuming he was still asleep. Quincey doubted it.

Jonathan pointed to a door under the stairs, his other hand on the gun at his side. Arthur pulled his specrays back over his eyes, switched them to flashlight, and started downstairs. The others followed, casting light as well. Quincey closed the door firmly behind

331

them, then took up the rear. The DetCen or maybe
CMS still had his xphone. Without a light of his own,
all he could see were narrow wooden stairs descending
into darkness. He climbed ahead, almost bumping into
Mina. He rested his hand on Mina's shoulder so he
wouldn't lose her. Mina held Jonathan's hand. Arthur
called out for Jonathan. They were all connected, in this
together.

"Clear!" Arthur called from the base of the stairs.
Then, "Is anyone else smelling that?"

"Yes," Jonathan said.

Quincey hadn't noticed before, but it did smell.
There was a thick, earthy smell of dust and rot, but
something else, something rancid. Quincey closed his
mouth, tried to block off his nose, but it gradually filled
the air.

They explored the basement in the same way,
Arthur leading, Quincey in the rear. The others shined
their flashlights from corner to corner, floor to ceiling.
The room was strangely small, empty except for a
vaulted doorway leading farther into the darkness. The
brick was old, rust red.

Blood red, Quincey thought.

"You could hide horrible things down here,"
Jonathan whispered, his thoughts echoing Quincey's.

"You could hide a whole army down here," Arthur
said, stepping through the entryway into the chamber
ahead of them. "Keep moving."

This space was cavernous with four more

doorways, one in each corner. But so far Anghen wasn't there.

Quincey stumbled and cursed. Arthur turned, his light bobbing. "You okay?"

"Just tripped. There's some sort of—" His voice died as Arthur shined his light over the floor. It was a metal chain with handcuffs at either end. Not shiny and new like what CMS had used but old, thick. Like what slave masters might have used.

They worked along the perimeter, Arthur beaming his light against the far wall. Jonathan held back, standing protectively at Mina's side. The smell grew exponentially worse.

"It's in there," Quincey said, gesturing at the far doorway. Somehow he could feel it. Either that or it was the fear, creeping into his brain.

"Dead raccoon maybe?" Arthur suggested. "Or bird? Something that ended up down here and couldn't get out?"

Quincey wanted to believe that. But as they peered into the brick entryway, everything appeared under the light at once. The smell was thick and there were flies buzzing around. The far wall was only a few feet away, like a basement closet. Or a tomb. There were metal cuffs hanging from the wall, evenly spaced. In the last was a human body, head hung down, scraggly hair hiding its face.

"God." Quincey exhaled the word. He didn't even think he believed in a god. But what else was there to say?

Arthur was braver in the face of death. He stepped up to the body, tilted its head to get a better view. "Dead several days, maybe even weeks. It's rotting."

Quincey grabbed at his stomach, but he was too late. Everything came gushing out. He crouched to the ground, heaved again. Globs of vomit trickled from his mouth. Yet all he could see, all he could smell, was that body. That person.

"A prisoner," he whispered.

"Dinner," Arthur said.

Quincey hadn't even thought of that.

"At least we know we're in the right house," Arthur said. "Mina was right. But look." Arthur turned his light on the floor. There were muddy footprints, dozens of them, along with hair, and a finger in a dried puddle of blood.

While this man was dead, there had been more, others. Were they monsters now?

"Maybe we should call the police?" Jonathan said from behind them.

Quincey shook his head. Why did the white guys always want to call the police? "They won't be on our side," he warned again.

"Let's keep searching," Arthur said.

They ducked out of the alcove and crossed to the other corner. A tattered curtain hung above. Quincey sneaked along the edge of the wall, looked inside. The alcove was small, like the other, but empty.

334

"Thank God," Quincey said. But his heart was still racing. His fingers clenched the knife hilt at his side.

"Quincey! Arthur!" Jonathan shouted.

Quincey jerked upright, his knife drawn.

Arthur cast his light across the room, but Quincey couldn't see a thing. "Where are you?" he called.

Across the darkness he could faintly make out another tattered curtain, and then Jonathan's face emerged in the gloom.

"Over here," he called. "We found boxes."

Quincey and Arthur hurried across the basement, ducking into the alcove with Jonathan. Arthur's light illuminated the whole room. There was a circle of ornate candlesticks, a lighter, and a box. The cardboard was dark with earth, implanted to the floor. Beyond the circle were several other boxes stacked haphazardly. Anghen's boxes.

"The tape's loose," Arthur said.

It was night; they knew Anghen shouldn't be asleep. But maybe they'd get lucky this one time. Arthur aimed his gun. Jonathan held his Star in one hand and kept his other arm wrapped around Mina. Quincey squeezed the knife hilt and crept toward the box. He ran his fingers along the cardboard, found the seam, and jammed the knife underneath. He looked once more at his friends, then yanked the flap up.

Nothing. Dirt. Arthur leaned in close, his specrays beaming light, and handed Quincey a broom he had found somewhere. Quincey turned the broom upside down and stirred the dirt. He shook his head. He should have known luck was not on their side.

Mina spoke abruptly. "He's not here."

"We can't jump to conclusions," Arthur said. "We should destroy his boxes, continue the search. Then—"

But Quincey heard the certainty in Mina's voice. Her arms were wrapped around her body as if she was freezing. Her skin looked pale even in the basement's gloom.

"I'm opening the next," Jonathan said, starting forward. But there wasn't anything inside.

Arthur opened the third, Jonathan the fourth. Arthur lined up the boxes, one after the other. They opened all of them. There was only dirt.

"Where is he?" Jonathan growled, kicking at the box closest to him.

"We'll finish searching the basement," Arthur said. "We have to be systematic, otherwise he might sneak up on us."

"Five." Quincey froze as he took in all of the room, the boxes, the dirt in front of them. "There're only five boxes. There were two more in the field house."

"There's eight in Jonathan's notebook," Arthur remembered. "We destroyed two. There's got to be another somewhere."

"His wooden box," Jonathan said.

They quickly checked the rest of the basement. They found a closet with suits, slacks, and a wallet stuffed with various ID cards. But no other boxes, no monsters.

"What now?" Jonathan asked, his voice cracking, desperate.

"We should head upstairs, search the first floor," Arthur answered mechanically. But he no longer sounded certain.

They had almost forgotten she was there until Mina spoke again, her voice tight, scared. "I hear him. In my head. He's laughing."

Jonathan cursed.

Something thick and heavy jammed itself into Quincey's stomach.

"He's not here anymore," Mina said. "It's a trap. We always knew."

Quincey remembered the car he had seen pulling away just as they arrived—he should have known. "Are we in danger?" he whispered, rising to his feet.

"We need to move," Mina answered. "Now."

"Here." Arthur handed his specrays to Quincey. "Message your brigade. Are they here yet? We need them."

"Sending out the message," Quincey murmured.

"Upstairs," Mina whispered. "Fast."

Quincey shoved the specrays back at Arthur. Jonathan took Mina's hand, and they raced back to the entrance to the basement, up the wooden stairs, and threw open the door at the top.

"You're under arrest," a voice barked. "All of you."

It was too late.

337

Chapter 63

Quincey

TWO COPS BLOCKED the basement doorway. The light from the chandelier reflected in their badges, against the gun one pointed forward, trained on them.

Quincey raised his hands in the air. In front of him, Jonathan did the same, though he kept one arm protectively around Mina. The police had arrived anyway, even though Quincey had insisted on not calling them. It was so ridiculously familiar. His gut churned and bile filled his mouth.

"You're under arrest," barked the female cop beside her male partner, both white, of course. "Breaking and entering. Trespassing. You have no right to a lawyer; however, you will have the opportunity to defend yourself in a court of law."

She kept her gun raised as she continued to recite the Revised Mirandas. The other cop patted them down, removed Quincey's knife, Jonathan's gun, all their IDs. Quincey waited for Arthur to step up, to say something, but he was quiet. Instead, Quincey could hear Mina's ragged breath, his own heart racing as he looked down the barrel of the gun.

"No." The urgency of the situation bubbled to the surface through Quincey's words. He tried to channel his inner Arthur: privileged, commanding. "This is the home of a known terrorist. There's a body in the basement as well as evidence of several other deaths. He attacked her"—Quincey gestured at Mina with his chin, without lowering his hands—"and we have reason to believe he's traveling to DC tonight. If you can't help us stop him, he will destroy countless others."

The male police officer, who had continued behind Quincey, froze. The female officer called for backup. "Unexpected situation here," she murmured at her screencast.

Did they believe him?

Quincey chanced a quick glance behind him. Arthur was gone! Had he escaped? Or was he in even worse danger?

"Out front," the female officer said, gesturing them forward with her gun. "We've gotten conflicting reports tonight. Let's sort out what's going on."

In the front entryway there were at least a dozen more police. Someone opened a door for Quincey and the others, and then the officer led them to the street. It should have been pitch-black. Uncle Leon said you could sometimes even see a few stars in Whitby's skies. But instead, the street outside Anghen's house had been transformed. Enormous floodlights shone right into his eyes. Newholm Police cars with flashing lights blocked the street. There was a row of dark, unmarked trucks beside them—like the one that had driven alongside the hospital when Quincey was arrested. Quincey's heart raced ahead. Was it the Alphas? CMS? And were they here to detain Quincey and his friends? Or to help Anghen? Maybe both.

There was an older officer on the front walkway. "Bring them over here," he commanded. He was flanked by two silver-uniformed officers. CMS again.

"Against the car," the female officer said, gesturing to the closest police car. "Hands behind your head."

"We need to know the facts, as fast as you have them," the older man said.

"There's a terrorist," Quincey said in language he hoped they would take seriously. "Wilhelm Anghen. He's behind the deaths at the Newholm DetCen last night. We followed him here because our friend is in danger, but inside the house there's a body and evidence of more deaths, perhaps dozens."

"You're accusing Dr. Anghen of these crimes? The executive director of Newholm Hospital?"

"And detention center," Quincey said. They were actually listening! "He was there last night when all those people were murdered."

The man crossed his arms. "How do you know?"

"Because he did this to her," Jonathan interjected, jerking Mina's body forward. Her eyes were closed. Her face was white.

Quincey's heart raced—Mina looked worse than he had thought.

"She's sick," Jonathan continued. "She might need a blood transfusion. We need to get her to a hospital."

"Wait here," the man ordered. "You're not to move, not to lower your hands." He strode across the yard, still flanked by the CMS agents. Quincey looked to Mina. She was slouched against Jonathan's body, her arms clutched her sides.

"What happened?" Quincey said.

"I don't know," Jonathan murmured. His hands were around Mina, propping her up, but the police officer didn't intervene. Just the same, Quincey kept his arms behind his head.

Jonathan kept talking as his voice grew increasingly panicked. "She's hardly responding to me. Her breath is shallow and she's pale. Maybe she's already turning—"

"Mimi?" Quincey leaned over her, rested his forehead against hers. She was ice-cold.

Beneath her awkward used glasses, Mina's eyes opened only partway, as if they each weighed tons. "He's talking to me," she whispered.

"Mina!" Jonathan said, shaking her, as if he could drive out the voice in her head. "Mina?" But she didn't respond. Jonathan covered his face with his hand.

Something inside Quincey died as he watched

Jonathan cry. He already feared he had lost Lucy for good. But after everything Jonathan and Mina had been through—their separation, their arguments, Jonathan's faith in God, Mina's doubt—Quincey had always hoped they would have each other. "Let me not to the marriage of true minds admit impediments." Quincey murmured the first line of the sonnet. Shakespeare had probably never imagined a relationship ending with a bloodsucking monster. Or maybe he had. Shakespeare was a pretty imaginative guy.

Snippets of the rest of the sonnet came back to him. With nothing else to do but wait, he recited the lines, trying to remember the whole poem. "Love is the star to every wandering bark." Quincey had always liked that line, the idea of a ship, alone in the night, following its star. "Love alters not with his brief hours and weeks, / But bears it out even to the edge of doom."

He couldn't remember any more. But Shakespeare had described it pretty well: the edge of doom as Quincey held his hands above his head while Jonathan huddled over Mina's body. He noticed Mina's hand, clutched around Jonathan's. So she wasn't unconscious. Her mouth was moving, murmuring. Almost as if she was talking back to Anghen. Or hypnotizing herself.

Quincey rocked on the balls of his feet. The Omegas would be here soon. He looked across the neighborhood, to the burned-out house next door, the crumbling brick wall alongside it. One of the unmarked trucks was parked in the grass with a bunch of people standing around. Something about the woman in front caught his attention. She was dressed in brigade gear but with no apparent insignias. Quincey stared down the street. He couldn't see his brigade yet. He wasn't sure what they would do, but if he could get free, Jonathan could rush Mina to the hospital, he could help the Omegas find Anghen, stop him...

A different man returned to the female officer. He wore a suit but no badge. Before he even opened his mouth, he made Quincey's skin crawl. Something was wrong with him.

But the woman spoke first, jamming her face in Quincey's own. "You care to tell me the truth this time?"

"Ma'am," Quincey started, then took a deep breath. There was no point in getting angry—it wouldn't accomplish anything.

But she wasn't done. "You mention terrorism, bodies... How do you expect me to believe any of that? No, never mind. Why don't you explain your detention?"

"What?" Quincey said even as his breath caught in his throat.

"Quincey Jordan, *Sir.*" The man in the suit growled Quincey's name as he held up his ID. "There's a warrant out for your arrest. Missing from the Newholm DetCen under mysterious circumstances, suspect in a murder investigation."

Something dropped in Quincey's stomach, fell all

the way to his shoes.

"You need to apprehend Anghen!" Jonathan said. "If he's not killed, she will die!" He was as tall as the man in the suit, level with his eyes.

"You're not going anywhere. We have a lot more questions for you," the female officer said.

"No." The man in the suit interjected, putting his hand up to stop her. More silver-suited officers had gathered behind him. "I've promised Dr. Anghen to take care of them personally."

His eyes flashed red. Sweat flooded down Quincey's back. Who the hell was this? The man reached a beefy hand for Jonathan.

Overhead, Quincey heard an unfamiliar buzzing like a swarm of hornets.

"He's coming for me!" Mina cried, waking in Jonathan's arms. But it was too late. Too late for everything.

Chapter 64

Arthur

November 22, Castle, Whitby

ARTHUR RETURNED TO the vaulted doorway, into the larger part of the basement. If it was a trap, he would find another way to slip out. He shined his light, found a window on the far wall.

He stepped backward, opened his mouth to tell the others.

But light flooded the room. Arthur deactivated his specrays and threw his back against the staircase, hoping to hide in the shadows.

"You're under arrest!" a voice yelled.

Arthur waited, listened. Only when the door had slammed shut, trapping him in the darkness again, did Arthur turn on his specrays flashlight.

The window in the far room surprisingly slid right

open. Arthur hesitated, remembering the windows in Jonathan's diary, how Anghen had used them to return to his lair. But like Jonathan, he had no other choice.

Arthur launched into the air, propped his hands on the sill, and rolled forward. Thankfully soccer season hadn't been too long ago.

The night was cold, thick with fog. The backyard was overgrown with bushes and scattered with garbage. A fence lined the property. Arthur saw no one.

"Clear," he whispered.

He crept around the side of the house, tight inside its shadows. From there, he saw the street was lined with flashing police cars and spotlights along with the more ominous unmarked trucks. Something was going down. Mina had been right about the trap.

A black truck drove down the street, then over the curb, onto the open land next door, parallel to the crumbling brick wall. The back rolled up, and a group of people rushed out. Arthur had expected CMS with their ridiculously shiny silver uniforms. But these people weren't government, certainly not military. They were dressed in a smattering of brigade gear, but there were no badges. They were in different shapes and sizes, some old, some young. And they weren't all white—in fact, most of them were people of color. They fanned out, as if in formation, behind the woman who seemed to be in charge.

Arthur pressed his back against the house. She looked familiar. She was dressed in formfitting black like the others, but she carried a gun at her side. Her hair was loose, long and dark and blowing in the wind. Something terrible turned in his throat. Jonathan's vampire woman. He recognized her from the field house, from last night. He ran a hand along his own gun, stocked with silver bullets. At least he would get her this time.

"We'll pull off a pincer move," Arthur mumbled to himself. The Omegas were on their way. If Arthur stayed on this side of the house, the Omega Brigade would approach from the other side. They could surround the vampire.

Of course, as one person, he wouldn't exactly surround anyone. He hoped Quincey's brigade showed up soon for backup. He hoped the police would listen rather than just arresting his friends. He hoped—

Something flashed overhead, traveling the night sky. Arthur could hear its faint, mosquito-like buzz.

That meant a military Kite, a four-person carrier pod for residential terrain. That meant someone important.

The buzz grew louder. It stirred the trees, sent the wind whipping. It was a sleek silver aircraft. The wings lifted in an arch above the body as it started its descent.

Headlights cut through the dark night. Arthur looked back to the street, hoping. But a black limo— like something out of an old-fashioned movie— stopped outside the house. The same car that had pulled away as they arrived earlier. It had probably been

347

circling the block, waiting.

"Right on time," Arthur said, shaking his head.

No one exited, no other cars arrived. The windows were tinted, impossible to see through. Then the trunk popped open. Inside was a long, wooden box.

There was nothing else to do. Arthur sprinted for the car.

"Stop!" a voice yelled. A searchlight beamed on Arthur. "Hands in the air."

"No!" Arthur yelled. "We need to stop that passenger!"

He made it to the limo, dove for the back passenger door.

Then a police officer was there. He wrapped his arms around Arthur, yanked him backward. "Hands in the air," he growled.

There was nothing Arthur could do. He stopped fighting. He relaxed his body. He raised his hands in the air. But the blood was thrumming in his ears.

"Step away from the limo," the officer commanded.

Arthur stepped backward. But he couldn't be silent. "There's a murderer inside that limo. He's killed dozens, probably many more."

"My orders are to allow a safe transfer onto the Kite," the officer said, even as no one in the black car moved. The buzzing died to a slow whine, then silence.

"You're not listening!" Arthur shouted. "It's not me you want! I'm Arthur Godalming, son of Colonel Godalming in the European-based forces."

More officers appeared, their guns trained on him.

But Arthur's words seemed to work. The lead officer lowered his gun, sent a message via his earpiece.

But out of the corner of his eye, Arthur saw her, the vampire woman. She was jogging toward the car, toward him. She grabbed the gun at her hip, raised it.

Arthur threw himself forward, but it was too late. A shot sounded out. Arthur collapsed.

Chapter 65

Quincey

"BRIGADERS! THERE'RE DOZENS of them!" The cops' earpieces all burst to life over the horrible buzzing.

"They're assembling on Charles Avenue, seem to be heading this way!"

Instantly the police started flicking their earpieces, casting screens. The man in the suit loosened his grip, looked over his shoulder. Quincey could see his fellow Omega brigaders on every screen. His heart started to race. This was what he had trained for.

Someone else yelled. "Sir, the dignitary! He's in danger! Security is—"

Quincey leaned into Jonathan's body and whispered, "Duck behind the car. Now!"

Quincey threw himself to the pavement, rolled behind the car. Jonathan crouched beside him, Mina pulled onto his back.

"Hey! You!"

Quincey didn't turn around. He kept moving, rushing along the backsides of the vehicles, away from eyes. If the police really cared, they'd come after him.

"We need to get to that limo!" Jonathan yelled, pointing at a sleek black limo that was now parked ahead of them. Mina was limp on his back. Her head lolled to one side.

Quincey saw the limo—the trunk was open, a wooden box resting inside. Jonathan was right; it had to be Anghen. But how to get to him? There were cops everywhere, interspersed with CMS agents, people yelling across screens and across the yard.

A gunshot sounded, reverberated above the din. Quincey froze.

"This way." Jonathan rushed to the willow, under its spread branches.

Quincey could see the limo parked directly in front of them. And on the ground beside it was a body. Arthur. His head was in a pool of blood.

There were other people there—police officers, giant bodyguards with guns, some woman in black. But all Quincey could see was the blood. Arthur. Motionless.

Quincey fell to the ground, screamed.

Chapter 66

Jonathan

Thursday, November 22

A BACK DOOR of the limousine flew open, and Anghen rushed out. His hair was dark, not gray, his face years younger. He must have prepared for tonight. He had feasted.

Anghen gestured to the police and silver-uniformed CMS agents rushing toward him. "Step aside, please. I have a flight to catch."

"Monster!" I burst out from under the willow's branches, carrying Mina piggyback, her limbs limp, as if she was unconscious, maybe worse. "I will kill you!" I screamed at him, my voice ragged in my throat.

Except for Mina—I couldn't put her at risk. I looked to Quincey. He needed to spring into action, do his brigader thing. But Quincey fell to his knees, his eyes fixed ahead. Arthur! His body was motionless, pooled in blood. The worthless revolver with its silver bullets hung loosely in Arthur's hand. I felt as if I had been punched in the stomach. My legs trembled beneath me.

"Mr. Harker," Anghen growled, "you will not be able to delay me. I have more important work to handle than your infantile grudge. In truth, the only lasting asset from this whole exchange has been your RAT."

I wouldn't have even known what he meant except he nodded at Mina, perched on my back. "Don't call her that!" I snapped, my hands curling into fists.

"It's true—your country has done a grave disservice to her. It was surprisingly clever how she used our mental connection to track down my home. It's too bad you're too late." As Anghen spoke, two burly men in suits filed behind him. Guns were strapped to their sides.

"Quincey!" I hissed. Our chance was slipping away.

"As you can see," Anghen continued, "it will not be you doing any killing tonight. My men can handle you. I'll collect your Mina and take her with me to DC."

A deep growl made the hairs on the back of my neck stand upright. The air reeked of musky animal. The police raised their guns. Next to the brick wall where the vampire woman had stood, backed by that random group of people, there were now three wolves, their heads chest high. *Vampires*, I realized.

"You're surrounded," I bluffed. "Give up."

Anghen laughed. "You think my people work for you?"

But then I heard something—the sound of boots thundering on pavement, voices chanting. It was the Omegas. My heart sped up as I calculated the marchers' rate of speed, how much longer Anghen would stand in place, how quickly the monster could run...

"Don't you understand?" Anghen laughed. "I always survive."

Arthur was probably dead. Quincey wasn't moving. I couldn't attack with Mina. I dipped to my knees, let her slide motionless to the ground. I chanced a final glance at her. Mina's eyes were closed, but her mouth was moving, murmuring. She was alive. Then, before I could think better of it, I dove for Arthur's gun. My fingertips touched the metal, but it was torn from my hand. A boot slammed on my chest. Then the wolves were on me. Fur filled my vision, musk, teeth. I curled into a ball, threw my hands over my face. One of the animals ripped into my arm with a burst of pain.

The animal flew aside and Quincey was there, screaming. He kicked another in its toothy mouth. Strangely, over it all, I heard Mina chanting Hebrew just as I had taught her.

A second gunshot sounded—loud, reverberating. Everything stilled. I raised my head in time to see Anghen stumble backward, Arthur's gun in his hand, pointed directly at his own chest. Then the monster ran.

Had Anghen shot himself?

"Stop him!" Quincey yelled.

The Omega Brigade was there; they rushed after Anghen.

I stood, tried to join them, but someone yanked the same arm the wolf had bitten. It sent a shock wave through my body. I wasn't fighting anyone.

"Police," a voice barked in my ear. "You're under arrest."

Chapter 67

Mina

IT HAPPENED IN an instant.

While Jonathan took in Arthur, studied his motionless body and the gun by his side, Anghen watched.

I knew. As I chanted Hebrew, I slipped into Anghen's head. I felt his heart thump, his eyes widen as he recognized the smell of silver. He knew it was coming from Arthur's abandoned gun.

Anghen kept talking, riling Jonathan up as he crept closer to the gun, as the wolves surrounded them. Still, Jonathan might have grabbed the gun in time, shot him first. Jonathan had a height advantage, and after years of soccer, he was fast. Except Jonathan turned around, looked at me.

When Jonathan jumped for the gun a second later, it was too late. Anghen was there. He grabbed the gun from Jonathan's fingertips, stomped on his chest. Then the wolves were on him.

I couldn't watch. There wasn't time. I kept my brain, my eyes, on Anghen as I imagined something different. After all, if I could see into Anghen's head, surely he could see into mine.

In my brain, Jonathan feinted for the gun, then dodged the other way, just behind Anghen. He sprang for Anghen's back. I made the images vivid, realistic.

Anghen grabbed the gun but jerked up as if something really were on his back. He raised the gun, shot behind him at the imaginary Jonathan.

Except Anghen didn't have my firearm experience. He wasn't as fast as Jonathan. Instead of flying harmlessly over him, the bullet slammed into Anghen's shoulder.

My body jolted along with Anghen's. The words I had been chanting died away. I could feel the bullet traveling through him, burning. The silver seared everything it touched.

It worked! I realized.

Fireworks danced through my brain as I let my head drop to the ground. I was exhausted, like I could sleep for a million years. But I had made him shoot himself! If the silver bullet worked, I could *live*.

That bitch!

I jerked upright. I could still hear Anghen in my head. I could feel the bullet in his body somewhere. His thoughts rushed like a fire, panicked.

357

Move, he thought. *Escape!* Then Anghen ran toward that military carrier, flanked on either side by burly security guards. CMS agents lined his path. Another set grabbed his wooden coffin from the limo.

But the Omegas closed in. I could hear people fighting, gunfire.

Anghen held his shoulder as my mind moved with his body. It was different than running as Mina. Anghen's limbs moved like pistons of a machine. His breath came in even, sure puffs of air. It was like running on a moving walkway. We went fast, faster, until we were flying across the yard.

As if the bullet wasn't even there.

Then, like a brick thrown at my head, I was jolted out of the vision. I was Mina again, facing the street so I couldn't see anything. I heard shouting, running feet, growls. I turned my head. Quincey was beside me, handcuffed. I looked at my own hands as my breathing became faster, panicked. Cold metal encircled my wrists. I could hear Jonathan talking, arguing. Then I heard scuffling and he crumpled in front of us on the pavement.

No! It wasn't supposed to happen like this.

"I told him to shut up," someone snapped.

Then Jonathan was shoved next to us, leaned into Quincey's shoulder so he wouldn't fall. His one arm was loose at his side, soaked in blood.

My mind flashed to Anghen's again. Thanks to his security and CMS, he had made it to the carrier's doors.

The door opened with a mechanical whir.

"Mina? Are you okay?"

I shook my head to clear my thoughts as Jonathan looked into my eyes.

"I'm in his head," I whispered.

I could feel the bullet lodging itself deeper inside, the silver burning his chest with each breath. But it wasn't enough. I hadn't stopped him. The bullet hadn't attacked any vital organs. I'd had one chance left to destroy Anghen, and I had failed. He grasped the handrail, pulled himself into the carrier. We were out of time.

I thought of Halloween, Lucy and I running through Newholm's streets. If only I could go back, we would run faster, run from everything, far away from those Alpha brigaders and the monster that stalked us. I could have protected her, watched over her. None of this would have happened. My best friend wouldn't have to die.

"Mina." Jonathan called me back, his blue eyes inches from my own. "Stay with us."

No, not Halloween... "Anghen's escaping," I whispered aloud.

I heard Quincey arguing. A cop barked something. Then officers were carrying me, hands pushing down my head, shoving me into a car.

"No!" Jonathan yelled, but it sounded so far away.

Anghen had taken his seat. It was comfortable, leather. One of the security guards in a dark suit settled next to him. A CMS agent boarded for extra security.

I clenched my hands around the leather seat's padded armrests.

I couldn't escape him. Soon he would be in DC. The bullet would be removed before it could inflict any more damage. He had already arranged a lair in the old city, stocked with his own staff, a physician President Evans had personally recommended. Soon he would be free.

The tension left my body. A second security guard helped load Anghen's wooden coffin into the luggage compartment, and then the door closed behind him. The aircraft's computer reported flying conditions: some clouds overhead, but a clear night in DC. Shots ricocheted off the siding, but it didn't seem to matter. The triangular wings lowered until they were parallel with the windows.

DC. But there was nothing I could do. I was a part of Anghen now. His creature. I felt his smile—red, toothy—and I smiled back. Together forever.

The plane rumbled. As its base lifted in the air, my ears filled with pressure.

I had never flown before. I tried to lift my hands to my ears to block out the sound, but something was holding them back. Handcuffs. I was trapped.

Anghen laughed at me.

I screamed.

Chapter 68

Jonathan

Thursday, November 22

THEY DRAGGED QUINCEY to a different car. Mina's eyes were closed, lost in some monstrous dream.

I should do it, I thought. *Before they handcuff me.* I had to do it. She had made me promise.

Instead, a hand clamped around my shoulder.

"Get moving, boy," the police officer said.

It was a relief. I didn't know how I would have killed her anyway. I had nothing on me, no weapons. I couldn't have laid a hand on her.

I looked back at Mina once. She was smiling, talking in her sleep. Her pointed teeth revealed themselves. My whole body shuddered. I had failed.

"Boy!" the officer insisted.

I followed her.

***

Police barked questions at me. Why were we here tonight? Who were we searching for? How did we know each other?

I answered truthfully. There was nothing more to lose, and I wasn't in the mood to play any games. The hospital could corroborate my story, along with Dr. Helsinger and the school, not to mention the others. Really I listened, waited for the buzzing that I knew would accompany the military carrier.

It came sooner than I expected. First as a tinny, mosquito-like drone.

Then as a thundering, pulsating buzz.

A scream echoed through the car. My head fell into my hands. *Mina!*

It was too late. We had done everything we could, fought in every way we knew. But we had lost.

Chapter 69

Mina

I WAS ANGHEN and he was me. I was centuries old. I had watched the Ottoman Turks annihilate the Armenians, the Europeans enslave the people of Africa's Gold Coast. I had burned witches at the stake and laughed. As I laughed now. It echoed through me, part of me. Soon I would rise further in this American government. I imagined more bodies, more blood. I imagined multinational armies at my command. Unlimited power. Never hungry again. And Mina would be by my side, orchestrating everything.

As the military carrier lifted from the field, my heart stopped. The silver had reached my bloodstream, found the way to my heart. I gritted my teeth together. I only had to make it to DC. I'd make sure my men were waiting there, make sure the physician was ready. There would be time tomorrow to have the beginnings of my army rejoin me along with Mina. I had months, years, eons.

My heart started beating again.

I watched the darkness swallow the carrier, the city lights flicker out of sight as we flew into the clouds.

Clouds shifted, blurred, formed into Lucy.

Lucy? I whispered, so confused.

Mina, she said, somehow in my head and in the buzz of the plane at the same time. *Pull away from him! Now!*

I can't.

He's injured, she insisted. *You can do it!*

No. I shook my head. *I failed. The bullet didn't do enough damage. He's too strong.*

But you're becoming part of him!

Lucy and Anghen had once shared blood. Now I shared their blood as well. Maybe that was how I could hear her. Or maybe she was only a dream. I didn't have the energy to puzzle it out.

Mina! You deserve more. You need to show the world what you can do.

I will, I thought. *Together. Anghen and I—*

No, Lucy said, and I was flooded with memories. I saw us dressing as a witch and pirate, slipping out of Florence, laughing together. I saw us curled on Lucy's hospital bed, me holding her while she cried.

You're saving me, she whispered.

No, I protested. Lucy had always been overly optimistic. But it was too late for all that. *I'm destroying you.*

No, Mina Bird. You're saving me. Actually, you saved me years ago, before we'd ever thought of monsters. You made me believe in me. You made me want to be someone. Because you were someone.

More images rushed through my head, too methodical to be any dream. My first report card, with straight As, and the realization that I was in the running for valedictorian. Lucy and I whispering across our Florence dorm room, unable to sleep we were so caught up in getting to know each other. Our first joint birthday party, surrounded by friends, a pile of presents. Lucy pinning the honor society sash to my dress.

I was someone, I realized. Without Anghen, before I ever met Anghen. I was a leader. I was smart. I had friends.

Look what you've done in the past few weeks, Lucy said.
I failed.

No. Her voice fought against the wind. *Never you, Mina. You found him, you trapped him, you even shot him. He preyed on us because he thought us girls were weak. But he underestimated us! Now it's his heart that's failing. Save me. Save yourself.*

My ears popped. We must have been high above the ground now, heading for the Eastern Seaboard. But Lucy's voice kept reverberating in my head, intermixing with the engine whine. *Save yourself yourself yourself.*

Save myself, I thought. I said it again, suddenly realizing I believed it. I didn't need Anghen. I could fight this. I could stand on my own feet, be my own person. I wasn't valedictorian, not anymore. Not even a high school graduate. I had no money to my name. But I was a leader, I was smart, I had friends. It was possible.

The plane gained altitude, soared above the clouds, thousands of feet above my body. Then his heart missed a beat.

I thought of Lucy. I thought of Jonathan. I thought of Quincey, and Arthur, injured, maybe dead. I thought about me. I yanked myself away from his dying heart.

A burst of energy soared through me like I hadn't felt in ages. My skin felt cool, not chill and clammy but refreshed, like the first spring day of the year and there was wind and—

I opened my eyes. I didn't see the plane. I didn't see Anghen. I only saw a grimy back seat, my cuffed hands, some officer standing at an open door.

"How are you feeling, miss?" she asked.

I reached up, ran my fingers along my neck. Completely clean.

Free.

Alive.

I jerked toward the open door. "Lucy!" I yelled. I had heard her. It was she who had talked me out of it, she who had pulled me away from Anghen. She had been awake, alert.

"LUCY!" I yelled.

***

366

Miles away, in an Irving suite, a brigader stumbled back in surprise as the blond girl opened her eyes. "Mina," she whispered, her previously dormant face turning out a wide grin.

Chapter 70

WHIT News

WHITBY ALTERCATION INVOLVES HOSPITAL
DIRECTOR
Nov 23, 2---

EARLY THIS MORNING, Dr. Wilhelm Anghen, the recently named executive director of Newholm Hospital and Detention Center, left Whitby via military carrier pod. Rumors speculate he arrived in DC for a meeting with White House officials, but this has not been confirmed. There was an altercation outside his aircraft as protesters and brigade members tried to prevent his flight. Several underage protesters were briefly apprehended and then released; however, an eighteen-year-old male was shot dead in the skirmish. It appears the deceased Newholm resident had no criminal record. There is speculation he was an

employee of the Newholm Detention Center.
Witnesses say he ran at Dr. Anghen and refused to obey
a direct order from police to stand down. Additionally a
woman, as yet unnamed, is in custody, although it is
unclear if she is a suspect. Authorities are investigating
the incident, and more information will be forthcoming
as this breaking news unfolds.

Chapter 71

Mina

Saturday, January 12

JONATHAN'S MOM'S CONDO was thronged with people, many wearing masks and gloves in fear of the latest outbreak. I pushed myself into a back corner, a pocket of space. After being downstate with my parents, out in the wide-open skies with the endless factories, everything in the Whitby suburbs felt too close. Dangerous.

"Breathe," Lucy murmured in my ear.

Lucy's lipstick was a smidge too bright for her pale face. She was thinner. She was also too close, right up in my personal space. But I wouldn't want it any other way. Finally we were together again. And her eyes were twinkling with mischief. I took her advice, forced myself to inhale for several seconds.

Across the way, a blinking, electronic banner screen

read CONGRATULATIONS! Jonathan and Quincey were wedged on either side of me and Lucy. Quincey shook out his arms, which were pinched in by a too-small button-down shirt. In the crowd, I could see Jonathan's soccer team, a collection of Irving teachers, some of his mom's friends and coworkers.

Jonathan's mom had pulled some strings, arranged for him to graduate early from Irving. He had enough credits and had even pulled off a last-minute admission to the University of Michigan.

"Did you get some cake, Mina?" Jonathan's mom asked, weaving by with extra plates.

"Yes, thank you."

Jonathan's mom smiled, pretended not to notice her son's hand wrapped around mine. She hadn't struck me as a smiler in the months I had known her. But she could finally relax. Tomorrow she would drive Jonathan up to Michigan to move into his dorm room and start his spring semester. It had been a compromise. Jonathan would go to a prestigious school, starting as soon as possible to make up for this past fall, but he wanted to study religion. No matter how people would look at his major, no matter that he'd never be able to get a job, at least officially, as a religious teacher, or worse, a rabbi. His mom probably hoped along the way he would change his mind about his major. She also probably hoped he would meet another, more suitable girl. The thought left a sour taste in my mouth.

"No sad thoughts today," Lucy chirped from my other side as if she could still read my mind.

"No sad thoughts today," I echoed. How could I when I was surrounded by the three people who mattered most in my life?

"To a future," Jonathan said, clinking his reusable bottle against mine.

"Future," Quincey, Lucy, and I echoed as we clinked our bottles together. But we couldn't forget who was missing. Lucy held her bottle out in front of her. Quincey followed her lead, then Jonathan and me, and we all clinked our bottles together again. We remembered Arthur, who gave up everything in his attempt to save us.

We were quiet after that. The memory of Anghen hung over us like an endless night. He was still listed as Newholm Hospital and Detention Center's executive director, but there had been no further news stories or public appearances. None of us had seen him since that night in Whitby. We told each other he had died. But regardless, I didn't go out at night. Even at home, several shuttle hours south, I barricaded the windows and carried a pouch of garlic in my bag. It didn't feel like a victory.

"Have any of you seen Dr. H?" Jonathan asked instead. "Mom invited her, but I haven't heard anything since…"

He trailed off. It was the first time we were all together since that horrible night in November when we had lost Arthur, when I had almost lost myself.

"I think she visited me in the hospital." I remembered seeing her, but so much afterward was hazy.

"I hope she's okay," Jonathan said. "I hope she doesn't think we blame her."

"I don't," I said. Dr. H had done everything she could to save me. If it hadn't been for her, I would have never tried to get inside Anghen's mind.

"Anghen found her weakness and used it," Quincey added. "Like he did for everyone else."

Out of all of us, she had been closest to Arthur. I wondered if Dr. Helsinger had known about Arthur's mom and her girlfriend. Probably. Dr. Helsinger made a point of knowing everything. I had certainly never known until the memorial service, until I had seen the two women together, holding each other upright. But then again, it wasn't the sort of thing you said publicly. Arthur and I had hardly known each other when everything began. It made Arthur feel even more distant, even more lost to me.

"I think I want to study politics," Lucy said abruptly into the silence.

"Politics?" Quincey echoed, like she had just signed up to join the local Alpha Brigade. After all, were the politicians really that different?

Quincey and Lucy were back together, but this idea must have been news to him. Lucy had been busy since she woke from her coma. Physically she was fine, although weak. Irving had arranged new housing for her—thankfully in a completely different dorm—and she and Jonathan had cleaned out our old dorm room. But she still had to clean out her mom's things, sort through her mom's finances, and figure out what she wanted to do with the house in Mayfield.

"I do think politics," Lucy said, nodding to herself. "I don't see any reason I can't get my diploma this spring. And then maybe college after all. I'd like to fight back. My way," she added, tucking a strand of blond hair behind her ear.

"I like that," said Quincey with a smile just for her.

"See, I'm making something of myself, Mina." Lucy poked a bony finger into my side.

"Of course you are," I said.

Jonathan and Lucy had both been pushing me to reenroll in Irving this spring, to finish my senior year properly. Lucy still wanted to do all the things: Midwinter Ball, the spring musical, the school newspaper. It was her way of processing her grief, her lost time, her mom. But beyond riding shotgun on her adventures, there wasn't really any point to my going back. After Anghen disappeared, I was admitted to a downstate hospital, administered a blood transfusion. But even once I had recovered, I couldn't go back to school. I told Irving and my parents that I was too far behind and dropped out. Irving would never count me as valedictorian again. Besides, my hospital stay had wiped out all of my parents' savings and more. I had been so close to perfect, but of course anything less wasn't enough.

"I have no clue what I'm going to do after graduation," Quincey admitted.

Quincey wasn't bothering to apply to college—

none of them would accept him. Without stellar grades, especially the past semester, not to mention his race, he'd never really had a chance.

"Didn't you get a job at the bookstore?" Jonathan asked Quincey.

After Arthur's death, when Quincey wasn't glued to Lucy's side, he had read, plowed through every text-message novel and digital book he could get his hands on. He visited Newholm's secondhand bookstore every day, surrounded himself with other people's words. I got the sense he had played those days in November over in his head a thousand times. He had invented dozens of scenarios, of what-ifs, that wouldn't have led to Lucy's attack, Arthur's death. While there was nothing more he could have possibly done, and even though Lucy was mostly back to normal, he desperately wished he had done more, had somehow found a way to save Arthur too.

Eventually the bookseller had started talking with Quincey about what he was reading. He discovered Quincey's family lived nearby, that he spoke like a poet and had no plans after graduation. The next week the bookstore had offered Quincey a job. First part-time, then full-time in the summer.

"I need someone who can talk to our community," the owner had said, gesturing around the empty store.

"But there's no one here," Quincey said.

The bookseller nodded. "But there could be. They could have space here."

"Will it be enough to keep you busy?" I asked.

"Trust me, I'll keep him plenty busy," Lucy said, her eyes dancing.

Quincey nodded. "And I'll still work with the Omegas every day. We have to continue the fight. But..." His eyes met mine. "I've been wondering—that digital file we put together—it still exists, right?"

"I haven't touched it. Do you want me to—?" I hesitated, then finally said, looking at each of my friends: "Should I destroy it?"

"No," Quincey said. "I want to be able to access it. If... if that's okay with all of you. I know it's painful and may be too personal, but... I feel like I've got a lot of stuff to work through. Maybe if I started writing..."

"You want to write our story," I realized.

"Maybe," Quincey admitted. "There's so much that people don't know, don't understand about our country today. If I wrote it all out, it could be my way of fighting back, continuing the revolution. And honoring him—" His voice got gruff as he again gestured to the empty space in front of us. Lucy wrapped her hand tightly around his. The rest of us grew silent, staring at the crowd of people around us, everyone except Arthur.

My xphone chimed. I cast my screen, stared at the caller's name: Irving Academy.

"Hello?" I answered tentatively.

"Miss Mina?" said an officious voice on the other end. She sat at a large desk, in front of a row of wooden bookcases filled with stuffy old books. So Irving.

"Speaking."

"This is Mrs. F," the voice replied through my earpiece. "Admissions director at Irving. You haven't put in an application to return for this semester."

"That's correct." Everyone's eyes were on me. I rolled my own. *Irving*, I mouthed.

"May I ask why?"

I sighed. Were they that hard up for my money? So much for the prestigious waiting list they always touted. "Well, for starters because I can't afford it."

"I suspected that might be an issue. We'd like to offer you the inaugural Arthur Godalming scholarship."

My breath caught in my chest. "No," I spat out.

The woman on the other end paused. "Of course, we'll give you time to speak to your family, consider your options, and discuss the terms and conditions of the award."

"No," I said again, like it was the only word I remembered. I didn't want to take Arthur's money, I didn't want to be beholden to any terms and conditions, I didn't want to go back to all the memories. "No," I said a third time, just to make myself clear.

"I'll give you some time to think about it. Arthur's mother herself recommended you. It would mean a lot to her to help you complete your degree."

"Okay," I found myself saying. See, I did know other words. "I'll think about it. Thank you." Something about knowing Arthur's mom was involved, that she was fighting for me, made it more palatable. Not right, but perhaps palatable. I disconnected the call.

All three of my friends stared at me.

"Arthur's mom is offering a scholarship for Irving students. They want me to take it and come back this semester."

"Mina, you have to!" Lucy said. "We could be roomies again!"

"Would you at least consider it?" Jonathan asked with something like hope in his voice.

"I don't know. I don't think so, but…" Maybe for Arthur. He had been making plans for a future that would never come, fighting to change his destiny, to become a doctor. Perhaps his mom wanted to support my plans in his place.

After Arthur was shot, we had spent the night in jail only to be bailed out the next morning by his mom. She had sued the Newholm Police Department. It would be months, if not years, until it came to trial, and even then, surely the government would build some case against us. But amid all that, not to mention the memorial services for her husband and son, she had remembered my situation.

"It's the perfect solution," Jonathan said.

He was right. Mina of a few months ago would have been overjoyed. So much had changed since then.

Chapter 72

Mina

LATER THAT AFTERNOON, after dropping Lucy off at her new dorm room, I walked through campus. The semester would start Monday, but already students hurried across the commons with stylish clothes, carefully done hair. There weren't many trees around campus, and of course they were all bare. But I knew in another few months buds would appear, leaves, green.

Behind Slains, I could see a light in the basement office. I pushed open one of the double doors and continued downstairs. Dr. Helsinger's office door was closed. She probably wasn't in. Even if she was, she probably wanted as little to do with me as possible. Hopefully she had returned to her regular life, been able to renew her ID. I should have just turned around, but I couldn't let it go. I needed to see her. I knocked.

There wasn't any answer.

I knocked again.

I had visions of her unconscious, bloodless. I grabbed for the handle. It turned. I burst into the room.

Dr. H looked exactly the same—hunched over her desk, several screens floating around her head.

"Yes?" Then she saw me: "Mina. Come in."

Technically I was already in, but I closed the door behind me.

Dr. H stood partway, as if unsure what to do. "I've been hoping you'd stop by."

"Really?"

Dr. H sank back to her seat. "Really." She pressed her lips together. "I need to tell you. I'm sorry."

"What?" This conversation wasn't going how I had expected.

"Sit down." Dr. H gestured to a chair, shifted her own to face me. "I misled you. That day, when Anghen stopped by, he told me to visit you, to egg you into chasing after him. Meanwhile, he was setting up his attack."

"But he forced you, didn't he?" It was what I had always assumed.

She shook her head. "The why doesn't matter."

"But it does," I argued. "You gave me that clue, about the connection in our blood, about dreaming. If I hadn't thought of that—"

"You think of everything," Dr. H said. "But if I had been straight with you then, or even earlier, we could've made a plan. Arthur wouldn't have had to die." Her

380

voice was gruff. She reached for a tissue, blew her nose, rubbed at her eyes.

"Sometimes," she murmured into her tissue, "you do things because you think they're the right thing to do. But sometimes you do something else and you hope it will be fine, that it won't matter in the long run…" She cleared her throat, continued. "He promised security. I don't care about myself, but Faven, my wife— He had connections. He was able to get CMS to reauthorize her ID."

I thought about when I had first met Dr. Helsinger, how she had wanted nothing to do with me, how she had feared her office was bugged. I thought about Jonathan and what I would do for him.

"And now?" I asked. "Is she safe? Are you?"

"We're safe," Dr. H answered but then frowned. "As if anyone could ever be safe in these times."

I didn't say anything. She was right. I thought about the revolution Jonathan had once promised. We hadn't done nearly enough. Who was I to be in here, demanding answers to my questions?

"Is it true you're not returning to school?" Dr. H asked abruptly.

I nodded. Even with Arthur's money, I didn't belong here. I had played the game well, but the system had beaten me in the end.

"Work for me."

She didn't say it as a question but as a statement, almost a demand. I was sure I hadn't heard her correctly.

"People in Europe are still dying. Japan is overrun by those supposed Filipino terrorists. I have a binder full of unsolved mysteries."

"But I thought... I mean, his heart stopped. Are you sure he's not dead?"

Dr. H shook her head. "At least in Whitby, there's been no further reports of wolves or other vampires. If Anghen did succumb to the silver bullet, all the undead monsters connected to him should have died as well. But the lack of a report isn't the same as bodies. The police apprehended a suspicious female on the scene, whom I believe was the other vampire Jonathan met in England. And I suspect there are others we don't even know about yet, both here and abroad. There's no proof Anghen is dead."

I didn't know what to say. My heart began to race as I thought of the implications. It was everything I had feared. Instead, I studied the rows upon rows of books behind her, the vast amounts of knowledge.

"You're always one step ahead," Dr. H said. "Always thinking. That's why you're here today. You had to figure out all the pieces of your puzzle."

She was right about that. I'd been thinking about Quincey sorting through our documents, writing his way through our story, and this was the one unknown in all of it. A big unknown. As long as Anghen lived, we'd never be safe again.

"So work for me. Let's do something right

together."

It would mean doing my part, just like Lucy going into politics. Plus Dr. Helsinger was brilliant. And she believed in me. It was my chance to put things right.

"How much?"

"That's my girl," Dr. H answered, smiling. Then she named an absurd sum. More than I had ever dreamed of making in my life. More than my parents made.

"But—" I didn't know how to finish my sentence, at least not politely. But that kind of money didn't square with Dr. H's job or her driver-required car or anything I knew about her.

"Let's just say I've met some people," Dr. H said, her smile widening. "Some people with deep pockets. But good people. People who want to get to the bottom of this."

"I don't have a high school diploma. I probably won't ever go to college. I can't—"

"You and I both know you're ready. And there're some skills—" She looked around the office, shaking her head. "There're some skills you can't learn in school anyway."

"But what about Faven?" I had to ask.

"We're done living in fear," Dr. H answered.

"Okay." I didn't need to think about it; I didn't need to talk to Jonathan. Everything in my gut was singing. "Okay," I said again, just to make it official.

"Welcome aboard."

Chapter 73

Mina

AFTERWARD, I HAD arranged to meet Jonathan at Newholm Plaza. His mom would pick him up that evening, and I had reserved a spot on a driverless shuttle back home, but we had a few hours.

While I waited, I thought about Jonathan. Sometimes it felt like we had spent more of our relationship apart than together. Of course, we had seen each other just a few hours ago, but before that I had been home recovering, and now he would be even farther away. We'd keep messaging each other every day. But our lives were about to diverge even further. Would we continue to love each other? When he looked at me, would he always remember a monster?

But as he got out of his mom's car, everything about his hair, his shoulders, his hands, was Jonathan. My heart filled to bursting and I could never imagine not loving him.

Later we walked toward Irving, weaving through the city streets, holding hands. We browsed in Quincey's bookstore, ate too-hot fries from McDonald's. I told Jonathan about Dr. Helsinger, about my job. He didn't push Irving on me again. Instead, he told me about the rest of his party, his plans for the drive tomorrow, his hopes for college.

We walked along Route 47, past campus, to the River Esk. The water was churning under the bridge.

I remembered Lucy and that horrible morning when I had discovered her dancing at the field house. Then I couldn't help but remember Arthur. His absence was still a hole in my heart every day. But as I watched the water, I wondered if he sometimes watched us. I knew he would be rooting for us.

Jonathan fell to his knees. I swung around, fearful, but he was looking up at me, reaching for my hands.

"Marry me, Mina Muto," he whispered.

I gasped. I took his hands even as I didn't know what to think.

"We're too young. You need to finish school. I've got Dr. H and—"

"But I love you. I don't know what next semester is going to hold, or anything about the future, but we have something and—"

"I will always love you." I knew that much. "And someday we'll get married. Soon. We'll have bucketfuls of kids, and all of them will be named Arthur, even the girls."

"Okay. But I don't want to wait forever."

I bent down, kissed him. "Nor do I."

When he stood up, he wrapped his arms around me, and I leaned my back against his chest. We stood there for a long time, watched the river and the darkening sky, and dreamed of a future together.

Chapter 74

WHIT News

NEWCOMER NOMINATED AS CMS DIRECTOR
March 15, 2---

IN A SURPRISE press conference, President Pro
Tempore Evans announced his nomination for director
of CMS, the Citizen & Migrant Security department
tasked with border control, immigration and
deportation, and the increasing number of detention
centers throughout the country.

"My candidate has innovative ideas and tools for our
country's fight against the plague of race terrorism. Plus
his medical background will enable him to seamlessly
join hospitals across the country in providing effective,
research-based treatments to detention center inmates.

I am delighted to announce this relative newcomer to you tonight. He's someone to keep your eyes on."

The president then stepped aside to introduce a young man with wavy dark hair: Dr. Wilhelm Anghen.

Acknowledgments

I'm so grateful to everyone who supported my first novel, *When Snow Falls Like Fire*, and kept asking when the next one would be out. It's here!

To my DW family, my fellow teachers, staff, and administrators, the community, and especially my students, past and present: thank you for showing up to my party. Your support continues to mean the world to me. And to Lori and Weldon Public Library—thank you for always hosting the party!

To my writing group, thank you for asking tough questions and pushing my writing to its best.

Anita Mumm at Mumm's the Word: thank you for championing this story from the beginning and seeing everything it could be. And thank you to Anne Victory at Victory Editing for making the words not only work but sing.

Carrie, the cover is beautiful, again. I'm so lucky to have you in my corner.

Thank you to the dog community for cheering on all my non-dog-related achievements. You're the best.

And thank you to Alicia for being determined to celebrate with me. I'm so grateful for your support and joy.

My family could not be prouder. Thank you for sharing in this with me: Erin, Kedar, Spencer, Savannah, Sally (you've always been family!), Dava and Jim, Holly and Kevin, Kari and Trish, Linda and Kevin,

Janet and Ted, Stephanie, Kalen, and Steve, Rachel and Bryan, Nathan and Isaac, and Mom and Dad.

Philip, thank you for always being there and always having my back.

Finally, thank you to all of you for buying books, for writing reviews, and mostly for reading. It's enabled me to keep telling my stories.

About the Author

Anne Leone spent her childhood getting lost in the woods and telling stories to anyone who would listen. Honestly, that still sounds like the perfect way to spend a day.

She currently lives in central Illinois with her husband and dog. By day she works as a high school English teacher. When she's not writing or teaching, she loves baking, traveling, dog sports, and—of course—curling up with a good book.